love

rekindled

MICHELLE LYNN

Love Rekindled
Copyright © 2016 by Michelle Lynn

Editor:
Hot Tree Editing

Proofreader:
Ultra Editing

Cover Design:
Perfect Pear Creative Covers
Cover photo:
© Shutterstock.com

Interior Design and Formatting:
Christine Borgford, Perfectly Publishable

Visit my website at www.michellelynnbooks.com

dedication

To my daughter
Always listen to your heart

one

Brad

I'M A CHEATER. THERE. I said it. Two years ago, I fell into a hole, and as fast as my fingers clawed to escape, the dirt continued to pile on me. I'm not saying it's an excuse. I'm not even saying she should forgive me. Although, I hope she does. But I can't live without her anymore. I tried. I found a girl and proposed to her, while imagining the delicate finger I slid the ring on belonged to someone else. No matter how hard I tried, I couldn't go through with marrying anyone but her. For sure, I never thought I'd say this, but I'm nothing without her. She brings out the good in me. That's why I'm here, in some small-ass town, to grovel my way back into her heart.

She's different now, and I'm not referring to the disappearance of her bleached blonde hair back to her natural brown. I loved her as a blonde, but the dark suits her better. I wouldn't care if she had rainbow-colored hair. I'm not sitting outside the hospital where she works, watching her walk to her car like some stalker, because she's gorgeous. I'm here because of her heart and kindness. That's what I'm fighting to get back. The package it comes in is just an added bonus.

Her ponytail swings back and forth as she laughs with what I hope is a co-worker, unless she's turned lesbian in the last two years. She waves good-bye to the girl and throws her purse into the passenger seat of her Jetta. The car has a little more rust than it did back in the day, but it's held up well. Still, it's old and she deserves something newer.

She pulls out of her parking space, and my heart constricts as I watch her drive away from me again. I should duck down so she doesn't see me, but my eyes won't veer from her. The beat-up Jetta passes and my stomach clenches. My hand itches to yank the car handle open. My feet beg to disobey and run to her. I don't have to, because she slams on the breaks and her eyes are locked on mine. Hope pours from mine while hers fume with anger.

She throws the car into park, thrusts the door open, and stomps directly to my door.

She bangs on the window and I jump. "Why are you here?" she screams through the pane.

As I lower the window, the smell of jasmine breezes in. Her perfume still has the capacity to calm me.

"Hey, Taylor."

"Don't 'Hey' me. Why are you here?" Her voice is sharp and cold, and nothing like I remember. Not sure why I wouldn't expect less though.

"I thought we could talk." My fingers move to the knob of my stereo to turn down the music.

"There's nothing to talk about. Leave."

She turns and walks back to her car.

I exit my truck and wrap my fingers around her wrist to stop her. She yanks it out of my grip.

"Don't ever touch me," she seethes, and I hold my hands up in the air.

"Taylor," I whisper, and she twists around. The look of fury heavy in her eyes.

She ignores the fact that I'm talking and climbs back into her car. I try to slide through the sliver of the open door, but she squeezes me out and the door rattles shut.

I knock on the window, but she shifts the car into drive. Her hesitation as she sits and studies the steering wheel, tells me my cause isn't lost. Maybe I have a chance. I knock again, softer this time. Her tear-filled eyes look up at me through the dirty glass, and my heart breaks for what I've done. If I affect her this much two years later, how bad did I destroy her then?

"Please," I beg, and she closes her eyes. I watch her shallow breathing falter.

As though she had a lapse of judgment, she shakes her head and the pain in her eyes disappears, returning to resentment once more. "Go back to your fiancée, Brad."

Her tires squeal before the rubber catches pavement. Within a minute, she's left me—again.

"Fuck!" I lift my leg in the air as my toes ignite with heat. She fucking rolled over my foot.

The pain in my foot is nothing compared to the pain in my heart as I watch her taillights disappear around the corner.

Looking up at the Hospital sign, I figure there's no better place to be. I limp to my truck to lock it up and grab my phone. My foot throbs as I step closer to the sliding doors, but Taylor Delaney occupies my mind with every excruciating inch. There has to be a way I can get her to talk to me and, hopefully, forgive me.

A half hour later, I'm finally in a room being fixed up by Edward Scissorhand's sister. You'd think they'd have some protocol about the length of a nurse's nails.

"Shit. My foot is still attached to my body?" I move the phone away from my ear, glaring down at the blonde. She shoots me a tight, insincere smile.

"Brad?" my sister, Piper, screams through the phone.

She's going to laugh her ass off. I roll my eyes while thinking about being her and Tanner's entertainment for the night and the two of them falling into a fit of laughter over my crushing situation.

"She ran over my foot when she left me in the parking lot."

I hear the snickering she's trying to mask.

"Go ahead and laugh," I say.

"Are . . . are you okay?" she asks around another muffled sound, which I suspect is her attempt at concealing her amusement.

"I'm fine. Thank God it was my left foot. Ouch!"

I pull my foot back from the hands of Hannibal, and glare down at her. I decide I don't need to talk to my sister, with her perfect life amongst my best friend. He's living my dream of being the fast-track Olympic swimmer with the love of his life to snuggle up to every night.

"I gotta go. I'll call you tonight."

I hang up the phone and toss it on the bed behind me.

The blonde nurse continues bandaging now that I've given her my foot again.

"Seriously, wasn't there a 'How to be kind and gentle' class in nursing school?" My fingers rip the paper under me from the pain she's inflicting.

"I'm barely touching you." Her eyes narrow before she heads to the cabinet to get God knows what.

Looking at my foot, I notice it's quickly turning black and blue.

The door opens and the scent of jasmine floats in. My head jerks up, and there she is, standing with her hands on her hips and her eyes on me.

"Taylor," I murmur.

"You know this guy?" blonde nurse says, sneering at me.

"Brad." Her voice is curt and to the point. Then she turns to Nurse Scissorhand. "I got this. Did he have x-rays yet?"

"Taylor, you were off a half hour ago."

"It's okay. We have unfinished business." She tilts her head my way like I'm a bag of her weekly garbage. I'm not going to argue her point.

"But what about Em? It's Halloween." The nurse's face glows with compassion as she pats Taylor's arm.

Who the fuck is Em?

Taylor shakes her head, dismissing her immediately.

"It's fine. This shouldn't take long." She points to my foot, and I notice her nails aren't manicured anymore. Obviously, she got a memo that Scissorhand hadn't. Actually, the purple nail polish is chipped and mostly worn away. Another thing that's unlike her.

"If you say so. X-rays are complete and there's no break. Dr. James said to put the boot on him for a few days. I printed off the instructions; they are on the counter. Have a great Halloween, and give Em a big hug, okay?" Miss Scissorhand wraps her arms around Taylor's shoulders.

"Thanks, Olivia."

She narrows her eyes at me with complete disgust, before exiting the room.

Taylor moves over to the counter to inspect my orders, disregarding that we're in this room alone together. God, her occupying the same space as me is like playing in the State Championship my senior year. Her perfume, the way her hips sway back and forth, and her pouty bottom lip, make images of our time together flicker through my mind. She sits on the rolling chair and lays an ace bandage on her leg. Those fingers are gentle when she grabs my foot to prop it on her thigh.

"I'm sorry," she mumbles, busying her hands with wrapping my injury.

"Don't be," I say, liking her touch much more than blondie's.

"You're right." She looks up, and I wish there was more anger than hurt swimming in her eyes. "You deserved it." She studies my foot once again.

"Well, you could be a little remorseful." A smirk crosses my face, but she doesn't bother to look at me.

"How is your fiancée, Brad?"

"She's not my fiancée."

"Oh, sorry, your wife?" Her voice is rough and completely affected, which only brings a smile to my lips.

"Nope. I called it off."

This earns me a look from her warm blue eyes. Is that disbelief or a tinge of happiness I see staring back at me?

"Caught you with another woman?"

Then again, maybe not.

"No. Who's Em?"

Her fingers tense and she stops wrapping my foot for a second.

"None of your concern." She winds the ace bandage tighter.

"Okay. Are you going to a Halloween party or something?" I ask, and the bandage pinches my skin.

"Again, none of your concern."

Finally, she's done and slides a boot over my foot. "You'll have to stay off it for a few days. Lucky it's your left, so you can drive."

"Taylor, can we go and talk somewhere? I'll buy you a cup of coffee." She busies herself at the counter, signing paperwork and throwing supplies in a bag.

"No, Brad, I can't. I don't know why you're here, but please go back home."

"I'm sorry," I say, my throat constricting. "I made a mistake."

"A mistake?" she screams, her fists clenching at her sides. She lowers her voice. "You cheated on me, Brad. I know we were having problems, but you slept with another girl. 'Sorry' doesn't fix that."

Her phone goes off, and she retrieves it from her pocket and quickly mutes it.

"I love you," I confess, anything to keep her here with me. She has to know how horrible I feel. How bad I want to fix this.

"No, you love yourself, Brad. Always have." She shoves the papers into the bag and hands it to me. "But if you care about me, even slightly, you'll leave Roosevelt."

"Taylor," I call out, and her hand stills on the door handle. Her back rises and falls with a deep breath and for a fleeting moment I think she believes me.

"Please, Brad, leave," she whispers and opens the door, leaving me on the hospital bed with the smell of jasmine surrounding me.

Taylor

MY NOSTRILS TICKLE AND MY throat's scratchy as I walk away from Brad. He still has that cocky grin, but his brown mop of hair is a little neater nowadays. I had convinced myself that, since his swimming days were over for him, his muscular build would turn into a gut that hung over his pants. I'd wished at least, but through his tight Henley, I could still make out the V-shaped torso. For a second, my hands remembered what it felt like to give him massages after each meet. The way his hands would rub along my legs, igniting shivers in the wake of his touch as I worked on his muscles. The times when he'd flip us over and capture my lips until I was dazed and only wanted more of whatever he was offering.

As fast as I'm back in that bed with him, the blonde comes to mind. Her shocked face when I interrupted them. How she slinked off him, pulling the covers tight around her chest as his glassy eyes tried to focus on me. I saw the signs of his drug use a mile away. My sister's addiction had taught me the telltale signals of a user. She trained me well. There I was again, trying to fix someone who didn't want fixing. To cheat, that was an all-time low, even for Brad.

"Bye, Taylor, for good this time." Dr. James waves and I smile. The fact that he let me come back and take care of Brad shows what a nice guy he is.

"I'm out. Em's waiting." I jog down the hallway as my phone rings again in my pocket.

I answer it quickly, my pace not slowing down. I can't be late for tonight. "I got hung up. I'm on my way."

"Hurry," Sam says.

"I am, I am." I hear Em in the background and my feet pick up speed a little more.

I click off and pull my keys out of my pocket, ready to unlock my door. By the time I'm safe in the car, I slam on the gas, noticing Brad made me late for the most important date in my life.

His Black SUV sits two spots down. A new car doesn't mean a new him. All those nights when we made out in his Mustang after a night at the bar flash through my mind. The days when our hands refused to leave each other's body. I shake my head at those happy memories, because what he did later negates anything good we had before.

When I met Brad, his reputation had preceded him. He slept with a lot of girls, and usually not the same one twice, but after he'd begged me to go out on a date with him, I thought maybe I was the girl who could change him. I could smack myself in the forehead for how stupid it all sounds. But for a brief time in our relationship, I felt like I was the magic girl who could tame the swimming stud, Brad Ashby. Until he didn't make the Olympics and everything crumbled around us.

Swallowing the pain those moments still bring me, I concentrate on the good in my life as I breeze by downtown Roosevelt. I pass Carolle's Tap, Bridger's Diner, and the mayor's office. Roosevelt is a town of six thousand, but you'd never know it had that many people with the amount of gossip that's whispered over the telephone lines and diner booths.

Unfortunately, the Delaney family is well-known in this town, but not in a good way. My sister has stolen something from practically everyone in town to support her drug habit, which Garrison Voight, the football quarterback, got her hooked on in high school. My dad's the town drunk, falling off his stool at Carolle's Tap most nights. Then I came home two years ago, any self-respect our family might have had in Roosevelt was destroyed to bits. In Roosevelt's eyes, an unwed girl who was pregnant with no father involvement—well, I became the poor girl considered a whore who couldn't keep her legs shut. The sad part is I believed them.

I pull down my street as kids fill the sidewalks in costumes, seeking candy. Parent's smiling faces and laughs echo in the cool, crisp air. Three houses down on the left is a red brick ranch-style home that contains two bedrooms and one bath. My car sputters to a stop, and I wait for kids to pass by our driveway before I pull all the way up behind the green pickup truck. My whole body buzzes with excitement because this is the best part of my day. Seeing Brad today might have thrown me for a loop and brought the resentment from years ago back to the surface, but it all goes away as I step through that back porch door.

"Hey," I greet Sam, who's stirring a pot on the stove. "Smells awesome." My eyes search Em out.

"Chili." He smiles up at me, continuing to stir.

Then I hear the squeal, and a second later, my girl rounds the corner, barreling right at me. Those soft chocolate brown eyes, which are a match to the ones I just looked into not twenty minutes ago, light up for me as her little arms wrap around my shoulders.

"My girl." I swoop her up and twirl us around, loving the sound of her squeals.

"Mama," she says, which I'm proud to say was her first word.

"Happy Halloween, baby." I kiss her forehead.

The doorbell rings and she wiggles to escape my arms.

I let her down and follow her short, small footsteps to the door. She learned to walk at ten months and hasn't looked back. I open the screen door to find a ninja turtle and a princess. Em grabs the candy from the bowl and puts one in each bag.

After the kids leave, she stares up at me. "Me go," she says, pointing to the street.

"Okay, okay." I pull her costume from the foyer table, and

we move into the living room to change her into her peacock costume.

"Change her diaper," Sam yells from the kitchen.

I move us to the floor, change her diaper, and get her dressed into her costume as a pang of guilt stabs me in the gut. Brad is here, in Roosevelt, and he has no idea he has a daughter. I convinced myself it was better this way after I'd caught him with the blonde. That he wouldn't be good for Em. He definitely couldn't be the father figure she needed him to be. Once news traveled back to me that he was getting married, I further convinced myself it was for the best. He'd forgotten all about me and would do nothing but disappoint her. But after today, seeing him and all those feelings surfacing back up, maybe I was wrong. I went back into that hospital room to ensure he keeps his distance, and to confirm he doesn't have a chance to rekindle things. Now, as I dress our daughter for Halloween, an annoying knot grows tighter in my stomach.

Em eyes Sam, who is leaning against the doorway. "I'm peacock," she says, and she holds my finger as she twirls around.

"You're beautiful," I say, and she grabs her bucket.

"Go, go!" She runs over to Sam and pulls his hand.

"I'll put the candy out on the table. Chili's in the Crock-Pot." Sam follows Em toward the door.

Apprehension fills my veins because of this guilt inside me, which refuses to quiet down. Suddenly, it seems terribly unfair that Sam has taken on Em's father role. Then again, a cheetah's spots don't change, and maybe I'm saving her from being hurt. Brad ignites flames of disappointment around his self-centered agendas. Maybe he'd want us now, but what if later, he decides something else is better? Where would that leave Em?

Anger at what he did to me quickly replaces that regret. Men like Brad care about only one thing—themselves. They step on everyone who loves them, and the same would be true for Em.

"You know there won't be any candy by the time we return." I glance at the overfilled candy bowl on the porch. Lucky for me, I purposely bought the candy I don't like. The temptation to eat the whole bowl is eliminated and saves on my already wider hips.

"Not our problem," Sam says, fussing with Em to put her coat on.

"No, coat." She stomps her foot, and I bite my lip to prevent from smiling. She's definitely got Brad's stubborn streak.

Sam blows a long release of air from his lungs, holding the coat up to me.

"It's okay. Let her go."

"If you're sure." He hangs it back up on the hooks by the door.

The three of us leave the small house, which is mine, all mine. I watch Em scurry up the sidewalk with our neighbor, who we'd ran into. Chelsea is eight and takes good care of Em, protecting her. She comes over while I clean sometimes to help me with her.

"So . . ." I kick the red leaves that have fallen from the trees. "Brad showed up today." I don't need to look at Sam to see how the news affects him.

"Really?" he asks, and my heart breaks because I'm not blind. I know Sam likes me and he adores Em. Unfortunately, after my sister left again, we've made our situation appear like a family, and maybe our roles have blurred slightly. Sam's my brother-in-law, still legally married to my sister, who left him over two years ago for her next fix. We haven't heard from her and, honestly, we stopped looking. It's hard to realize some people just don't want to be found, which is more gossip that runs the stools of Carolle's Tap.

"He apologized," I say, shrugging my shoulder as though hearing those words didn't patch my heart up somewhat. There are still a lot of empty holes, but his apology was nice.

"Anything else?" I know what he's asking—did I tell him about Em?

"No. I asked him to leave town."

His body relaxes and I hear his sigh of relief. We're going to have to have a conversation about our situation soon. I could never repay him after all he's done for me these past couple of years, but to be honest, I'm not over Brad. Maybe because when you still look into the same eyes of the one you love every night, it's hard for your dreams not to be filled with thoughts of a love gone wrong. If only I could convince myself that Brad and I didn't have something special at one time, then maybe Sam would be enough for me. If I hadn't experienced such a deep love for Brad, I wouldn't know the difference, but sadly, I do.

two

Brad

THE APARTMENT I SHARE WITH Dylan is dark. Dylan is my best friend, Tanner McCain's brother. He just graduated from NYU with a degree in advertising. He got a job at what Forbes has called an up and coming firm. Hard to believe anything in Detroit can be up and coming. There's rumors it will be moving to Chicago if all goes smooth, which means he'll be gone and I'll be solo once again.

My sister, Piper, and Tanner left for Colorado six months ago so Tanner can train for the Olympics—the Olympics that I didn't make the cut for. It was the reason I departed on a drinking and drug binge my senior year of college, two and a half years ago, which had found me in bed with someone who wasn't my girlfriend.

I toss my keys on the kitchen table and plop down on the couch. I should call Piper, but she's busy with the love of her life while I wallow in the loss of mine. Mindlessly, I watch some cooking show until I'm jarred from my numbness when the door opens.

"Forget it. It's not my problem. What do you want me to do?" Dylan's voice raises the more he talks, and I look up to find his tie already loosened and his hair disheveled. I guess that's what an executive looks like all stressed out.

He notices me and shakes his head. "We'll talk later." He

disconnects the call, and I watch him switch the ringer on vibrate before dropping it on the table next to my keys.

"Who's that?"

"Bea," he says, opening the fridge, grabbing two beers.

He walks back to the couch, handing me one, and then throws himself in the chair.

"I thought you said you were staying out of that?" Dylan and Bea, my sister's best friend, have been flirting with each other pretty heavily since my no-go wedding six months ago. I'm fairly sure he's nailed her, but Dylan doesn't kiss and tell—not that I want details on how Bea kisses or anything else for that matter.

"There's something about her, but she's going crazy." He crosses his feet on the coffee table and I feel his eyes burning into the side of my head.

"What's up?" I ask, continuing to look at the television.

"Jackass, you didn't show up . . . again. I'm fairly sure you're getting fired tomorrow."

Dylan found me a job at Deacon Advertising, but I hate it. My ex-fiancée's dad got me fired from Lincoln Industries. I guess all the big people know a hell of a lot of bigger people. Turns out the owner of Lincoln Industries and Bayli's dad were fraternity brothers. So, when I dumped his daughter, Lincoln Industries dumped me.

"I'm not made to work in an office," I say, and he rolls his eyes. Dylan doesn't understand. He wasn't a swimmer like me, Tanner, and Piper. He was always cooped up in his room, playing video games. He was a loner, really, until he came back from NYU a geeky tattooed God who girls fawn over, especially Bea.

"You have to do what you can before you find what you want to do. The job pays you money, which in turn pays your bills," he lectures like he always does, and it's starting to become white noise to me.

"I pay my bills, okay. That cubicle is like a prison. I can't breathe."

I'm not even sure why I bother talking to Dylan. He doesn't understand and never will. He's in his element at Deacon, always kissing ass and appeasing everyone.

"Maybe it's a blessing if you get fired."

I shrug. "Maybe. But then I have to find something else."

"True." He downs a long pull of his beer. "What did you do when you played hooky today?"

"I went to see Taylor."

He bolts up, his tatted forearms leaning on his thighs. I can even admit the guy is intimidating as hell. How he went from wimp-on-a-stick to bulk-as–a-brick is beyond me.

"Whoa. What happened?" His eyes check out my foot. "Shit, man. Never mind. I take it things didn't go well?"

"You think?" I hold up my foot. "Shit, that hurt." I slowly lower it down to the pillow.

"Do you want to talk about it?" Dylan asks. For being such a tough-ass, he hasn't minded me babbling on and on about Taylor these last months.

"Nothing to say. She asked me to leave town." I shrug, downing the rest of my beer. Man, that went down fast.

"And you listened?" He cocks his eyebrow at me and leans back into his chair. "And here I thought you wanted her back." He relaxes into the chair, his phone buzzing along the kitchen table.

I know what he's thinking, but Taylor doesn't want me. She made that clear by running over my foot.

"You going to get that?" I ask, nodding to the phone tee-tering off the edge of the table.

"No, she can cool off a bit," he says, rising to his feet and venturing into the kitchen. He grabs the rest of the six pack from the fridge and comes back over. "Might as well numb it, bro." He places the cold beers in front of me, takes one, and sneaks off into his bedroom. Without the annoying buzzing of his phone going off, my eyes check the table. Sure enough, the bastard grabbed the phone. He's such a damn pussy.

I sit there for a little longer, thinking I should make the half-hour drive back to Roosevelt. Crazy how I never realized she was this close to me all this time. For months I asked about her around Michigan's campus, only to be told people had no idea. After graduation, she vanished into thin air, or people were hiding her from me. From how bad she wanted out of the small town she grew up in, I hadn't thought she'd go back there, not in a million years. But she had, and I'm still curious as to why she would return to a town she so deeply despised.

Knowing getting drunk isn't going to help me, I put the beer back in the fridge and snatch my keys off the table.

I drive the fifteen minutes to Creadle's Aquatic Center, my foot killing me, reminding me I won't be swimming today, but I can sink into a hot soak in the therapy pool if need be.

Creadle's is right between my town and Roosevelt, and the closeness to her isn't lost. It's a sign that we're meant to be and live together happily ever after.

I park and grab the packed bag I keep in the trunk. Heading inside, I walk into the locker room and change.

The smell of chlorine eases my nerves. I dip into the therapy pool, envying the people swimming laps. How I would love to relieve the anxiety with the exertion of a good freestyle. Water has relaxed me since I was young. Once I knew how to channel my crazy behavior in the pool, it became my serenity.

"I'm not sure I've ever seen you in the therapy pool." Cami bends down, her blue-tipped hair falling forward, tickling my bare shoulder. Cami is the manager of the Aquatic Center, plus the owner, Wes's, girlfriend.

"Hey, Cami. I hurt my foot today. Taking it easy." I lift my bruised foot.

"What happened?" Her mouth cringes as she looks at the black and blue skin.

"I was in someone's way." It's the best way to describe how my ex-girlfriend ran over my foot because of a dick move

I made years ago.

"Sorry, it looks nasty." She clasps my shoulder before moving over to the lap section. She grabs a towel and waits for Wes to climb out of the fourth lap lane. He shakes his head and she backs up, making him have to wrap her in his arms, completing his mission of soaking her. The two of them laugh, and pang of jealousy stabs my heart. I did the same thing to Taylor so many times back at MU.

Wes's arm is swung over Cami's shoulder as they walk toward me.

"Hey, just the man I wanted to talk to." He stops, handing the towel back to Cami. "Give me ten?" He kisses her cheek and enters the pool down the steps.

"Why on Earth are you looking for me?" I ask, and his chuckle echoes off the walls.

"You were the hotshot at Michigan, right?"

I huff. "No. That would be my best friend, Tanner," I say. He was the swim god, always has been.

"Hey, man, not many people make the Olympics. That doesn't make you bad."

"It doesn't make me great either." Time to end feeling sorry for myself. "What do you need, Wes?"

"I had two swim instructors quit today. No notice. I'm in a bind." His arms move through the water and I take a long breath. Swim lessons isn't exactly what I'm looking for.

"What kind of swim lessons? Like the swim team?" I look up at their flags hanging, showing The Sharks are a team to reckon with. At least in the four years the facility has been open.

"Hell no, that's me." Wes is another swimmer who never continued after college, but found coaching was his drive to keep him in the water. "Lessons, man. Just until I can find replacements. It's nights, so you don't have to worry about missing work."

"Okay," I agree, and his eyes widen. Guess he thought

I would say no. But since I'm getting fired tomorrow, what choice do I really have?

He rubs his hands together. "I thought that would take a hell of a lot longer. Be here at five thirty tomorrow. They're private, so it's one on one."

He wades through the water, clasping his hand on my shoulder. "Thanks, man. You're a lifesaver."

"Does that mean I get my membership for free?" I ask, and he laughs.

"Half-priced, okay?" Behind me, I hear Cami squeal and can only assume she's wrapped up in Wes's arms. "Done, baby. Let's go home," he tells her, and I close my eyes, missing what they have. At least with Bayli, I hadn't been alone—well, physically anyway.

"Bye, guys." I wave my hand in the air.

"See you, Brad. Thanks again," Wes says, and then it's silent again.

At least I'll be in the water, I remind myself, and not choking for a breath in that cubicle.

Taylor

I HUG EM TIGHT TO my chest, pressing kisses to her face. "I love you," I whisper. I can't shake the bad feeling hounding me ever since Brad's reappearance this afternoon. Suddenly, I want to pack our stuff and run away again, but I know we can't. I need to face him this time. After trick-or-treating, we sat around the table eating chili. Me feeding it to Em and Sam making her laugh, so I could barely get a spoonful in. It all hit me: it's not fair that I have these moments with her and he doesn't.

Way to go, Tay. You really screwed up this time.

I lay her down in her crib and she searches for a pacifier and sticks it in her mouth. Every night, I swear I'm going to try to break her of that habit, but I don't want to take something away from her she apparently needs so much. Maybe because I know how horrible it is to live without what you want.

"She's fine, Tay." Sam appears at the bedroom door and I inch back. He usually stays on the couch when he's still here as I put her bed. It's terribly intimimate if both of us put her to bed.

"Ssssm," Em calls out, standing up in her crib. She holds out her pacifier, and when Sam tries to approach her, she puts it back into her mouth.

They have such an easygoing relationship that there have been times I've been jealous of it. He lays her back down and I can't help but envision this exact scenario with Brad. I always thought he'd be halfway to homeless by now. Never thought he'd clean his act up. With a sister who constantly promises but never delivers, it's something I've never considered. Brad did just that, and he showed up at my hospital asking for a second chance.

"I got it. Thank you, Sam." I bump my hip with his, scooting him out of the way. He tilts his head in confusion and then blows a kiss to Em before escaping the room.

"Good night, my little bug," I whisper and press my hand to her forehead. Those brown eyes peer up at me, and I see her lips curl around her pacifier. My hand smooths out her chestnut hair and she rolls over on her side.

I turn on the monitor and nightlight, sneaking out of the room.

Sam's waiting for me on the couch, his arm stretched above his head, watching a game of some sort. I see the exposed patch of his stomach and a trail of dark hair disappearing down to his jeans.

"So," he says, and I know he felt the tension when I pushed him away a minute ago.

I sit on the farthest cushion I can from him. He observes me with those hazel eyes, and his arms drop to his lap. "I guess

I should be going." He moves to stand, but I lean forward and touch his thigh. He freezes and relaxes back down.

"Sam." I take another breath. "I'm afraid I've put you in a bad position when it comes to Em and maybe us."

"I have no problem helping you, Tay. You owe me nothing." His words are always the same. He doesn't help me for payback, but I've always felt guilty for somehow taking advantage of his time and generosity. He has a life to live, and our situation only delays the fact that we both need to move on.

"You should have a date or party to go to, instead of being here with us," I say, and he huffs.

"I'm happy here." His eyes stay focused on the television and shame washes over me. *Can't I do anything right?* "You can't live your life for us, Sam. She's never coming back." By she, I mean my sister. God, he's tried to heal her, but she's gone, and I doubt we'll ever see her again.

"I'm not waiting for her to come home."

"Okay. That's good." I sit forward, crossing my legs. I catch his eyes looking over, and if I'm the woman I think I am, it's time for me to be completely honest with the man. "I'm telling Brad," I spit it out fast as if he won't catch it. That somehow it will ease the pain I'm sure he'll feel.

"I figured. Can I ask why?" From the hesitation in his voice, I know he's hurt. Tears prickle behind my eyes.

"It's not right. He should know."

"He didn't seem to care about you when he slept with that whore." I'm taken aback by the anger in his voice.

"I think, over the years, I've convinced myself he'd end up drinking and drugging himself to obliteration. Then once I found out he was engaged, I just figured he didn't care." I'm pouring my heart out here, and he flips around to face me.

"He's just going to hurt you, Tay. I'm not sure why you would put yourself through that."

"I'm not going back to him. But she's his daughter. It was his decision as to how he'd handle it, and I took that away from him, and I had no right." I turn to face him and his hand grabs mine on the back of the couch.

"I don't want him to hurt either one of you." Sincerity shines from his eyes, and I wish for the same thing I do almost every night. Why can't the heart take advice? Weigh the pros and cons? Because I know Sam's love has a ton more pros than cons, whereas I'm unsure about Brad's.

"He won't hurt me, and as far as Em, I have no control over it. Two and a half years ago, I thought, by stripping her away from him, I was saving her from the despair I was positive he would inflict on her, but I can't. Because as she gets older, she's going to ask."

"Oh, yeah, I guess I can see that." His hand lets go of mine. In this moment, I know he thought he'd fill that spot for her.

"I'm sorry, Sam."

He stands, straightening his jeans, and down to his work-boots. "You have nothing to apologize for. I should really get going." Without so much as a backward glance, he rounds the couch, grabs his jacket, and walks to the front door. "I'll pick her up from daycare after work tomorrow."

"It's okay, Sam. She has swimming lessons tomorrow."

"Do you want me to go with you? I know you hate having to get in the water."

Sure, let's bring up the ten pounds I'm self-conscious about, which I haven't been able to lose since Em was born.

"I want you to go out tomorrow. Don't worry about Em and me, okay?" I follow him to the door, and his knuckles turn white on the knob.

"I've never wanted anything different," he whispers. "Catch you later, Tay." He swings the door open, and the squeaking screen door opens and shuts behind him.

I watch his truck pull out of the driveway as I worry about him. He's a great man. He doesn't rev his engine or leave skid marks on the road as he speeds off in a trail of hurt. Instead, his truck slowly moves back, and he doesn't turn on his headlights until he isn't facing Em's bedroom anymore.

I shut the door and lean my back against it. "I'm a complete and utter bitch," I whisper to myself.

I venture back to the kitchen and busy myself with the dinner dishes as my phone, laying on the counter, plays havoc with me. I wonder if he has the same number, or if he's changed it. *No,* I think to myself, *I cannot contact him.* All those reasons I never told him I was pregnant rush to my mind, seeming like excuses now. Justifications for being spineless. Then a bowl slips from my wet hands and shatters to the floor, and I'm back in that room.

My eyes were blotchy and red from crying most of the day, because I knew Brad wasn't ready for a child. His dreams had just crashed around him weeks before, and it spun him into a tailspin, like a damn fighter jet hit by the enemy. He wasn't even looking for an eject button. He was happy to spin, uncontrolled, letting the alcohol and drugs kidnap him far away from everyone he loves, including me. Tanner had skipped walking in graduation and left for Colorado the week before. Their apartment was filled with fast food, empty cigarette boxes, and an array of beer and alcohol bottles.

Finally gaining the nerve to approach him after the fight we got into the night before over the cocaine I'd found, which he swore was someone else's, I used the key he'd given me a week earlier. The door softly opened and I dropped my purse on the breakfast bar. His Mustang was parked outside, so I figured he was home and probably asleep. In my mind, I imagined sliding into bed with him and finding some way to tell him we were going to be parents. The news would sober him, make him have something to live for.

I walked into his bedroom, and within a second, moans filled my ears. A blonde was straddling him as she rocked back and forth. My water bottle dropped from my grip and crashed to the floor with a bang. Brad sat up, his eyes glossy, his pupils pinholes. It wasn't the Brad I loved.

"Taylor," he mumbled, barely audible, and my heart shattered in my chest. This was it. The moment that sealed our love for good, and of course, Brad did it with finality. Didn't he always do everything over-the-top?

"I'm pregnant," I whispered. At least I think I did, but maybe I said it internally to myself, because after I fled the room, he never came after me.

Tears escaped my eyes, as my feet scurried out of the room. I grabbed my purse and slammed the door behind me. We graduated the next week, and he never even approached me. Just stood in line and got his diploma as though all was right in his life. Delaney and Ashby weren't that far apart in the line of graduates. Piper tried to talk to me to see what happened, but I just confirmed what she assumed. Her brother wasn't meant to be with one woman. Her brown eyes, a mirror image to Brad's, tried to figure it out, but with her being heartbroken over Tanner, she didn't fight it. Neither one of us believed much in love at that point.

Now I see her and Tanner on that laundry commercial—a happy couple ready to be wed. It's no doubt a sponsorship since he's going to the Olympics next year.

Reliving the single worst moment of my life is never good for my ego. I pick up my phone, and without thinking, I text.

Me: Can we meet tomorrow to talk?

I wait a few minutes, figuring his number would have changed.

Brad: Name the time . . .

Me: Seven o'clock

Brad: In the morning? I'm still not a morning person, but for you, it's worth it.

23

I press my hand to my stomach to demand it stop flipping.

Me: Evening. Come to my house. 6453 Valley Rd. in Roosevelt.

In my mind, I rationalize the situation. He'll meet Em, and then I'll put her to bed and we can talk about what will happen now.

Brad: Can we make it eight? I would normally ditch my commitment, but I promised someone.

Jealousy takes residence in me, wondering if it's another girl. Then I slap myself, because if he was seeing someone else, he wouldn't be coming after me, right?

Me: Sure. We can meet another day instead?

Brad: No. Tomorrow.

Me: See you then.

Brad: I'm sorry.

My thumbs rest on my screen and I have no idea what to type back.

Me: Me too.

Tomorrow will be the day he'll find out he's a dad and hate me for stealing over two years of his child's life from him.

three

Brad

THE OFFICE IS EERILY QUIET when I step through the glass doors. Liz, the snippy secretary, rolls her eyes. "Nice of you to show up." The twenty-year-old packs her plant in a box. Maybe her incompetence got her fired. Should I remind her now how she hit on me during her first month here? Nah, who gives a shit. After today, this place will be in my rearview mirror.

I weave past the abundance of men carrying desks and chairs to the elevator.

"What the . . . ?" I press my back to the wall as two guys carry Jim's, my boss, desk out of the corner office.

"Excuse us," the one says.

My eyes dart around the fourth floor office, noting the cubicle walls lined along the window and stacks of desks piled on top of one another on the opposite wall. I find my cubicle spot and see the only thing left is my latest Sport Illustrated, laying abandoned in the middle of the floor.

Dodging the men, I roll up the magazine and shove it in my back pocket.

"Brad?" Jim questions, as though I shouldn't have reported for work.

I break the distance between us and he waves me into what

25

used to be his plush corner office. Now, it resembles my college apartment when I moved out. Papers lie sporadically on the floor, and an array of paperclips were spilled in one corner; even the dust bunnies look confused on which way to clutter together.

"I hadn't expected you to return." Jim leans against the ledge of his office window.

"Did I turn in my notice?"

His eyes pierce into mine, not thrilled with my attitude.

"You've missed, what, five days in the last few weeks, and usually come in late or skip out other days." His suit sleeves pull as he crosses his arms over his chest.

"I've had a few personal problems."

"Maybe that's why you never made it to the Olympics. Can't commit."

This jackass is going to go there? By his lack of muscles, I'd say he shouldn't be pointing a finger to others for not pushing themselves.

"So, I'm guessing I'm fired." I change the subject before I add jail time to my list of regrets.

"No. You're laid off. We're moving to Chicago and only bringing a select few with us." My jaw drops to the floor, because somehow I'll bounce back on my feet, but what about Dylan?

Just as the worries for him flicker to mind, I hear his voice past the door. "No, I'll take that myself," he tells the movers and grabs one of his small plane models. I shake my head at how many hours he wastes putting all those things together. At least it appears he still has a job though.

"Sounds good, Jim." He stands right before I wave him off.

"Brad?" he calls out, but I ignore him, wanting to catch Dylan.

What more can Jim really say? The unemployment line will be waiting for me. I could stay around and let him insult me a little more, but fuck that. The asshole is a weak son of a bitch, who's enjoyed glaring down at me way too much over my short time here.

"Dyl," I holler, and he stops in his tracks, turning around.

His smile fades and he nibbles on the inside of his bottom lip.

"Don't bother feeling bad. It's probably for the best," I say, catching up to him in the hall.

"Still. It sucks. Not only do you lose your job, you lose your roommate."

Shit, I hadn't thought about that.

"It's good news for you though." I plaster on a fake smile. Not that I'm upset that he gets to keep his boring-ass desk job and I get the boot, but because he's finding his way and I'm still roaming around town trying to find a goddamn map.

His fingers thread through his wavy hair. "Yeah. I'm pretty stoked." He shrugs, but the perma smile on his face speaks much more than his timid eyes.

"You deserve it. You bust your ass here." I clasp him on the shoulder. "What about Bea?"

I no sooner ask and she appears—her blonde hair colored with pink tips for Breast Cancer Awareness month.

"Heard you didn't make the cut, sorry, Brad," she says with fake concern. Everyone knows Bea and I aren't exactly friends in any sense of the word. She's Piper's, my twin sister, best friend.

"At least you get a few hundred miles closer to my sister. However, I'll add again how happy she is with Tanner."

Her fake nails pinch the flesh of my arms, and I step out of her reach. "I'm not a lesbian, jackass."

"Really? Could have fooled me?" She narrows her hazel eyes like she's conducting some voodoo shit on me.

Honestly, I don't think she's a lesbian, but for some reason, it riles her up, and that's enjoyable to me.

"So, you guys are moving to Chicago?" I ask, raising one

eyebrow to Dylan.

He shrugs, and Bea's lips cringe like she ate a bug.

"Somehow we're both supposed to be working for the same person." Bea snatches a pad of Post-it notes from a departing box as a mover walks by.

"You can never have enough of these." She raises them in the air, and Dylan rolls his eyes.

"You can. I swear, if I get one more damn Post-it note on my office door . . ." He holds his model steady with one hand and digs out his phone with the other. "See this? You can text, email, and even call someone on it." He jiggles it and Bea seizes it from his grip.

Her thumbs quickly move through the screens.

"Whoa now," Dylan says, reaching for it, but Bea pivots, and unless Dylan wants to take a chance of losing his prized model, his hands are tied. "Help a brother out," he softly says to me.

I read over Bea's shoulder, but she turns on her heels again. The girl has better moves than most wide receivers in the NFL. "Who's Kali?" She raises her voice and enunciates the I.

"No one. Give me my phone back." He holds his hands out.

From what I know, Dylan and Bea aren't a couple, and not from Bea's lack of trying. It's Dylan holding up the process, and for the life of me, I can't figure out why. I might razz Bea, but she's a hot piece of ass. Too much of a smartass for me, but Dylan and her have this odd turn-on with it. I could ask Dylan why he hasn't tapped that, but I don't give a shit. If Dylan wants to talk about it, he knows where to find me.

"She wants to meet you before you leave for Chicago."

I shake my head at Bea for intruding on Dylan's text messages.

"What? It popped up when it was in my hands." She holds her hands up in the air in a defensive pose.

"It's not her." Dylan speaks only to Bea, and suddenly I'm caught in what should be a private conversation.

"I think you're lying." She turns her eyes to me—sad eyes with a hint of anger. "Sorry you got the boot, Brad, but I figure you can find someone else to bug the shit out of at a new company you never show up for. See you, boys." She waves and grabs a slice of pizza from another co-worker walking down the hallway.

"Bea." Dylan's voice actually sounds like a lost baby calling after their mother. Pussy.

She never turns around, and the last we see is her finger up in the air.

"I'm guessing that's directed at you," I say, and Dylan scoffs.

"I don't want to talk about it." He turns on his heels, heading back to his empty area. "We'll talk tonight about another roommate."

Quickly, I'm alone in a hallway of a company that had just fired me. Oh, sorry, laid off. But that's okay; I've got better things to do.

SIX HOURS LATER, THE HUMIDITY and smell of chlorine wraps me in a blanket and calmness fills my veins. This is where I'm meant to be. Not in some stuffy cubicle smelling tuna fish from my cubicle mate's lunch.

Wes is waiting on me by the time I walk out of the locker room. My trunks feel restrictive because I'm used to speedos, but no need for that today.

No matter how much I push the thought of meeting Taylor tonight as far away as possible, it keeps resurfacing. She shocked me so much with that text, I almost thought it was a prank from Dylan. I googled the address right away. Taylor's done well in the past two years. She lives a small two-bedroom house. From the bird's-eye view, it's cute with perfectly trimmed shrubs around the front door; it suits her. I can't deny the twinge of jealousy I felt in my heart when I saw the life she's made for herself. I guess it was both jealousy and relief that I didn't scar her forever.

"Ready?" Wes pats my back, and I smile over at him.

"Yeah. I saw the schedule you texted me. So four lessons. My last one's at seven?" I clarify, because as much as I'm convincing myself I've got this whole thing with seeing Taylor tonight under control, there's no way I want to screw up and be late.

"Yep. Today's the younger kids, but some of the other days you'll have older kids where you can work with them more." He goes into the glassed off office and I follow.

"The younger ones? How young are we talking? Five, six?"

"Try eighteen months." He scans a sheet of paper on his desk and sits down.

Seriously, that young? I'm not even sure I know what do with a kid that young. Maybe I'm not built for this job.

"Oh, wait." He raises up his head, and I'm thankful he's wrong about the age. "You have a cancelation. Yeah, your five o'clock cancelled and re-scheduled for next week." He swivels around in his chair. "Sorry, man, that leaves you a gap, but I'm sure you can find something to do."

He stands and makes his way to the door. "Wes, hold up?"

He turns around, leaning on the table covered in forms. "What's up?"

"I got laid off today, so I can pick up extra lessons if need be." Although the thought of holding a baby in the water scares me a bit, I have no other choice. With no job and a roommate soon to ditch town, I'll need the money.

"Really?" His eyes light up, and I'm hoping this is a good thing. "Actually, I've been debating on starting a younger team. Usually I only do eight and up, but I have some seven-year-olds who I think can start training to compete.

I rub my hands together. The excitement already buzzing in me. "I'm game."

He chuckles. "Good. Let me get it organized."

His hand touches the door handle and I think about babies in water and what the hell I'm supposed do with them.

"Wes?" I call out before thinking my question all the way through.

He turns around, a question in his eyes.

"How do I teach a baby to swim?"

He laughs that hearty laugh again and shuts the door before taking a seat in the unoccupied chair across from me. "All you have to do is get them used to the water. Make them comfortable without drowning them."

I nod, while my insides knot into tight balls. I try to grasp onto that cocky arrogance of mine, but still, the thought of holding a slippery baby in my arms scares the ever-loving daylights out of me.

"Relax, you'll do great." He smiles, and this time he does leave out the door. I sit in the solitude of the office and wonder how I got here, especially when I should be training for the Olympics.

I wish the sadness that encompasses me would leave. One day, the fact that I'll never be an Olympic swimmer should sink in. A guy can hope.

Not about to sit around and continue to wallow in self-pity for myself, I walk out to the pool. Wes is busy on the sidelines of the lap section, hollering at his team. Watching the bodies skim the surface at a fast pace almost makes me revisit my younger days. But I shake it off before the feeling of loss consumes me again.

"Brad." Cami walks up to me with a mom and a baby. "This is your four o'clock."

I turn and my heart pounds in my chest. The boy is so small, and *is that a diaper around him?* "Hi," I greet, swallowing my fear.

The mom's eyes scan my body. I'm sure I'm a hell of a lot better looking than her husband, so I'll let her take full advantage. "I'm Brad." I hold my hand out, and by the time she sees it, her face is flushed.

"Hi. I'm Melanie and this is Austin." She points to the baby, whose hands are being swallowed by his mouth.

Great.

She holds Austin out to me, and I almost deny the drooling little bugger. There's no way she should trust me to hold her pride and joy on concrete.

I clench my fists for a second, willing them to stop shaking as I take Austin from her arms.

"Hey, buddy. You ready to get in the water?" I ask, and his mouth releases his hand only so his bottom lip can quiver.

"Brad," Cami steps closer, whispering in my ear, "Try to pull him to your chest. Holding him at arm's length is scaring him."

My eyes snap to his mom, and the look of fear in hers alarms me. I bring Austin to my chest and his grubby fingers begin to play with the small hairs on my chest. It's still odd to have those after shaving my body for so long due to competing.

"Right." I smile, and the mom returns a tight hesitant one back, her body tense.

I walk him over to the stairs of the pool and his mom wanders over to the bench, I'm sure to watch me like a hawk with her young.

The warm water swooshes around my legs as I move through it. Austin's fingers dip down and I'm thankful he's not one of those kids who scream bloody murder as soon as their toes touch water.

The more I allow him to let the water move through his fingers, the more relaxed we both become. I gain confidence, and with every smile, I become more comfortable.

Obviously, Melanie feels the same since she's now busy

on her phone. I take the opportunity to plunge the two of us in the water. Maybe too soon, because when I bring Austin back up, tears are streaming down his face and his little hands are splashing the water.

I'm not sure where the instinct comes from, but I draw him into my chest and circle us around the water, making small waves. His fingers grab onto my ears and he squeals in delight.

Thank fuck it worked.

I hand Austin back to his mom at the end of our lesson, and Melanie's hand strokes my arm.

"Thank you so much, Brad. He's never done so well in the water."

I'm positive she's lying, but I'll take the compliment.

"He's a great kid."

She smiles and walks toward the locker room. Her eyes glance over her shoulder one last time before she disappears through the door.

"An admirer?" a feminine voice says behind me, and I turn to find my next lesson.

"Hello." I hold my hand out for the attractive girl. She's in her early-twenties with red hair and knockout tits.

She's holding a baby in her arms. This one is squirming, and I fear she's about to drop her.

"Brad, I presume?"

"Yours truly." I hold my arms out. "Is this," I glance down at the sheet on the clipboard, "Ava?"

"No, Quinn." I tilt my head and check my clipboard. "I have an Ava next." I scan the few names, and there's no Quinn.

"Oh, Ava." She lets out a flirtatious giggle. "This is Ava." The little girl raises her hand. "I'm Quinn," she introduces herself and lets the little girl down so she can shake my hand, but the girl runs over to the water.

"Ava," I call out, but the girl doesn't stop.

"I guess we're starting the lesson," I say, having no choice but to ignore Quinn's outstretched hand.

"She's a handful," she yells out.

I think I figured that much out.

Ava is bold enough that I don't have to worry about getting her used to the water. She has no problem going under, rather she actually enjoys it. The girl never stops laughing and splashing. If her mom's eyes would just stop looking at me as if I'm a decadent piece of chocolate cake after a long stretch of dieting, I'd say she's my favorite client. Usually, I enjoy a good-looking woman's eyes on me, but Quinn is creepy. She doesn't even turn around when I catch her staring.

"Down!" Ava screams and I dunk her again. I'll need to do more research on how to move another step ahead when the babies are ready. I'll call my sister, Piper. She's been taking classes for instruction in Colorado. The nerd she is, I'm sure she has some helpful tips.

Wes sits down on the ledge of the pool and I watch the boys file to the locker room. Jealousy zips through me because I would much rather instruct a swim team than a bunch of babies.

"Hey, you're five-thirty is coming in early. So your gap will be later."

"Okay." It doesn't really matter to me either way.

"You're doing good," he says, and I cock my head at him, while Ava smacks my cheek.

"It's my dream in life to get hit by little kids."

He laughs and nods toward Quinn.

"I see you met the nanny," he says, a smirk evident across his lips.

"Nanny? I never got that far when this one decided she was ready."

"Yeah, she sure seems to like you. Warning, she's only eighteen." My head instinctively moves her way. Her eyes bore into mine, no care that I caught her. Then I look back at Wes.

"No worries, man. I'm taken."

"Long distance? You're here every night; I just assumed

you were single."

"I am." Ava hits me again, and I dunk her. She comes up laughing.

He tilts his head, clear confusion in his eyes.

"I'm trying to get my ex back." I'm not sure why I'm telling Wes this, but he doesn't know my past, Taylor's and my history, which is nice for a change.

The others don't think I hear their tones, the one that insinuates Taylor might be better off without me, and they don't even know I cheated on her. I've kept that hidden because I'm too ashamed to admit it. Tanner's the only one who knows, and if he's the best friend I think he is, he hasn't shared that piece of information with anyone.

"Then you shouldn't be here so much. Win her over somehow." He glances over his shoulder. "Cami was my ex once and look at us."

"Really?" I give Ava a toy to put in the water and pull back out.

"Yeah. We were young, and I didn't want to commit to just her. We broke up, and then I heard she was dating someone else, so I went after her. The hurt Cami buried was tough to get through, but we did." The bastard smiles so wide, jealousy ignites in me. "Don't hold back, just go for her."

"Thanks. I'm going over to her house tonight."

He pulls his feet from the water and moves to stand. "That's a great start." He smiles. "Good luck, man."

My eyes veer to the office and I see Cami standing there, talking to another instructor. Her eyes lock with Wes's for a second, and he's like a magnet, walking directly to her. Taylor used to look at me like that, as if I was a fucking rock star and she couldn't believe I was hers. One look from her made me come alive.

Pushing back the past, knowing she won't be looking at me like that tonight, I swim over to the side and hold Ava out to Quinn.

"She did great. See you next week," I say, and Quinn takes Ava in her arms.

"You're great," she says, her eyes not leaving mine for a second.

"Thank you."

"No, I mean really, you are so good with her."

I smile again. "Thank you."

She pushes out her tits to me a little more, but I turn my eyes in another direction.

"See you next week, Ava." I disregard Quinn. Eighteen, fuck that. Even if I wasn't after Taylor, that's way too young.

Quinn stands and straightens her back before walking away. Her ass sways back and forth as she steadily makes her way to the locker room. The door swings open, almost hitting Quinn in the face. I snicker to myself at the look of disgust she gives the person. The two must exchange words, and then my heart plummets to my stomach, and my breathing stops altogether.

Taylor steps through the doors, holding a little girl in her arms. I watch in awe as she saunters up to Wes and Cami. Cami reaches for the girl and spins her around in a circle while Wes talks with Taylor. Taylor swipes her long dark hair off her shoulder, listening intently to whatever Wes is saying.

My whole body freezes in the pool, unable to move a muscle. She's breathtakingly beautiful and still has that self-assured posture that made me want her from the start.

Wes turns and my heart slams against my ribs. Her eyes find me and panic flares in those blue beauties. As I stare at her, her eyes quickly dart to the little girl. She shakes her head adamantly and says something to Wes, and at the same time, she plucks the girl from Cami's arms.

My feet move through the water, and Taylor backs up toward the locker room. Wes tries to reach for her, but Taylor shakes her head. Cami's eyes volley between me and her. The little girl starts crying, and I'm guessing it's from how hard

Taylor has her face pressed into her jacket.

Taylor looks at me with a small shake of her head, but I'm not staying away this time. Then she turns around and bolts to the locker room.

four

Taylor

MY HEART POUNDS AS I run to the locker room. Em cries in my arms and I hate how this whole situation is affecting her. If my keys weren't locked in the locker with my purse, I'd have escaped this place by now.

"Taylor." His deep voice sends a tingle throughout my body.

I unlock the locker and grab my purse before throwing Em's coat over her small body. She tosses it to the floor, and I bend down to pick it up. My fingers reach for the down fabric and his feet appear right next to it. As I grasp it, my eyes skim up his near-naked body. I take in his strong calves, now covered in dark hair, and his taut waist, rising up into a chest of chiseled, contoured muscles. Our eyes lock, and his bear nothing but confusion.

That easy smile I had grown used to years ago isn't there, but the lines on the outside of his eyes are becoming evident, showing the passage of time. We're no longer the young, carefree college kids we used to be.

"Mama," Em screams, and I'm jarred back to Earth.

"It's okay, baby," I soothe her, my hand holding her protectively against my chest. I look to Brad as he steps closer.

"Taylor?" he repeats.

My heart breaks. I don't want to tell him he's a father in the middle of this locker room. I had the whole thing planned for later this evening. Having Em's usual swim instructor quit and finding her father as the replacement wasn't part of the plan.

"I can't," I stutter, backing up while he steps forward.

"Who is that?" he asks, and I'm fairly sure we both know the answer, but he's willing to act ignorant on my behalf.

"Can you just come over tonight as planned?" I take another step, and my back presses against the hard wall. Brad moves closer, and the smell of chlorine coming off his body is sweet torture. Reminding me of all those late nights when he'd promised me I was the only one.

"Who is the girl, Taylor?" He's careful to move slowly as he inches closer, but remains far enough away as not to scare Em, who's still tucked against me.

I swallow, feeling my pulse quicken. "Please, Brad."

"No. Answer me." His voice is casual and sweet; however, there's authority in it as well. He's not going to let this go.

The words are about to come out of my mouth when Em peeks out from under my chin like a joey kangaroo out of their mother's pouch. Brad steps back, distancing himself from us as his eyes widen with disbelief.

"This is Em . . . well, Emerson actually."

Seeing the man is not a threat, Em sits up more on my hip, intrigued about who he is. Could it be instinctive?

"Her eyes," he softly says. The similarity in their eyes isn't hard to miss. The gold flecks are a little more prominent in Em's, but warmth shines from both. The long lashes only seal their commonality.

I inhale a breath, grasping for an ounce of courage, which I'm not sure I have. "She's . . ." The words lock in my throat.

"Mine," he finishes for me. Although there's certainty in his tone, his voice breaks over the one word.

"I'm sorry," I say, unsure of why the hurt in his eyes is

affecting me to the point I'm apologizing, when he's the one who ruined us.

His bare feet back up another step, and then his eyes finally leave Em and meet mine, switching from confusion to disgust. "How could you not tell me?"

His retreat has my arms tightening around Em, as though I can protect her from her father, who isn't so enamored by her he swoops her up in his arms. Those few steps back spurs a rage so fierce, I want to run away and hide her in a tower, so she never experiences the sting of rejection.

"I told you," I say. He might have been drunk and my voice might have been soft, but I did tell him.

"I think I'd remember you telling me." He crosses his arms over his impressive chest and widens his stance.

"You were high on either drugs or alcohol and too busy scooting the blonde off your lap."

Em's hand reaches for my necklace, playing with it. I'm thankful she's distracted. The diamond and emerald necklace is the last possession of my mother's that my sister didn't sell. Em always enjoys how the diamonds shine in the light.

"You could have—"

"Could have what, Brad? Stuck around to watch the two of you . . ." I glance to Em, "finish?"

He winces. *Yeah, the truth hurts.* "I tried to see you after."

"You tried once, Brad. One time, and you were still high as a kite on my doorstep."

His head drops between his shoulders, shaking lightly back and forth. "I was in a bad place."

"I know, and that's why I made the choice I did."

"Which was to deceive me." His eyes fly up to meet mine again.

"My only option was to raise my daughter with love. You wouldn't have stuck around, and eventually, you would have resented me."

"No, I—" He stops, because we both know it's the truth.

41

Two and a half years ago, Brad would have never wanted to settle down. I doubt he wants to now. He's always chasing something, and it was a hard lesson to learn.

The locker room doors open and a family shuffles through, looking between us.

"I should go." I glance at Em and Brad agrees with a nod. *Some things never change.*

"Can I still come by tonight?" he asks.

My body stiffens as I think about him being a part of her life now. Suddenly, my decision to tell him seems worse than any choice I've ever made where Em is concerned. I'm not sure I can share her. Then, without knowing what's going on, Em reaches for him, and my heart shatters and soars at the same time.

He takes it, and her little hand gets buried in his larger one. A smile creases his lips, getting wider the longer he admires her.

"Hi, Emerson," he says.

She looks at me then back to him. "Hi." Her voice so small and low, but interest fills hers eyes. She wants to know who he is.

"You have our address," I tell him, shifting her to my other hip, ultimately making their hands separate.

Brad nibbles on the inside of his cheek, watching me back step to the door.

"I'll be there." He waves. "Bye, Emerson."

"Bye." She smiles as her small hand goes up in a wave of her own.

I exit through the locker room doors, glad to have a reprieve, to suck in oxygen not shared by Brad. There's relief that the secret's out. He knows he's a father, and he didn't run away, which is what I had imagined would happen when I thought about this moment. Could he have changed? The old Brad would have, at least, had to process the information before dealing with such a serious revelation.

Setting Em on the chair, I throw on her leggings and wrap her coat around her.

"Swim!" she screams, and I shake my head.

"No swim today," I whisper.

"SWIM!" She becomes louder, and I know from prior experience, she's about to have a meltdown.

"Not today, baby."

"SWIM!" Her voice rises another octave, alarming the girl behind the desk.

"Taylor." Cami walks out of the locker room.

"Hi, Cami. Sorry. I'll pay for today, but we're not going to have the lesson."

"I know Em really liked Kevin, but Brad's good. He has a lot of experience."

Do I even bother telling her?

"It's not that. It's just—"

"SWIM!" Em yells again, and my face flushes with embarrassment.

"See, she wants to swim." Cami holds her hands out and Em immediately goes to her.

"Cami." I try to stop her, but she trudges through the locker room doors.

"Come on, Taylor. I'll make sure Brad does a great job."

I follow the spunky girl with my daughter, not stopping at the lockers this time. I'll have all my belongings should I need to hightail it out of here. Under different circumstances, I'd grab my daughter and never return, but Cami was my sister's friend since childhood. We've been through a lot over the years. Unfortunately, she knows Em's the product of a college relationship gone bad, but she doesn't know that the man is now her employee.

Brad's leaning on a table with his ankles crossed casually while talking to Wes when we appear again. For some reason, I thought I'd shaken his world up by telling him he's a father. Confusion swarms inside me as I wonder what he's expecting from Em. Either he's indifferent, making that the reason he can stand there unfazed, calmly, as though I'd just told him Em was a little girl I was babysitting. Or he's confident, and figures he'll patch everything up.

Cami approaches, holding Em out to him.

"Your next client," she says, and Brad, having no choice, holds Em out at arm's length, studying her from afar. I almost chime in and pinpoint each of his feature our daughter has. Her lips, her cheekbones, and even the lobes of her ears are all him. Sadly, she only has my nose and hairline.

"I thought. . . ." His eyes seek me out, and they still make my heart gallop in my chest. I nod slightly, and he rests Em on his hip.

"You ready?" he asks her.

"SWIM!" she yells, and he chuckles.

"Okay." He looks back at me one more time for approval and I nod again.

He kidnaps her to the water. At least that's what I refer to it as, because she's my baby and I can already tell he could very well be the person she's calling out for in the middle of the night. Maybe it's true that there's an unbroken bond between parents and children.

"See, she likes him." Cami places a hand on my shoulder and I sidestep. I fear telling her the truth of who Brad is because I can see her firing him, and there must be a reason he's teaching swimming lessons. He was working at some advertising agency not that long ago. Google has been my friend over the years when it's come to checking up on Brad Ashby. I'm guessing I didn't cross his mind since he knows nothing about me or his daughter.

"Yeah," I mumble. Wes eyes me for a second. He suspects something, but I'm going to ignore him with the hope that, if I give him nothing to work with, he'll let the subject drop.

"We have to go," Cami says, pulling me in for a hug. "He's a hottie, and I'm positive he's single," she whispers in my ear.

I hate the feeling of being deceitful. Why do I care if Brad needs this job? I should just blurt it out. Hell, I need the friendly advice she would give me.

Wes comes out of the office with his keys in his hand. "We're going to Carroll's later if you want to join us."

My eyes scan Brad, who's currently handing Em a ring to play with.

"I have Em."

"Ask Sam or find a babysitter. You should get out more, Tay," Wes says.

"One day I'll have a life again. You guys have fun." They nod. Cami leaves to talk to Brad, and I'm alarmed when Wes wraps his arms around me. That same cologne he wore in high school is embedded into his white T-shirt. We went on one date when we were seniors, and I'm fairly certain it was to make Cami jealous. Needless to say, nothing happened, except I was left at a party while he drove off to chase after her.

"Try to hide the fact that you still love him," he whispers, and my body tenses, but his hand rubs up and down my spine. "It's him, isn't it?" he asks, and a tear falls down my cheek. "I won't tell Cami yet, but you'll have to eventually." He pulls back and his hands grip my upper arms, holding me steady. "I hope, for his sake, he's changed. I'd hate to beat the ass of someone I consider a friend." He laughs and I discreetly rub away my tears.

"Thanks, Wes," I say, and he nods. Cami's busy helping Em get acquainted with Brad, but from what I'm witnessing, Em's just fine, smiling up to her—Brad.

"Talk to me anytime."

I nod.

"Babe!" he calls out. "Time."

Cami ruffles Em's dark hair, which has yet to be wet.

"Coming," she says. When she reaches us, she kisses my cheek before the two of them leave me stranded alone with Brad.

The locker room doors slam with a bang and my eyes scan the pool area. There's a father sitting on the bench waiting for his child's lesson with another instructor. A group of gossiping moms are huddled together on the other end while their girls and boys swim in the group lesson.

Brad and Em are busy getting used to one another. I notice she still hasn't been dunked, and I wonder what Brad's intentions on teaching her really are. Does he even know what he's doing with a twenty-two month old?

I mosey on over to the bench and drop my bags next to me. The father looks over and smiles.

"Hi," I politely say. He's new or his wife usually comes, because I've never seen him here before. Then again, Sam brings Em sometimes too.

Brad hasn't let go of Em once, nor has he taught her anything. I look up at the clock and see it's only ten minutes into the lesson. I watch his biceps bulge from the small weight of Em in his arms. His jaw's more chiseled than years before. I've never seen his body with hair on it, but it suits him. Nicely.

"Is that your daughter?" The father scoots next to me, and I back up for some personal space.

"Yes," I answer, hoping that's the end of our conversation. Doesn't he know I'm busy ogling my ex's more mature and developed body?

"That's my son. It's my week to have him."

I smile and nod. "That's nice."

"His mom is a real bear." He looks down at my hand, his eyes lighting up when he notices there's no ring. "How's your ex?"

Right in front of you.

I gage Brads smiling face, blowing bubbles in the water to Em. He's treating her like a porcelain doll.

"He's not really involved in our lives too much."

"Oh." He slides back over to his side.

I'm sorry, is that code for something I don't know about?

But I don't ask any questions, because he's gone and I prefer it that way.

Brad's eyes glance in my direction, and I bite back my smile, hoping he caught the dad interested and maybe he's jealous a guy was showing me attention.

"You know she's been taking lessons since she was six months," I holler over to Brad, and he swims the two of them over to my side of the pool.

"She has?" Shock flutters on his face.

"Yeah. Cami was her teacher first, then Wes, and finally Kevin before you. You can dunk her," I urge him, but he cringes.

"Maybe next lesson." His hopeful eyes question mine, asking me if there will be a next time.

"Do it, Brad. She's great." I push the issue more.

"Nah. Next time."

"No, now," I urge, and he cocks his head at me, probably wondering what I'm trying to do.

"Okay." He gradually lowers her under the water and pops her back up.

She squeals in delight, and Brad chuckles.

"Again," Em says, and he obliges.

He looks over to me and smiles. "Thank you." He nods and the two continue on.

I watch them for the remaining fifteen minutes, trying to concentrate more on Em than Brad, but it's hard. Every time his eyes find mine, my heart flutters and I'm thrown off my stable axis again. How can he still have this effect on me after all this time?

Another parent comes over, checking the schedule, and I already know it's Tyler. He's right after us. Sadness washes over me that our time with Brad is over. Brad will never be ours, what am I saying? Never will he be a constant in our life, and I need to remember that if he sticks around to raise our daughter. Brad has the capacity to leave us high and dry in the middle of the night. He's not one for commitment.

He swims her over, placing her on the edge of the pool.

"My next appointment is here." He eyes Tyler and his mom.

"I saw." I wrap Em's princess towel around her.

"I'll see you tonight." His eyes never leave Em.

"Yep."

"Bye, Emerson," he says, holding his hand up for a high five.

She steps forward and hits his hand with hers.

"Bye."

I pick her up.

"Bye, Brad," I say, balancing all our bags on my shoulder.

"Bye, Taylor." His voice quivers.

How is it just as heartbreaking to walk away from him now as it was before?

five

Brad

I DRIVE MY TRUCK DOWN the streets of Roosevelt. I spy
Wes's Camaro parked out front of some tavern in the downtown area. My palms are sweaty and my heart thumps against
the wall of my chest. I press on the gas a little harder in my
eagerness to get to Taylor's.

I think I'm still absorbing the fact that I'm a dad. Tonight,
I'll get to the bottom to why Taylor thought it was okay to keep
her from me all this time. I've missed two years of my daughter's life. It's hard not to be angry, but at the same time, a small
part of me understands Taylor's reasoning. I was a different
person back then, and I'm not sure what would have happened
if she'd told me. That's considering she would have found me
sober and coherent at some point.

My GPS tells me I've reached my destination, and I pull
along the curb, spotting her beat-up Jetta in the driveway. It's
a small house, but the cute Halloween decorations in the yard
show how homey Taylor probably makes the house for the two
of them.

I climb out of my truck, shoving my phone in the pocket
of my jeans. My footsteps drag because I'm not sure I have the
strength to deal with this. Trudging up the asshole I was two
years ago isn't a pleasant thought, but if I want Taylor back,

along with a daughter I just discovered, I have to man up and talk this shit out.

My shaky finger reaches for the doorbell, but the door opens before it connects.

Taylor stands there in jeans and a sweater, different than the scrubs she was wearing earlier. Her hair is pulled in a messy ponytail on the top of her head, but her make-up is still flawless. Her rosy lips make me want to kiss her until we're both desperate for air. She's perfect and gorgeous as always.

Em squeals from behind her and Taylor opens the screen door.

"Come in," she says, her hand urging me inside.

"Thanks." I slip off my boots, and she shuts the door behind us, flicking the lock.

Em is sitting on the floor, playing with some toy that sings over and over again. Taylor walks over and switches a button on the toy, softening the noise. "You'll thank me later when the song replays over and over in your head."

"I think I can thank you now." I stand there, still in shock that my daughter is sitting at my feet.

"Do you want anything to drink?" she yells on her way to what I assume is the kitchen.

Beer is the first thing that comes to mind, but I shouldn't drink around my daughter, right? "Water would be great," I answer.

She comes back into the room, her ponytail swinging back and forth. Her face bears no smile. She hands me the water and our fingers brush as it changes hands. Electricity surges between us.

"Come sit." She ushers me to the couch, and I look at Em and then back to her. "She's fine. Everything is childproofed here."

She falls to the couch, tucking one leg under the other.

I mimic her, my eyes watching Emerson. Her face lights up and she giggles each time the toy drops through the hole.

"She likes that one?"

Taylor nods. "She likes all her toys, but that's her favorite."

I watch in awe, unable to tear my eyes away from her, searching for myself in her every mannerism. She's beautiful, just like her mom, the one who's now staring right at me.

"I don't want to talk about it with her here," I say, the words escaping my mouth before I can process them through a filter.

"Okay." She accepts my wishes. "She's ready for bed. Do you want to come up with me and read her a bedtime story?"

"Yeah. I'd like that." I stand as she bends down to pick her up. She's so at ease with her, every muscle probably trained to hold the weight of our daughter. Em whimpers, but Taylor continues on her path.

"Tomorrow, baby girl. Now, it's sleep time," she tells our little girl.

I follow them up the stairs and notice no pictures fill the walls. In my house when I was growing up, it was overflowing with pictures of me and Piper. Taylor turns right at the top of the stairs, stepping over a box in front of the door.

"Sorry, I haven't gotten to clean up here this week," she excuses a non-existent mess.

Still, no pictures occupy the wall space, and I wonder why there aren't any personal decorations. Back in college, Taylor had her damn high school tassel hanging from a corkboard filled with pictures of her high school friends. She'd rushed to get our first picture framed, and I hung it on her wall for her. So, now, with a daughter, why would those pictures in frames not adorn every wall for everyone to see?

The white crib sits against the far wall, and "Emerson" is hung in pink letters above it. The whole room is decorated in gray and pink. Taylor stands next to rocking chair in the corner, holding Em in her arms.

"Go ahead and sit," she instructs. Once I'm seated, she positions Em on my lap and hands me *Goodnight, Gorilla*. "This is her favorite right now."

I wonder how many other favorites I've missed. I tamp down the anger that wants to rise out of my throat. Taylor isn't the only one to blame for the awkward position we're now in.

Emerson rests her head on my chest and her legs splay out on my lap. She stares up at me, waiting for me to start reading, but my voice catches in my throat from the unbelievable feeling of love that's brimming inside of me.

I start reading the story, and she laughs at the gorilla sneaking the keys, and when I change the voices of the animals, she laughs harder. I close the book and she plucks it out of my hand. "Again," she says.

I look over to Taylor, who shakes her head in amusement. She gives me the green light to read it another time. So I do. Another three times, actually.

"Okay, Emelem, it's time for bed." Taylor plucks her from my lap, and I miss the weight of her small body on my legs instantly. "Give Brad a hug." She holds Em out to me and her small arms wrap around my neck loosely. I deny the urge to tighten my hold and never let her go.

I'm in love with a child I met only hours before.

Taylor lays her down and Emerson rolls onto her side, facing the back of the crib quickly. Taylor busies herself turning on a nightlight and some lullabies from the stereo in the corner.

I lean against the wall, watching the mother in Taylor go about a routine she thinks nothing about, I'm sure. It's amazing that she's raised her all these years without any help.

"Let's talk." She walks down the hall, shuffling a box into a corner. My eyes intently watch her ass as we walk down the stairs. How I loved it when my hands molded to her hips as she rocked back and forth on me.

She sits back down on the couch and switches on a white box; instantly, I hear Emerson's cooing and her light lullabies through the speaker.

Taylor's back straightens and she inches closer to the far

corner of the couch. "Speak your peace, Brad," she says—defensively, I might add.

"I get why you did it, but all these years, did you ever think about contacting me?" I ask the question the way I'd practiced on the way over—calm, cool, and collected.

"I did, but I was worried you wouldn't want this responsibility, or worse, you'd hurt her." Her consistent honesty is refreshing, and I'm glad she didn't lose it. Otherwise, we'd be beating around the bush right about now.

"I'm not your father," I grind out.

"I know, but I also know what it's like to have a father who despises you."

Taylor was honest when we'd dated, but she wasn't an open book. Little things here and there, and I put the puzzle of her childhood together, but I'd get just shy of the final piece, and she'd shut down. Her dad's an alcoholic, and her mom died when she was young. Her sister would show up on campus occasionally, but never stayed more than one night. The only other thing I knew was that she hated her small town, so imagine my surprise when I found out she came back here after graduation.

"Was it because of Emerson that you came back here?"

Her eyes stare intently at the bottle of water in her hands. "I needed help."

A sharp pain jabs through my chest.

"I wish you'd have come to me. At least at some point." I fiddle with my own bottle.

"I am sorry for that, Brad, but you destroyed me that day."

My eyes remain down, unwilling to see the hurt I assume is flashing from hers.

"I'm sorry. You shouldn't forgive me, but, Taylor, I wasn't me then. I was so upset about the Olympics, I went into this tunnel of depression."

"Brad—"

"No, Taylor, let me get this out. I don't even know half the shit I did then. Most of it is a blur. It started with enhancement drugs, and then when I didn't make it, my dealer gave me some harder stuff when I asked to not be in the present." I scoot closer, needing to look in her eyes when I apologize. "I understand if you never forgive me for cheating on you." She winces, but I hold her eyes. "I had to give this a chance, because you are my future. I was positive of it then, and I'm positive of it now."

"I won't keep Em from you." A tear drips down her cheek.

"Taylor, I came here before I even knew Emerson existed. I want both of you," I beg, but I see in her eyes she's shutting down. Her lips are shut tight, and she doesn't believe me.

"It's not just my heart I'm risking, Brad." I cradle her head in my hand, thankful she's letting me touch her. Her skin is warm under my touch. My thumb brushes away the tears dripping down her cheek.

"I know, but I promise you are both in good hands."

She shakes her head and her eyes once again move to the bottle, but she doesn't pull away from me. "I wish I could believe you. There was a time I believed in us, but that time is long gone."

I urge her face back up, so she's meeting my eyes. "Give me time to prove myself."

"I don't know." The fact she hasn't moved and my lips are mere inches from hers tells me she still feels our connection.

"One week."

This grabs her attention.

"All I need is one week to make your feelings for me resurface and prove to you I'm not going anywhere."

"I can't promise anything," she relents, but at the same time, there's a knock on the door.

She slides back and my hand falls from her face.

"Are you expecting someone?" I ask.

She shakes her head no and rises to her feet.

"I'll get it," I say, beating her up and making my way to the door.

"Brad, you don't have to be protective of us. We're in Roosevelt." She follows right behind me, and I look through the peephole.

A tall guy with a John Deere cap low over his eyes stands on the porch. A big jacket covers up his upper body, and worn in jeans with a pair of work boots clothe his lower half. Taylor unlocks and opens the door without even looking.

My hand splays on the door and I shut it before it fully opens.

"You're going to open the door without looking?"

The one side of her lip quirks up. "You just looked through the peephole. I'm fairly sure if there's a man with an axe, you'd have said something."

The knob twists in her hand, but my hand holds it firmly closed.

"It's some guy with a John Deere hat." Her lip turns down.

"Tay," a guy slurs on the other side of the door. "Open up, Tay."

I remove my hand and she opens it up, ignoring my objection. The man falls into the house, landing on his face.

"Friend of yours?" I ask. She peers out the screen door, waves to a truck. It then pulls away, and I'm guessing there's more than one reason for her apprehension and her hesitation to give us another chance.

"This is Sam."

"That's me," the man raises his hand. "That hurt."

Taylor kneels down and helps him sit up. He leans against the staircase and rubs the tip of his nose.

"You reek," she says, waving her hand in front of her face. He captures it and kisses the top. My veins explode with rage.

"Marry me?" He laughs, but anyone can tell he's dead serious from the admiration overflowing his eyes.

She pulls her hand away, and looks at me nervously. "Sam is my brother-in-law," she informs me, and I shove my hands in my pockets. Sam looks at me, judging and appraising my size. I'm doing the same, but a little more discreetly since I'm not drunk off my ass.

"Oh, I forgot the deadbeat was coming over tonight."

I inhale a deep breath, hold it, and count to ten before I lose all control and beat the shit out of him in front of the girl he loves.

"Sam, don't say that." Taylor gets up and grabs her bottle of water, handing it to him. "Have some water."

He takes it easily from her hands and starts drinking.

"I should probably go," I say, moving to grab my jacket hanging on the knob of the staircase.

"Back to wherever you came from," Sam sneers.

"Excuse me?" I turn around, but Taylor shakes her head, and I clench my fists at my sides.

"You obviously prefer blondes, right?" He grabs a strand of Taylor's dark hair. "She's a brunette now, so beat it." He stumbles to his feet and Taylor helps to hold him up.

I can't deny the fact that she told him about my indiscretion hurts, but whatever relationship she has with him isn't my business. She agreed to one week, and I'm going to hold her to it.

"I'd appreciate it if you didn't allow drunk men around my daughter," I say, swinging my arm through my jacket.

"Oh, fuck off. She calls me daddy," he says, and this time I can't restrain myself. My fist flies out my pocket and cracks along his jaw. His head hits the floor, and Taylor looks up at me, her eyes pleading. This isn't the first fight she's seen me get into.

She's down on her knees at Sam's side again, but her eyes are on me. "That's not true." She's defensive. "I swear."

"Is she close with him? And where the hell is your sister?"

She swallows deep, and I watch her panic. "She is. He's helped me out since she was little, but I swear I've always been clear that he's Uncle Sam and nothing more."

"Your sister?"

"She disappeared right after I delivered Em. I don't know where she is. Probably shacked up somewhere half unconscious."

I close my eyes and inhale a deep breath to gain control. I bend over and pick up the piece of shit, who's just protecting his spot in my family. *My family.* I drop him on the couch, and he falls into the cushions.

"Thank you," Taylor whispers. "I swear he's a good guy. He's just hurting."

I nod, not wanting to hear anything else. I've processed as much as I can tonight.

"Are you okay with him here by yourself?" I look around, finding nothing for me to sleep on besides the floor. Not that I wouldn't consider waking up with a backache in the morning.

"I'm good."

"I can sleep on the floor," I offer, but she shakes her head.

"Thank you, but no. He'll sleep it off, and I'll drive him home in the morning."

"I hate that he'll wake up where I want to be," I softly say, surprised I'm revealing my envy to her. Taylor moves closer, her hands moving up my face until they mold to my cheek.

"I know it hurts, and I can never fully express how sorry I am for that. I made the best choice I could at the time, but I know now it might have been the wrong one." Her body heat is so close to mine, I struggle to not grab her and smash my lips to hers.

"We both made mistakes," I say, hoping we can somehow find a way to forgive one another, because in all honestly, I haven't forgiven her yet.

She nods. "She has your arrogance." She smiles.

"I'm not sure that's a good thing," I mumble, still trying not to kiss her. Those lips are so full and inviting, the memory of them causes a flash of heat to spread through my body.

"My nurturing side evens it out." She laughs, and at the sound of her happiness, I yank her into my waiting arms, securing her body to the length of mine.

I kiss the top of her head, smelling the jasmine shampoo I've always loved. I smile at the memories that flood into me from just one smell.

"I never stopped loving you," I tell her, and she looks up at me through her eyelashes.

"You've always been sweet." She kisses my cheek. "Can I ask you something?"

"Anything."

"Are you clean? I mean, are you still using?"

Her eyes flicker with worry that she's offending me. I want our relationship to be honest and whole, with no secrets from one another.

"I don't use. I went into counseling about a month after you left me. I've been tested and I'm clean. Promise." I hold up my hand with the Boy Scout's salute.

"Okay."

She slides out of my arms, and I miss her immediately.

"Goodnight, Taylor," I whisper, my hand fiddling with the door.

A small smile crosses her lips and she remains planted in her spot, watching me leave. Hopefully, she's afraid if she comes closer, that kiss I've been trying to ignore will happen.

I leave the house, shutting the door behind me. She flicks the lock, but turns on the porch light for me to see my way. Small steps . . . baby steps if we need to, but I have no doubt we'll get there.

six

Taylor

THROUGH MY WINDOW, I WATCH Brad walk down my driveway to his truck. Sam moans and rolls over on the couch. Brad's back is stiff as he shoves his hands in the pockets of his jacket—the jacket I'd bought him for his birthday our senior year. I didn't remark on it, and I wonder if he even remembers. He'd passed out early that night and Piper helped me carry him to bed.

Piper.

I've thought about her plenty over the years. She should know she's an aunt—well, I'm guessing she knows now. If Brad didn't tell her directly, I'm guessing Brad told Tanner and he informed Piper of the news.

Brad climbs into his truck and flicks on the interior light. The shadows on his face worry me. He's processing the news of Em at such a fast pace. I assumed he'd get furious and storm off, and maybe he'd come back, maybe he wouldn't. But the electricity that hung between us two years ago hasn't fizzled out in the slightest. If anything, the time apart made it fiercer.

Before he left, I willed my hands to stay at my sides, but I had to reach out and assure him Sam hasn't taken his spot. Even if he never would have shown up, he's always been Em's father. I hate myself for waiting until now before I figured out that running away had been the wrong choice.

Right before he turns off his interior light after fiddling with his GPS, he glances at our house. The longing and hesitation in his movements breaks my heart. I've had a soft spot for Brad Ashby since the first time I met him. He flicks off the interior light and darkness consumes his truck, obstructing my view. As his truck slowly pulls away from the curb, my arms wrap around myself to sooth the knots tightening my stomach, as I watch his truck's taillights dwindle into the darkness.

I turn around, my back firm against the door as my body loses all control and slowly crumbles to the floor. My heart aches already, and he's only reappeared in my life in the past two days. My eyes scan the home I've made for Em and myself. I've let Sam wiggle in, welcomed him, even when I shouldn't have.

Two days ago, I thought my life was good—not perfect by any means, but solid and firm. Now I feel like I've transplanted into someone else's and all my mistakes are lined up in front of me.

I rise to my feet, grab the blanket hanging over the chair, and I lay it across Sam. His cell rings in his pocket, but I don't pull it out. After turning everything off and double-checking that the doors and windows are locked, I climb the stairs. Em is fast asleep, so I turn off her lullabies and stare down at the little girl who has no idea she just met her daddy today.

After changing, washing my face, and brushing my teeth, my feet slide under my covers and I pick up my e-reader. My finger swipes the screen to scan the books I've downloaded, but I'm not into it. My usually dead tired body is now consumed by a bustling of nerves that refuse to let me rest. Instead of reading, I turn on the television. I'm struck right off with that damn laundry detergent commercial with Piper and Tanner. I roll my eyes at their adorable and loving smiles at one another. Envy rings loud and clear in my heart. They've forgiven each other after what Tanner had done, giving me hope that

Brad and I have the same odds. It's a little harder with Em, and cheating on me with some bimbo isn't the same as what Tanner did, but love can prevail. I hope so, because as many times as I'd begged my heart to stop loving Brad, it wouldn't. So, here I sit, reading these romance stories filling my e-reader, dreaming of Brad at night.

While I'm watching some episode of *Friends* with Ross and a monkey, my phone rings and I jolt.

Fiddling with it until I can grab a good hold, I quickly slide my finger across the screen to answer before Em wakes up.

"Hello?" I say softly and leave the comfort of my warm bed to shut my door completely.

"I hope it's okay for me to call," Brad says, and I can tell from the outside noise he's driving.

"It's okay. What's up?" I slide under my covers again, unable to deny my smile. What can it hurt? No one can see me.

"I just wanted to hear your voice. I wasn't ready to say goodbye."

The pit of my stomach warms like I just indulged in a gooey chocolate lava cake at hearing his words.

"Okay."

"I wanted to expand on a few things too. Is it okay if we do it over the phone?" I hear the ticking of his turn signal, and wonder if he still has the nervous habit of tapping his thumb on the steering wheel. On the way to meets, that thumb would tap to the beat of *Eminem's* Till I Collapse, his go-to song to fire him up.

"Okay."

"You know you can say more, right?"

"Okay." I snicker, and he chuckles lightly.

"After you left me, I continued to get really messed up until Piper finally informed my parents. They got me to a counselor. It took about two months and living with my parents, to get my act together. I enrolled in business school to get my master's."

He pauses and I continue to wait for the entire story.

"That's where I met Bayli."

"You don't need to continue. I don't need to know."

"You do because, Taylor, I should have come after you, and please believe me, I regret that decision every day. But I truly thought you were better off without me."

"What's changed? Why now?"

"Me. I've changed. I know it will take time for you to believe me, but not one day has ever passed where you didn't occupy most of my mind. I have a whole fucking list of regrets, but you're my biggest, and I'm here to make amends now."

I release a breath, my feet rubbing together for warmth from the shivers he just ignited. "I'm scared," I admit.

"Me too, but I think we're scared of different things. You're scared to trust me, and I'm terrified you won't."

My hand lands on my heart to stop it from opening. *They're words, Taylor, that's all.*

"You can hurt me, Brad, but promise me you won't hurt her. No matter what, I have to know you'll be in her life forever."

"I'm going to prove it, Taylor. I promise I'll show you I'm back for good and I'm not that piece of shit anymore."

"I fell in love with that piece of shit." I wish I could stay silent and allow him to knock himself down, but I can't. He may have faults, but he is a good person deep down.

"Well, if I wasn't a piece of shit, you'd still be in love with me."

Who's saying I'm not?

"I'm going to extend a branch, Brad, but that's all." He doesn't need to know I'm close to giving him our whole tree.

"That's all I need. Just give me a chance."

"Okay."

"But, Taylor, I'm warning you; I'm not going away."

I nod, even though he can't see me. A small part of me likes it that he's going to be fighting for us. I just have to trust him enough to let him. That's the hard part.

"Okay."

"Please give me another word."

"Yes."

"Taylor," he pleads, and I hear his turn signal go off again.

"Tell me something I don't know about you."

"Hmm . . ." I can imagine he's nibbling on the inside of his cheek, thinking about it. "Do you want to know about Piper and Tanner?"

"Nope. Something about you."

"Okay, I like long walks and candlelight dinners."

I cover my mouth to conceal the burst of laughter that's threatening to pour out. "Seriously."

"I am serious," he argues, but he's laughing as well.

We talk for another hour about how he got fired and his roommate Dylan, Tanner's brother. He touches on Piper and Tanner, their problems, and how they reconciled at his wedding, but I can tell he's hesitant about sharing because of the fact he was going to marry someone who wasn't me. He's moved from his truck to his apartment, and I waited on the line while he took off his shirt to climb into bed. What I wouldn't do for a selfie of him right about now.

"I guess I should get to bed. She wakes up early." I yawn, stretching my limbs.

"Okay. If you can't sleep, call me back because I'll be awake." He doesn't sound groggy at all.

"Brad, I have to work late tomorrow. Would you like to pick Em up from daycare?" I bite my nail, because as much as it frightens me, I have to extend the branch. Some might think it's too soon, but I know Brad. Plus, I want this to be as amicable as possible.

"I'd love to. What time?"

"Five o'clock. I'll text you the address. There will be a list of instructions on the counter for you when you get here."

"I got it. I'm an adult." He laughs, but whether he knows it or not, this is a huge step for me.

"I know, it's just . . . Okay, I'm going to tell her daycare provider you'll be picking her up."

"Sounds good. Get some sleep."

"Good night, Brad." I wish I could stay on the phone with him all night, but I can't let him in completely, and after talking with him for just a little bit, I know it would be too easy. He'll slide back into my heart without me even knowing it.

"Good night." I move to hang up.

"Wait, Taylor?"

"Yeah." I bring the phone back to my ear.

"Thank you." His voice is humble and gracious. Everything I'd hoped for in this moment.

"You're welcome."

We finally hang up, and I lay in bed wondering if it's even possible for me to fight my feelings for him.

"MAMA!" A SMALL HAND SMACKS my face.

I bolt up, my heart racing. My eyes fly to the monitor to see it's disappeared from my bedside. Then I find a tall figure in my doorframe, still dressed in his clothes from the night before and a smirk plastered on his boyish face.

"Good morning," I say to Em, pulling her small body to mine.

"Sorry." Sam's voice is low as he walks into the room and hesitantly sits on the edge of the bed. "I made you breakfast." His eyes cast down to the floor, and I hate the fact that I'm part of the reason he feels this way. Us Delaney girls have taken his heart for granted too many times in his life.

"Okay. I have the late shift today."

He looks up with hurt in his eyes. "I know."

Of course he does, he probably knows my schedule better than me. The room quiets, and lucky for us, we have an almost two-year-old to break the silence.

"Play!" she demands, jumping on my bed. I hold her hand as she catapults from my mattress and falls down into the softness.

Sam smiles at her. "Let's give Mommy time to get ready." He holds his arms out for her and she bounces over to him until she's secure in his arms.

"I'll be right down," I say, covering myself as much as I can. No need to show off what little cleavage I have.

They leave and I throw off my covers and move into my bathroom. I grab some yoga pants and a T-shirt, figuring I'll shower during her naptime.

By the time I reach the bottom of the stairs, Em is laughing uncontrollably and Sam is doing his elevator impersonation where he disappears around the wall. It's like a jab to the chest knowing Sam will have to step back in order for Brad to come forward. I've worked the angle, and there's no doubt about it. Then again, ultimately, Sam knew his time with Em was going to be cut short.

Looking around, I notice the blanket is folded up nicely and swung over the chair again. Em's toys are strewn around, and I wonder how long they've been awake. Sam catches me coming from the corner of his eye, and he rushes over to give Em a kiss on the cheek.

"Gotta go, I'm late."

"Sam, wait." I eye Em to see she's busy trying to use her fork to pick up her pancakes.

I follow him to the door, but he's moving so fast, I barely catch him before he escapes.

"Sam," I plead. He inhales a deep breath and looks over my shoulder instead meeting my eyes. "We need to talk."

"I get it, Tay, and I'm sorry for barging in last night."

"He's her father."

He looks outside to the lawn covered with fallen leaves.

"That's not all," he mumbles, probably hoping I don't hear

him.

"Don't, Sam."

"Don't what, Tay? Don't call you out for still loving someone who threw you to the side for a piece of pussy." His eyes meet mine, red and fierce. I step back and he shakes his head. "It's the truth. You never even thought about us because you might have run away from him, but you were running away from yourself too."

"Me?" My fingers jam to my chest. "What about you? You're still hung up on my sister. Clue in, Sam. She's fucking around just to score drugs. You're the laughingstock of Roosevelt."

"Takes one to know one." He twists the knife a little more. I can't fault him for spouting the truth. The Delaney family has been the joke of Roosevelt for as long as I can remember.

"Well, aren't we the fucked-up ones then?" I glance to Em, finding her still enthralled with her fork and pancakes.

"It's just . . . whatever. I shouldn't have said that. I'm sorry." His distant eyes look everywhere but at me.

"Me too."

Silence fills the small space, and he looks at his watch.

"I'm late. We'll talk tonight." He steps onto the porch and I hold the door open.

"Sam." He turns around, and I know I'm about to crush him. "Brad's picking her up."

His lips straighten and I watch the emotions cross his face before he gives me a simple nod.

"Gotcha." He turns and steps off the porch.

"Please, Sam, try to understand," I say, but he waves his hand in the air.

"Mama!" Em screams, and I turn from Sam's retreating back to find her wiggling to stand up in her high chair.

"Hold on, baby." I close the door, run over to her, and catch her right before she falls to the floor. "No standing. You wait until Mommy can get you." I semi-scold her. I've never been good at that whole strict parenting role.

I place her down and she scurries over to the window. "Sm." She hits the window and my heart breaks. The little girl has no idea she might lose Sam to gain her dad. It's a hard lesson for a two-year-old to learn.

Just then, my phone dings and I retrieve it from my back pocket. Brad's name shows on my screen and my heart leaps.

Brad: Good morning to my girls.

Not such a good morning for me, but it's getting better.

Me: Good morning.

Brad: I hope that lump is off your couch.

Me: That would be none of your business.

Brad: Hmm . . . I don't agree with that line of thinking. When it comes to you and my daughter, it's my business.

Me: Here's the address. Pick her up at five. I'll be home around eight. I'll lay out her pajamas and her sippy cup of milk will be in the fridge.

Brad: Hey, what do you think of me? I got this. I'm a damn baby whisperer.

Me: I'll bet money she's up when I return home.

Brad: Bet taken. She'll be fast asleep. What is her bedtime anyway?

Me: Seven. Directions will be on the kitchen table.

Brad: Pfft. I don't need directions. I'm Brad Ashby.

Me: Arrogant as always. See you tonight.

Brad: You love my ego, don't try to deny it. See you.

I place my phone down and Em walks back through the

family room, her head down with a stuffed animal in her hand. It's the elephant Sam bought her this past summer at the zoo.

"Sm," she says, and my lips turn down, as I hold my arms out to her as an invitation to come. She shuffles her limp body into my arms.

"He'll be back." I soothe her hair.

After a second, she forgets and squirms to break free of my hold. I miss the days when she'd let me hold her for hours. That ended once she could walk.

"Let's play," I say, cherishing the small amount of time I'm blessed with her due to my work schedule. These five day, eight hour shifts are a killer on my quality time with her. But that's a small hospital for you.

She smiles bright and runs behind the couch where all her toys are stashed.

seven

Brad

DYLAN SITS AT THE KITCHEN table putting together another model car. At least it's a 1969 Chevy Camaro. He's working remotely for two weeks before packing up and moving to Chicago. Talk about no notice. How nice of the shit company.

I plop down in the chair across from him, watching his precise fingers fiddle with the small pieces. He's been building these things since we were little, and I never understood the point. While Tanner and I would be playing basketball or swimming, he'd be inside with one of his kits. I thought he'd grow out of it when he went to college, but from the amount scattered around the apartment that didn't happen.

He peeks up at me. "You look like shit," he remarks and continues what he's doing, which I believe is attaching the muffler.

"Well, thank you." I slouch down in the chair, the cold air chilling my bare chest. Winter in Michigan sucks.

"Is the heat on?" I shiver and Dylan shakes his head in annoyance.

"Put on a damn shirt for once," he mumbles.

"You have a girl over?"

"No."

"Oh, I figured you didn't want her jumping at me after seeing your scrawny chest."

Truth, Dylan is anything but scrawny, but he's my best friend's younger brother. Isn't it mandatory to razz him?

He shakes his head, never coming back at me with a smart ass answer himself.

"Can we talk?" I lean my elbows on the table.

His green eyes flicker up at me and he nods. "What's up?"

"You can't talk to anyone else, got it? This stays here." I tap my finger on the table.

"Okay."

"No, I mean it. Not Tanner, not parents, and not Bea." I point to him and he chuckles.

"I said okay."

He places the small tube of glue to the side and leans back in his chair.

"I have a daughter," I divulge, my heart swelling with the words. I thought for sure it would scare me beyond belief, but after being up all night, I'm at peace with it. My only concern is that I have no job provide for her. Swimming lessons aren't exactly going to put a roof over her head. Then again, her mom's already done that. Taylor . . . she's amazing.

His lips quirk up. "Figured one would pop up eventually. Who's the mom? The brunette from last month, or that girl from the bar last week. Shit." He runs his hand through his dark, wavy hair. "Please tell me it isn't Bayli."

"No, no, and hell no. Don't make shit up." He knows full well, I've been celibate since Bayli.

He laughs, dropping the small piece of metal in his hand.

"Taylor," I say. Dylan doesn't know Taylor, but he's heard about her. Probably hears me calling her name as I jack off at night.

His green eyes widen and he expels a long stream of air.

"Shit." He's as stunned as I was. Well, I might have almost fainted. I am the father after all.

"Yeah."

"You tell anyone else?" He moves the model over to the

side and stands. Grabbing two beers, he slides one across the table.

"It's eight o'clock. No thanks." He twists his open and downs a hefty sip.

"Brad Ashby, Dad. Doesn't seem to fit."

I pick up a piece of his model and throw it at him. "Fuck you, man."

He laughs, catching it in his hand.

"I'm kidding . . . kind of. And don't throw my shit." He sits down, placing the beer next to him. "What are you doing about it?"

"What do you think I'm going to do? Raise her."

"With Taylor?"

"That's the question of the night. I hope so, but we have a lot of shit to work through."

"I'll say. She never told you? That's cold, man. I get it, you cheated, but she purposely deceived you."

"So did I, in a way." I move my hand to the back of my neck and squeeze, relieving none of the pressure plaguing it. "If I could go back in time—"

"Everyone thinks that. FYI, you can't."

One corner of my lip lifts. "I know, jackass. I'm not a moron."

"Just making sure. Didn't want you looking for some time machine. As far as not being a moron, you did cheat on a girl you loved." He raises both his eyebrows at me.

"Fuck off."

"Gladly. Leave me alone then."

My head falls to the table with a thud. "How am I going to raise my daughter? What if Taylor doesn't forgive me, or worse, doesn't love me?"

"Those are all good questions and ones you need to find the answers to." He pats my head. "It's time to grow up, Bradley."

He slides his chair out and he moves into the kitchen. I'm not sure what I expected Dylan's advice to be on my descent to fatherhood. Damn sure, I can't bring my family into this yet. My mom would descend like a vulture, showing up on Taylor's doorstep.

"When are you out?" I murmur into my arm.

"Bea and I are sharing a moving van. We're driving out the Saturday after Thanksgiving." He leans on the counter, crossing his ankles. Is that another damn tattoo on his leg?

"You can cool it with the ink," I say, wondering why he wants to mark his body constantly.

He shakes his head and walks across the room.

"It doesn't make you cool anymore. Imagine when you're a wrinkled old man," I holler and he shuts his door. I swear I can't get a reaction out of him to save my life. I think Tanner and I conditioned him too well when we were younger.

More important than Dylan's tattoos is the fact that I have to find a roommate or be out by then too. Dylan said he can get out of the lease because of the transfer clause, and it would work for me too. But where would I go? Home? I don't think so.

I KNOCK ON THE DOOR of the small, white house, and hear screaming and hollering before a million little feet stomp to the door. A middle-aged woman with short dark hair opens it, bearing no smile.

"Hi, Mrs. Allen, I presume?" I wave my hand in the air, but still no uplift of her lips.

"You must be Brad." She pushes the door open, reluctantly letting me in. "She just woke up from her nap."

I glance at my watch. Five o'clock and she's sleeping. Must take after her daddy.

The children swarm around my feet, some grabbing at my jeans and others standing quietly, staring up at me with curiosity.

"Sorry," she says and claps her hands. "Children, go into the playroom. Your parents should be here soon."

They scurry off into a room to the left. I rock back on my heels, waiting for her to retrieve Emerson, but she continues to stand there. Her eyes rack over my body, but not in a sexual manner. Her lips curl and disgust washes over her face.

"Don't come into town and break their hearts," she says, and it takes me a second to realize she's speaking to me.

"No, ma'am."

Who is this woman and how well does Taylor know her?

"Taylor left the key in Em's bag, so you can let yourself into the house."

"Thank you." I nod and smile, but she doesn't.

"She's taken very good care of that girl while you've been galloping around God only knows where."

I nod again. "I know. They are both quite amazing."

"There's no quite about it." She turns around before I can correct myself.

"Jesus," I whisper.

"We don't use the Lord's name in vain under this roof," she says, never turning around.

"Sorry," I murmur, not even sure if she heard me.

What seems like a lifetime later, she comes out of some back room with Emerson in her arms. Her cheeks are rosy and her eyes are watering.

What did this lady do to my baby?

"She's usually emotional when she wakes up. Give her a little time and she'll be back to her old spunky self." She turns her attention to Emerson. "Won't you, baby girl? Yes, you will," she coos like a toddler herself.

Mrs. Allen holds Emerson out for me and she easily comes into my arms, laying her head on my shoulder.

"Hi, Emerson," I whisper as her small hand rests over my heart, piercing it with love. At least that's how I imagine the scene.

"Thank you, Mrs. Allen." I shift Emerson in my arms to pull out my wallet. "What does Taylor usually pay you?"

A wry laugh escapes her. "Taylor pays me monthly, boy. Maybe you could buy some diapers or food for them, since you've been gone for two years."

Obviously, when Taylor was tossing the whole single-parent role around, she forgot to mention she choose it.

"I will." I take the highroad before Roosevelt's only sheriff gets called for a domestic disturbance. Nice Jesus lover she is and all.

With my daughter in my arms and her diaper bag swung over my shoulder, I leave the cold confines of her daycare. I place Emerson in her car seat and she leans her head to snuggle with the elephant in her hands. Thank goodness I decided to buy the car seat first. It took me all day to figure out how to install the thing in the truck.

Emerson is quiet in the backseat as darkness fills the street. She has to be hungry, and I know there's a list of directions on how to care for her at the house. Pain echoes through me that I need directions on how to take care of my daughter. Shouldn't a father just know how to nurture his child? Anger surfaces at the fact that Taylor stripped me of that, but then I look in the rearview mirror and find Emerson beginning to smile.

"Hey, do you want to go to the store?" I ask, and she claps.

"Taget," she says, and I nod.

"Sure, we can go to Target." I passed it on the way into town. It's closer to the pool house. I wonder how many times we've missed each other, since I'm sure we've both shopped there.

I drive the twenty minutes to the Target and Emerson's personality is alive and shining as I unbuckle her. A mom and her son park at the same time and we follow them into the store. Her eyes keep diverting to us, and I smile to appease her. When we enter the store, I follow her movements. Grab a cart, wipe it down with the cloth, then put the child in the bucket part, and buckle the seatbelt. Her son happily begins to rock back and forth after being strapped in. Easy enough.

I put Emerson in the cart, but she refuses to bend her legs. I reach down to help, eventually winning the battle of wills. While reaching for the two straps, she tries to stand up.

"No!" Her little hand smacks mine over and over again.

"Emerson, you have to be strapped in," I say calmly.

"No!"

The mom looks at me and shrugs. Guess I'm not that attractive anymore when my child isn't behaving.

"Come on, Emerson," I say, pulling the two sides together. Each time I get them close, she twists and I lose the grip. "I'll buy you a toy."

"No!"

"Candy? You want some candy?"

"No!"

"If you sit down and I can strap you in, I'll get you whatever you want," I beg, trying to ignore the scrutinizing eyes directed at us from all areas of the store.

"Me stand."

"Not unless I want your mom to kill me."

"Kill?"

Shit. "Don't say that."

"Kill," she repeats and my face heats with embarrassment.

"Excuse me." A young girl comes over in her red shirt and khaki pants. *Great, she's going kick me out.*

"Sorry, she doesn't want to be strapped in."

"I see that." Her eyes look me over, curiosity etched in them. "Who are you?"

"Who are you?"

She points to her nametag.

"Cindy, okay. Why do you care who I am?" Emerson is busying herself with the strap she so adamantly doesn't want across her stomach.

"Why do you have Em?"

75

"You know her?" I ask, and she stealthy steps between me and Emerson, pushing the cart behind her and away from me.

"Yes, and Taylor. So, I'm asking again, who are you?" She looks past my shoulder, so I follow her line of sight to find a security guard five steps behind me.

"I'm Brad, Taylor's friend and Emerson's father," I spout, upset that this whole scenario is happening to me right now.

"You're her father?" She looks questioningly at the security guard, who I could probably take down with one punch. He's not much older than Cindy. "I thought Sam was her dad," she says.

Great, another one for Team Sam.

The security guard comes over. "They are on their way."

"Who's on their way? Jesus, tell me you didn't call the police." I run my hand through my hair and my teeth grit together.

"We don't know you and Em seems upset."

"She's throwing a fit because she doesn't want to be buckled in." I point to her and everyone's eyes shift to her. She's still enthralled with the belt, now trying to strap herself in.

"It doesn't appear like that, sir."

I dig my phone out of my pocket, click on Taylor's name, and hand Cindy the phone. "Here."

She looks down at it and then holds it up to her ear.

"Hi, Taylor. This is Cindy Gregory. I'm working and there's this man here stating he's Em's dad."

I wait, my eyes on Emerson the whole time as the pimply security guard stares me down. As if he could intimidate me.

"Oh, okay." Now her eyes appraise me in a whole other way. As though Taylor caught herself a fine stud or something. "I thought Sam was her dad." Another pause. "Okay, I'll have Billy call them right now. Just watching out for Em." Cindy smiles at me, her one finger twirling a lose strand of her blonde hair. "Yeah, gotcha. I'll tell him." She laughs. "Bye."

Cindy hands me the phone. "Billy, call off the police. He's legit." Billy walks away, pulling his phone out of his pocket. "Sorry about that. I live down the street from Taylor and thought you were a kidnapper or something."

"Okay. Mind if I get my shopping done now?" I motion toward Emerson, who almost has the buckle fastened.

"No, but Taylor said she's sorry," she says, and a smile creases my lips.

"Sorry, huh?"

She chomps on her gum. "Yeah, sorry."

I nod. "Thank you, Cindy." I place my hand on her shoulder to slide her away from the front of the cart. "I'll be doing our shopping now."

"Yep, have at it. There's a sale on diapers," she calls out, but I help Emerson finish the clasping and we cheer as though she did it all by herself.

"Let's go check out the sale," I tell the small girl and lean over the rail of the cart. Her small hands rub along the prickly one-day beard growth. My heart has never felt as full as it does in this moment, and that's without her mother admitting to herself we belong together. She'll get there in time, though, because I know I'm supposed to be right where I am.

I mosey around the story, enjoying my time with Emerson. She fiddles with the belt, I buy her a pretzel, and we buy those diapers on sale. Finally, I make my way to the toy section. Emerson instantly starts pointing to toys, repeating want over and over again. She wiggles her body, swinging her legs through the openings, trying to pry herself from the restriction of the belt.

"Hold on." I unclip her and pick her up. Reluctantly, I place her feet on the floor and she scurries over to a bin of stuffed animals. She sits down, pulling each one out on the floor. She's so excited, it makes me excited for her.

Crap, I'd buy her the whole lot if I didn't think Taylor would shoot me. Then my mind flashes to two lost years. Years when she grew into this amazing little girl, and I missed it. I sit down next to her and she climbs into my lap. Could my life be any better in this moment?

She picks up little princess characters with pink crowns and purple hair. Each one is adorned with a sparkly dress and fancy shoes sewn on.

I pluck each one that's different and put them in her arms.

"I get?" she looks up at me, those small teeth shining, eyes bright with question.

"Yep." I kiss her forehead and she pulls them into her body, hugging them tight. I scoop her up and place her back in the cart with her array of new friends.

As I make my way to the check out, I intently watch her play with the dolls, and there's this proud feeling bursting inside me because she loves something I bought her. She doesn't know who I am, and as much as I hate to admit it, she probably does think Sam is her dad, but damn this warm feeling in my heart just grows more intense the more I'm with her.

By the time I snap Emerson into the car seat, unload the cart, and drive back to Taylor's, I realize, other than the pretzel, I haven't fed her. I'm sucking at this dad thing already. Not knowing what to feed a two-year-old, and not wanting to call my mom or sister, I opt for Dylan. He's a smart guy and should have some knowledge.

The ringing sound over the car's Bluetooth gains Emerson's attention. She peers at me through the rearview mirror. I'm not sure I'll ever get used to seeing my eyes staring back at me. I should already be because of Piper, but it's somehow different with Emerson.

"Yo," he answers, and there's a ton of noise in the background.

"Where are you?"

"At Bea's. She insists on singing with the contestant on The Voice." Then I hear her squealing in the background.

"What's going on with you two?"

They've been at this friendship, not friendship thing for a while, and Bea isn't shy about wanting him, so I wonder what the holdup is.

"Nothing. We're friends and co-workers."

Bea bellows another note and Emerson covers her ears.

I laugh at my little girl. "What can I feed a two-year-old?"

"The shit if I know. Call your mom." I hear muffled voices and Bea's singing has ceased.

"You know I can't. Not yet anyway. She'd scare Taylor. What do I feed her?"

"What on Earth would give you the slightest idea I would know? I'm a twenty-three-year-old bachelor, who is the baby of the family." He whispers to Bea, and so help me God, if he's letting my secret out, he's going to get it. "Bea says stop and get chicken."

"Did you tell her?" My hands tense on the steering wheel.

"She says that kid you're feeding after the swim lesson should be happy with chicken."

"She bought that lame-ass story," I ask.

"Would you prefer she didn't?"

"No, thanks."

"Talk to you later. Remember, times a ticking." The line clicks off and I look back at Emerson.

"Do you like chicken?"

"Cluck, cluck," she says, and I purse my lips to keep from laughing at her serious face.

I continue to ask her the sounds of animals through the drive-thru and she nails each one of them. I got myself a genius.

An excruciatingly long time later, I pull into Taylor's driveway. I stand outside Emerson's door, wondering how to get everything inside, and including her. She can't be left alone either place, but I figure she's safer strapped in her car seat.

"I'll be right back, baby," I hold my finger up in the air and she continues to play with her dolls.

Rushing, I grab the diapers and bags from Target and drop them on the front stoop. My feet hammer back to Emerson and I dig through her diaper bag for the key. With the key in my hand, Emerson in my arms, and the chicken hanging from my forearm, I've accomplish getting all of us into the dark and quiet house.

Emerson hurries over to her toy bin with her four plush dolls, as though she's introducing them to the old toys. Five minutes later, I'm in the house, completely exhausted until it dawns on me I still have to feed her and she probably needs a diaper change.

Crap, diaper change.

Taylor never showed me how to do it, but it can't be that hard, right?

eight

Taylor

THE BITTER AIR RUNS THROUGH me like I'm a loose piece of paper on the way to the car. I pull my jacket tighter across my scrubs, preparing for a cold ride home. The heater will never be warm enough to heat the car before I get home.

Home.

In all my twenty-five years, I've never felt like the house I was living in was a home, but that changed after Em. She's my home, and the house I bought for us is a nest of love created by us. Now, my thoughts linger on Brad being a part of us. His body stretched on the couch after a long shift watching a football game at a quiet volume so as not to wake our daughter upstairs. It's a nice thought, but a thought I can't fully absorb yet. There are issues between Brad and me. Issues I'm not sure even the greatest love could overcome.

In the meantime though, I'll embrace this happiness that makes my step a little giddier from the image of Brad waiting at my house for me.

My car rumbles to life. Half dying, half the cold weather making it struggle to life, but it doesn't fail me. It never has, and I'm crossing my fingers it never will.

By the time I pull up to the house, my fingers have warmed

slightly and my nose tingles. The living room light is on, but the drapes are drawn, hiding what's behind them. Em's light is off, which could be a good or bad sign.

My key fiddles in the lock, and when I push the door open, Brad's sitting on the couch watching television.

"Hey." He smiles, but I catch his quick inhale of breath.

"Hi. How was your night?" I inspect the living room, finding all her toys tucked away. It's immaculate. Not that I'm organized and a clean freak, but . . . did he dust? My fingers rub along the foyer table, bringing up a pile of lint. Too bad.

"It was good. She's been out for a while now." I glance at the monitor, the red dots are blinking rapidly up and down, revealing she's awake.

"Was she hard to put down?" I unwrap myself from my scarf, coat, and gloves, hanging them by the door.

"Not at all. You know I have a magic touch."

All too well, and I usually relive those memories with my vibrator.

"I'm just going to go check on her." I move toward the steps, but Brad stands.

"No. She's fine. Come and let's talk." He looks down at the empty seat next to where he was just sitting. "I have some chicken in the fridge. I can heat it up for you if you're hungry."

"Chicken sounds great. I missed lunch. Do you mind heating it up for me?"

"Not at all. Sit down." He moves to round the couch to go toward the kitchen, and I act like I'm going to sit down, but at the last minute change directions toward the stairs.

"Taylor, she's fine."

"I just have to check." He follows me, so my steps quicken, but so do his. He has longer legs than me, and I feel his breath tickling my neck.

"She's good." My stomach flips when his hands grip my hips and slide me out of the way at the top of the stairs.

"Brad." I tilt my head as he forms himself as a human

block to my daughter, who is laughing to herself in her crib.

"She's asleep," he says at the exact moment, Em squeals in delight and Brad's eyes close. "Maybe she's dreaming."

"Doubtful." I step forward, my chest rubbing against his. My hand sneaks through his arm to find the handle of the door. He pushes harder against me and my nipples tighten under my scrubs.

I open the door and my daughter's hands are on the railing of her crib as she bounces up and down.

"Emerson," Brad sighs. "You woke up?" He stays by the door, probably afraid to step forward.

I eye him and he raises his hands in the air like he has no clue why she's awake.

"What are you doing, sweetie?" I walk to her and her arms stretch out for me to pick her up.

"Mama," she coos, and my heart breaks that I have to be away from her all day like today.

I pick her up and Brad stays quiet in the corner. Her good night book sits on the ottoman of the rocking chair. "*I Love My Daddy*," I read the title and eye Brad.

He shrugs with a sly smile across his lips. "Figured she needed a new favorite book."

I touch the princess doll's yarn hair. "And a new favorite stuffed toy." My eyes search, finding Elephant stuffed in the corner under a pile of toys.

"I like my daughter to have new stuff." He moves closer as I sit down on the chair, laying her on my chest.

"He got me," Em says, and I'm impressed by the three words she managed to string together.

"I figured," I say, unable to stop smiling.

I lean back and she lays her head on my shoulder. The chair rocks back and forth and she lulls slightly, holding that princess doll to her chest. After a few minutes, she's out and I move to get up, but Brad gradually sneaks his hands between us, grazing my breast at the same time he takes her from my arms. Damn that felt oddly good.

He kisses her forehead and gently places her down in her crib. I don't interrupt his moment with her, but instead stay back and admire the man I've loved for so long as he puts his daughter down to sleep. Tears threaten to fall, but I hold them in, not wanting to pour all my emotions on the table.

After a few minutes, he turns to me and begins to tip toe out of the room. I follow him, flicking off the lights and shutting the door behind me.

In the hallway, Brad waits for me to walk down the stairs first, and I pray my scrubs don't cling to my ass showing off how big it's become. That small pocket hopefully conceals how it stretched out while I was pregnant.

"Sorry. I tried, but she was wound up. If it helps, I think I bruised my side when I heard your car pull in the driveway."

"What did you do, throw her in the crib and run downstairs?" I laugh, imaging the thought.

"Yeah," he admits, shame written on his face.

"It's okay, Brad. Not every night is perfect. She's two and finding her own personality."

I jog down the steps, hoping the faster I go, the less time he has to notice my gigantic ass.

"I got a glimpse of that personality at Target," he says behind me, and I can't stop the smile from crossing my face. After Cindy, our neighbor down the street, called from his phone, I felt bad, because it must have devastated him to have someone question his relationship with Em. Then I couldn't stop laughing, picturing Em's very bad outbursts and the panic he must have been burying inside.

"She has quite the willpower." I round the end of the staircase and head to the kitchen. My stomach growls from hunger. The winter cold has hit Roosevelt and the overfilled hospital rooms proved that there are no lengthy lunches to be had in my future.

"Willpower? She switches on a dime." He gently touches

my shoulders and leads me away from the fridge right to a chair.

"Yeah. It's the terrible twos," I comment, rubbing my foot.

He busies himself in the fridge, pulling out the chicken and the plastic containers filled with mashed potatoes and macaroni and cheese. A girl could get used to this treatment.

"I read about them last night. Someone said three is worse," he mindlessly talks, dishing up spoonfuls of mashed potatoes onto the plate as my voice catches in my throat. I stare at his back, well-sculpted even through the T-shirt. The grooves of his perfect swimmer's muscles haven't faded.

"You read?"

He glances over his shoulder and shrugs. "I wasn't going into this blind. Had to find what I was up against."

The fact that he searched out information about two-year-olds elates me more than I wish it would.

"Up against?"

"The stories had me a little worried." He moves to the microwave and then leans against the counter, looking right at me. "But she's great, Taylor. You did a great job." His smile reaches all the way up to his serenity filled brown eyes.

"Thanks," I choke out because tears are welling up in my eyes from his praise, and I refuse to look like I needed the compliment. I know I'm a great mom, but hearing him say it confirms it somehow.

"No, thank you. I can't imagine what it's been like for you."

I shrug as though the late night feedings and recovering from a C-section weren't excruciating. The job searches while requesting time to make sure I could find fit daycare. The student loans that never seemed to go down, and still haven't been paid in full because I had to choose to keep my good credit or feed her. I'm not ashamed of those unpaid loans, because my daughter is perfect and healthy.

"I know I've said it a zillion times, but I'm sorry for not

telling you." I pull my legs up to my chest as though they'll protect me from the wrath he's yet to give me for stealing years with our daughter from him.

"Why didn't you?" he asks, and I busy my thumbnail digging into the cracks on the oak table I bought at a secondhand shop.

"You changed before me, Brad. I had no idea who you were, and I had flashes of my dad, my sister, and their own addictions. Then the girl—"

"I'm sorry, Taylor. You're right, I wasn't me then. Not that I'm excusing myself."

I nod. I understand it, I do. The anger of him cheating has faded over the years, but I'm not sure forgiveness has happened yet either.

"Do you remember that night?" I ask, my voice as shallow as a kid's pool.

His eyes look everywhere but toward me. "Not much until you walked in. You sobered me up fast."

I fight with myself, searching for something I'll never get answered. Why did he do it? I'm not even sure he knows why.

The microwave dings, and he turns around and grabs silverware from the drawer. He moves around my kitchen like he belongs here, and I wish I hated him more than I do. He places the dish in front of me with a napkin and silverware right next to it.

"Eat. Your stomach has been making noises since you walked in that door."

My hand falls to my stomach, embarrassed that he's heard the rumblings. He sits down in the chair next to me. This whole scenario is intimate and I love it. Maybe I shouldn't have let him get Em and should have made him prove himself more, but that demon I cast him as for two years isn't inside him anymore. I don't know who he is, but there isn't one part of me that doesn't feel safer with him near.

I pull apart the breast of my fried chicken, and he leans

back in the chair, his long legs casually swung open. The dark circles under his eyes a testament to the fact that he is as exhausted as my tired limbs from a day on my feet.

"Can I ask you a question?"

He tenses, his water bottle stills on his lips.

"Sure."

"Why did your engagement break up?" Truth is, the fact he'd proposed to someone who wasn't me hurt worse than him sleeping with the slut in college.

He sits up, his shoulders ridged. "How did you know I was engaged?" It's a fair question.

"I ran into Sara one day when I was in the city. She said she heard and asked how I felt about it."

Sara was one of Taylor's sorority girls, who was known to gossip. I guess, even after college, she keeps tabs on people.

He shakes his head. "I'm not sure how she even knew." His eyes peek up at me, realizing what he sounds like. "Not that I wouldn't have told you. I would have." He insists he'll be truthful with me, and I want to believe he will be.

"She was really pretty." Why stop now? I snooped.

"You saw her?" The shock in his voice isn't hard to miss.

"I may have crept on Facebook a little."

His lips quirk up, finding great pleasure that I cared enough to snoop.

"I deleted my account after I graduated."

"I know. Me too."

"You tried to find me?" The hope in his eyes breaks my heart, because even if I had found his page, I doubt I would have made contact.

"I saw some pictures of you with your fiancée."

"Ex-fiancée," he clarifies, but that fact does nothing to ease my anxiety.

"Why?" I ask, ignoring him.

"I don't know. I still wasn't in the best place with Bayli. We started dating, and before I could get a handle on what was

87

happening, she was talking marriage. I thought if I pushed a new life hard enough, I'd forget." He twists the water bottle in his hands, his fingers fiddling with the label.

"Forget what?" My fork moves around the mashed potatoes, I'm suddenly not very hungry.

"You, Taylor. Forget you."

My eyes sting as they fill with tears. I can't compose my emotions fast enough. My fork drops with a ping on the table and I lean back in the chair. Brad takes the opportunity to capture my hand and wrapping it securely between his.

"I was afraid to come back and apologize. I was afraid I'd hurt you again, so I stayed away and tried to force you out of my mind. But I promise you this and your heart can trust it: You are the only woman I've ever loved." I swallow the golf-ball-size lump in my throat at his confession.

My hand drops and I close my eyes, trying to bury the exhilaration pumping through me. Failing, I abruptly stand from the table and grab a hold of the counter. The edge digs into the flesh of my palm and I concentrate on that pain instead of the one ripping at my heart.

"It hurt so much, Brad." One tear leaks out and I continue staring at his truck in my driveway through the small window above the sink. "You hurt me."

I hear the sliding of his chair against my linoleum floor and his hesitant footsteps padding toward me. My heart pounds a little harder in my chest, waiting for him to say something, anything, but he doesn't. He rests his hands on my shoulders, his chin on top of my head. More tears fall from my eyes, dropping into the sink. He doesn't verbally promise me anything; however, his silence says enough, that maybe it hurt him the same way it hurt me.

"How do we overcome our past?" I whisper.

"Together." His fingertips clutch my shoulder a little tighter and his lips kiss the top of my head. "Together."

nine

Brad

IT'S BEEN FOUR DAYS, AND Taylor's worked every one of them. She's allowed me to pick up Emerson from daycare. Lucky for me, the only late day I have lessons is the one with Emerson on my schedule. All others are during the day. Taylor and I haven't grown much closer since she's usually exhausted by the time she returns home. She eats and drifts off to sleep on the couch. Last night, I carried her to bed, wishing like hell I could climb in right next to her. But I can't. She's not mine. Yet. Truly, I need a night out with just her if we're going to move on from our past.

The most recent terror in this whole 'I have a daughter and want a family' is that I don't have a job which enables me to provide for them. So, that's why I'm here, outside the building where my dreams shattered. The same place my darkest demons continue to hide.

Trying not to let the feelings of inadequacy I struggle with surface, I hurriedly swing the doors open. There's Coach, screaming with his hands clasped to the top of his head. I lay low, watching him coach by insult. It's his tactic, and I can't deny it worked. He can claim he coached an Olympian now. That's a killer on a resume. But then again, he coached a cheater too.

Coach's eyes find me leaning against the wall and a smug smirk crosses his lips. He knew one day I'd come groveling back. The whistle moves to his lips and he blows it long and hard to grab the guys' attention. All swimming stops and the waves slow to ripples.

"Well, boys, looks like we have a visitor," he announces and turns his body my way like I'm today's entertainment. The heads twist and recollection flares on a few of their faces, while others are blank. I'm sure my reputation isn't dead. In the 'don't do this shit' category.

I kick off the wall and break toward them, careful not to slip on the wet concrete. At least I took off my shoes before coming in. If not, Coach would have had my head for sure.

By the time I make it across the pool, the guys are whispering to one another. The ones who know me tell the ones who don't about my past. Coach looks me up and down.

"You put on some weight, Ashby?"

I glance down at my well-trimmed body and laugh. I don't bother arguing his point. He's a life line for me right now.

"Maybe a little."

"I can assure you it's more than a little."

I eye the stomach straining over his blue athletic shorts, but I don't comment on his weight gain over the past two years.

"Give me fifteen minutes and we'll talk." He blows the whistle and I tilt my head, covering my ear. Shit, I know he did that on purpose.

Still popping my jaw to retrieve my hearing, I slide back and squat down against the wall. I cannot watch these guys swim their laps and not remember when I thought my dreams were an arm's reach away. In the early years, Tanner and I would go from swimming practice to the bar, all the girls fawned over us and treated us like college royalty. Hell, they practically begged to come over to our place. Then came that frat party when Taylor spilled her drink all over my shirt.

At first, she was just another sorority girl that I'd flashed my eyes at, shown my muscles to, and flirted my way into her bed. Truthfully, I did. I promised her later, I'd never tell anyone how she slept with me that night. It didn't take much to persuade her, but afterwards, when we were laying in my bed, her vulnerability about how scared she was of what others would think of her stuck with me. In the past, all the girls I slept with practically texted their friends before they got dressed, but her, she didn't want a soul to know that she'd allowed me to take her home.

That night, I kissed her good-bye, and assumed I'd never see her again. My life was too busy and my dreams too big to be tied down to one girl. In a campus of tens of thousands, how would our paths ever cross again? They hadn't before that night, at least from what I knew. How foolish that thinking was though, because the next day, when I turned around after buying my coffee in the student center, there she was, biting her lip as her eyes glowed with seduction like she was remembering the highlights of the night before. I asked her to sit with me and she accepted. By the time our coffees were cold, I'd asked her to dinner. Like everything else up to that point, she'd accepted my invitation without hesitation. She'd never played hard to get, and I loved how she'd wanted to spend time with me as much I did with her. Quickly, we were inseparable. She's all I thought of, all I wanted, and I even nestled her into my future plans. Then, I fucked it up.

Hands clap in front of me. "Ashby!" Coach screams, pulling me from the memory of Taylor and me.

"Shit. Sorry." I shake my head to surface back to the here and now. The swim team is shuffling to the locker rooms, some glancing back at me and whispering to others. I feel like I should raise my hand and just announce myself like I'm in an AA meeting.

"Let's go back to my office." He swings his clipboard down, and doesn't offer me a hand up. I expected as much.

I follow him past the pool, through the locker room doors,

and straight to his office. The whole time, memories are coming back to me, and I miss Tanner more than a guy should. Half our college years were spent here razzing each other.

The slap of the clipboard on his desk startles me. His office chair squeaks when he sits down, propping his feet up on the edge of the desk, his eyes peering over at me.

I slide into a chair in front of him after I close the door. The air in the small room tenses. I rub my sweaty palms down my jeans and attempt to hold his pissed-off gaze. The worst part is it's not as much pissed off as it is disappointed.

"What are you looking for?"

"An opportunity." I'm honest.

"Why should I give you one?"

"Please, Coach. Do you know anyone who might be looking for an assistant? I miss the water," I beg for any opportunity, inching forward in my seat.

"I can make some phone calls, but your reputation proceeds you." He reminds me of the nightmare of a life I made for myself two years ago. "But I'll see."

He's being a hell of a lot nicer than I thought he would be.

"Thanks, Coach. I truly appreciate it."

He nods and then puts on his reading glasses and studies the paper lying on his desk. He tosses a piece of paper and pen my way.

"Write your name and number down," he mindlessly instructs, concentrating on whatever he's reading. "Then you can excuse yourself."

I do what he says, and my hand is on the doorknob before he speaks again. "You look good, Ashby. Whatever you're doing, it's working," he mumbles to the newspaper and a small smile creases my lips.

"Thanks, Coach. You look good too," I say, and he huffs.

"I've gained thirty pounds and developed high blood pressure, but thanks for the bullshit as always, Ashby."

I shake my head and sneak through the door, crossing my

fingers he can find a lead of something where I can coach or do anything in the water. I'm not meant to spend my days behind a desk inside some stifling office building.

The door clicks behind me and I weave through the locker room, again with the whispers at my back, but I can't be upset. I'm the one who gave them the ammunition to fire my way.

I'm out of the pool house on the way to my truck when my phone dings in my pocket at the same time someone hollers my name.

"Brad Ashby?" they question, and I pull my phone out of my pocket, seeing a number I don't recognize. Clicking ignore, I wait for the young kid in shorts and a T-shirt to catch up to me. His hair is black and wet, his face flushed and red. There's something familiar about him though.

"That's me." I stuff my hands in my pockets, hearing the ding of a voicemail on my phone.

"Hey. I'm Cayden Mendes. I'm Greg's brother." He pants, catching his breath.

Greg was my teammate and a year younger, which means he must have graduated last year. In the haste of my life's turmoil, I lost track of everyone on the swim team, but Tanner.

"Really. How is Greg? I haven't talked to him in years. He was going for Architecture, right?" I recall the small fact I remember about a guy who was my drinking partner at parties.

"Um . . . he died." The kid's face pales at the same time my stomach drops.

"What?" I lean closer, as though I didn't hear him right.

"He got in a car accident last year right after graduation." His voice lowers and my heart breaks for this kid. Thoughts of if anything ever happened to Piper wiggle into my conscious before I can shut them down.

"Jesus. I'm sorry, Cayden. He was a great guy." He was always ready to stand beside me in the fights between us and the football players. You always knew he had your back. "Please give your family my condolences." I place my hand on his shoulder, and his chin falls to his chest.

"Thank you. He always bragged about you. What a great swimmer you were."

"Not that good," I correct.

"I'm sure you have a really busy life, but can I ask you something?"

The hope in this kid's eyes has me agreeing before he asks.

"My brother had been working with me. I think I'm about to be cut, and I need someone to train me. Even if it's only one time, would you be willing to work with me? Tell me where I need improvements—?"

I laugh and hold up my hand to stop his rambling. "Sure."

"Sure? Really?" His body starts fidgeting and I wait for him to take flight somehow he's so damn excited.

"Yeah. I have some time." More time than he knows. I pull out my phone, seeing that voicemail button marked with a one. "What's your phone number?"

Cayden tells me and I type it in my phone, then text him so he has mine.

"Message me your schedule and we'll work out a time. When are cuts?"

"Three weeks."

"Okay. Don't sweat it. We'll get you there." I clasp him on the shoulder again. "I'm really sorry about Greg, Cayden. He was a great guy." I repeat what I'd said, unable to form words that express my sincerity.

"Yeah, he was. Thank you, Brad." His eyes light up and a smile crosses my lips at how happy my agreement made the kid.

"Sure. Text me tonight and we'll get a time down." I back step to my truck as the kid rushes back inside to the warmth of the building.

Pressing my voicemail key, the first thing I hear is Emerson's screaming. It's Mrs. Allen.

"Hi, Brad. This is Mrs. Allen. Emerson has a fever and I

can't seem to get a hold of Taylor. I can't have her here with the other kids. I'll wait for a minute, and then I guess I'll call Sam."

I click off to not listen to the message anymore. Like fuck she's calling Sam.

The phone rings as I jog the last steps to my car, climbing in, and start it up. Finally, after numerous rings, she picks up.

"Hello, Brad. No worries, I called Sam and he's on his way."

Bile rises my throat. I guess when she says a minute, she means sixty seconds.

"No, no. I'm coming." I look at the clock, realizing I'm more than an hour away. "Can you just keep her there for like an hour?"

"An hour?" Her voice shrills. "I'm sorry, I can't. The other children. We'll just have Sam come, and then you two can meet up."

I have no choice. The lady won't budge as much as I wish she would. "Yeah, thanks. I'll get a hold of Taylor."

We say our good-byes and I can't dial Taylor's number fast enough. While I wait for her to answer, my anger brews more intense. I hate this vulnerable feeling. The protectiveness that she's my daughter pores through me and quickly my vision narrows into one line. I'm her father, not Sam.

"Hi," she answers.

"Where the hell have you been?"

"Hi, Brad."

"Taylor. Where have you been?"

I repeat my question in the same accusative voice.

"I'm working. If this is about Em, I know. Sorry, she shouldn't have bothered you."

My anger boils, spilling out everywhere.

"No, she should have. I'm her goddamn father. Fuck, Taylor."

I hear her suck in her breath over the receiver, and I take a deep breath, but it doesn't calm me.

"What is wrong, Brad?" she asks, and I hear the receiver muffle as she talks to someone else. "Okay, sorry. I'm going outside."

The sliding doors of the hospital alert me she's outside. "What's wrong? How about the fact that some guy is picking up my daughter. Or that you said she shouldn't have bothered me. She's mine, Taylor."

"And mine, Brad. And it isn't some guy. It's Sam. The guy she's known—"

She stops herself and I'm thankful, because I might just throw my phone out the window of my truck, which is currently going seventy-five miles per hour.

"Don't say it, Taylor," I seethe.

"I wasn't going to. She's sick, Brad. I know you were going to the University to talk to Coach Kass. I was only apologizing because I didn't want her to interrupt you." Her voice lowers, and I wonder if she has someone around her.

"The fact that you think I wouldn't want to be bothered that my daughter is sick pisses me off, Taylor. Straight up. I can't believe you would say that." I inhale another breath, considering the thought that's been lingering in my head the past few days. The same thought Dylan told me to hold off on and not mention to Taylor. But I can't sit back and not have any control over it anymore. Still Dylan's voice, *'Give it awhile. It's only been a week,'* rings in my mind, but I can't wait any longer.

"I want custody," I rush out, my voice much calmer than before.

Silence seeps over the line, but I hear her breathing.

"Brad, we need to talk more," she says, but I'm shaking my head, even though she can't see me.

"No, we don't. Taylor, I really hope things work out between us, and I want you both in my future, but I need to know Emerson will always be." My heart breaks because I'm sure

I'm shattering Taylor again, but I can't idly sit back and let another man take care of my daughter.

"Let's just talk about it, work it out between us. It's only been a short time, Brad."

I pull over on the side of the highway, needing to calm down.

"I don't like him around her."

Another long pause of silence on the other end.

"Please, Brad. We can handle this together."

I'm surprised on how even keeled my voice is when I open my mouth to respond.

"I need an answer to a question, Taylor." My car rattles as another truck breezes by. I take her silence as a sign to keep going. "Would you have ever sought me out and told me about her?"

She gasps, and I don't think I'm going to get an answer from her.

"I don't know."

"I'll take that as a no."

"God, Brad. Can we please not do this over the phone?" I hear how upset she is, but all rationality I have is slipping away from me.

The thought of Sam having my daughter is like fifty knives stabbing me. "Tell Sam I'll meet him at the house. I'll be there when you get out of work. We'll talk then." I hang up, unable to hear the bullshit she's spouting. She was never going tell me I had a daughter, but she's mistaken if she thinks I'm going to let Sam try to slide into my spot. I've missed two years, and I'm not missing anymore, even if I have to pay through the nose in attorney fees.

ten

Taylor

U NABLE TO IDLY SIT BY while a brawl breaks out at my house between Sam and Brad, I beg Dr. James to let me go early. Lucky for me, he's in a real good mood and we've slowed down dramatically in the past hour. There's only an hour left in my shift, so Olivia agrees to cover my patients.

I park alongside Sam's truck in the driveway. Inhaling the deepest breath, I climb out of my beat-up car and walk through the back door. Em isn't anywhere, and the two men are sitting on opposite ends of the couch watching television. What in the world could I have missed?

"Hi," I announce myself, approaching the back of the couch.

Sam's eyes light up and Brad's roll.

"She's sleeping," Sam says, moving to stand. My guess isn't to leave. He circles around the end of the couch to meet me. Leaning over, he kisses my cheek, and I draw back, questioning why he would do that. "Welcome home."

"Jesus," Brad whispers under his breath. He stands and his hurt eyes find mine, bringing a ripple of guilt. "I guess we'll talk later, so you can have quality time with lover boy." He moves over to door, grabbing his coat from the hook.

The words stay locked in my throat because I can't have the conversation in front of Sam. I've already hurt him so much, but I've hurt Brad too. I'm stuck in a lose-lose situation.

"Are you leaving?" I step forward, closer to him, but Sam follows.

"Yeah. We'll talk another time." He slides his arms through his jacket and then peers down at me, his caramel eyes swimming with defeat. "Can I have her a night? Take her to my parents?"

Sam coughs out, "Yeah right." I look over my shoulder, scolding him with my eyes.

"Brad," I sigh, moving closer to him.

"Can I talk to you outside then?" he says. Not waiting for me to answer, he swings the door open and steps out to stand on my front stoop.

"Stay here," I instruct Sam as though he's my dog. Why not treat him like one, he's peeing a circle around me and Em.

I zip my coat back up and follow him outside.

My feet barely hit the snow-dusted concrete before Brad starts talking, "Taylor, I'm sorry for earlier. I acted rash. I was just thrown off." He shakes his head, drops his gaze but instantly picks it back up, his eyes locking with mine. "But I want time with her."

I nod, knowing I'd have to share her, but it doesn't make it any easier. My nose tickles and I fear with all the emotions stirring inside me, I'm going to declare every fear and hope I have and dump it for him to deal with.

"Okay, but she's never been away from home."

"I'll only be at my parents'. They live an hour away."

We never got to that step in our relationship where one meets the parents. I imagine they're wealthy, poised, and caring people. Complete opposite from my family.

"It's hard for me, Brad. That's asking a lot."

"Asking a lot? You didn't tell me I had a daughter for two years, and I'm asking for one night. You're refusing?"

I exhale a breath in a slow stream, delaying my answer. "I didn't refuse."

"You didn't say yes either." He steps closer to me, the familiar scent of his cologne invading my senses. "This isn't up for debate. I want her for a night."

I hold my hands up, his heaving chest giving off heat. I quickly remove them before I lose all willpower. "Okay, okay. I'm off the next two days. That's when I really get to spend time with her. Would you mind if I came with?"

He backs up, stares up at the star-lined sky, and his chest rises and falls. "That defeats the point. I want to take care of her by myself."

My hand brushes his arm and he jolts, finally peering down at me. "Maybe we could talk too?" His sadness about our situation is stirring something within me, something that's telling me to give us an honest chance, at least for Em's sake.

"Okay." His shoulders fall and his eyes burn with something other than sadness now. It's desire, and it's pointed right toward me. A small smile creeps the corners of his lips and my stomach flips. Suddenly, we're back where we were two years ago and he's kissing me goodbye outside my door. "I'm going to hold you to that."

My hand falls to my stomach, relieved we're back to where we were before Mrs. Allen's call, or at least, he's acting like we are. I'll take either at this point.

My body shakes from the cold wind whipping around us. Brad pulls me into him and my hands easily slide around his back. His lips drop a kiss on the top of my head. Comforting and safe. Brad's the only one able to bring those feeling from me.

"I don't want you to leave," I whisper into his jacket, half hoping the wind gust will carry my confession away.

"I don't want to." His arms tighten around me and warmth spreads to the pit of my stomach. "But I won't sit in the same room as that douche."

I draw back, and his hands cup my cheeks.

"He's helped me so much. Can't you guys just try to get

along?" The fight inside of me to keep them both in my life shows and his hands drop to his sides.

"He told me you two were 'together'." He puts up air quotes.

I blink, processing the information. I take full responsibility that lines might have been blurred between us, but I always stayed on my side. He's my sister's husband, and I would never see him as anything but that.

"That's not true." I swallow down the anger. "I swear—"

His finger presses against my lips. "I know." There isn't a sign on his face that tells me he believes otherwise.

"Now, I need you to go." My fingers grab his jacket by the fistfuls to hold him in front of me. "I have to talk to Sam. I thought I had cleared this up a few nights ago, but I'm guessing I didn't."

"I'll wait out here." I should have expected nothing less.

"No. We're going to take this night away from one another. Then you're picking Em and me up first thing in the morning, and we'll go to your parents' for the weekend." I smile and a slow grin spreads across his face.

"Okay." His head slowly nods and his eyes focus in on my lips for a second.

My tongue snakes out of reflex and his breathing becomes shallow. Unable to hold back, I rise on my tiptoes and lightly press my lips to his. Not wanting to allow it to go any further, I fall back on my heels. He blinks, those caramel eyes glimmering like he's a thirteen-year-old boy who'd just had his first kiss.

"I'll be here at nine," he says. "She can nap on the way."

My stomach somersaults because he already knows my— our daughter's schedule.

"We'll be waiting."

His blazing eyes studies mine, and his hand slowly rises, grazing my cheek as his thumb swipes back and forth. "Good night, Taylor."

My body shivers as I watch his retreating back round the corner of the house toward his car. He never looks back, and I wait for his truck to pull out, wishing it were coming, not leaving.

After he reverses, he waits on the street. He motions for me to go inside, and I nod, remembering he likes to make sure I'm safely inside before he leaves.

When I open the door and step in, Sam is relaxed on my couch, his legs outstretched on top of my coffee table. I've seen him in this position plenty of times and it's never brought up the clenching sensation in my stomach it does right now.

"We need to talk," I say, and break the distance between us.

His legs swing down and his elbows rest on his knees. He expected this conversation, which is evident when his head falls between his shoulders before I say anything. "Why are you giving him another shot?"

The distress is clear on his face, and I could smother myself for being the one who put us in this position. I should have never leaned on him as much as I did. I should have kept some distance between us, especially since he really isn't family, what with my sister leaving him for some jackoff, who could score her more drugs.

"He's her father."

He inhales a deep breath and his eyes follow me while I slide into the chair opposite him.

"It's not because of Em that you're giving him a chance."

I nod.

"Do you still love him?"

My fingers knot together and I look down at the carpeted floor. I'm not going to shatter him.

"Do you?" His voice rises and my shoulders shake from the surprise. I thought I would be unable to be that truthful to him, but with his voice rising, he's asking for it.

I lift my head and allow my eyes to lock with his. He will

not intimidate me. I might feel guilt for allowing him to accept a role that wasn't his in the first place, but I never stepped over that line. Not even an awkward hug was exchanged between us. I'm not going to pretend otherwise.

"I do."

His eyes darken as he stands up, snatching his coat from the arm of the chair. All his movements sharp and deliberate.

"Figures. Don't women always want what they shouldn't?" he mumbles and stalks toward the door. "I promise you, Taylor, he'll hurt you again. But now it's not only you, it's Em, too. What are you going to tell her the next time you find him with some trash?"

I swallow down the words that I still fear every day.

"You don't have to worry about it if it happens. I'll handle it."

"Damn right you will. Seriously,"—his fists clench in the air, his knuckles whitening, and it's the first time I've witnessed this side of him, when his control is hanging on by a thread—"why do you Delaney girls want these boys, who treat you like shit? What's wrong with the good guys, who cook you dinner, take care of your kids, and want to spend evenings wrapped up in only you?"

My breathing stutters, because if this world made sense, I wouldn't want a guy who cheated on me with some girl, whose name he probably doesn't remember. I'd want a man like Sam—reliable, caring, and loving. But I can't help but remember Brad has those qualities too. Most of all, I can't deny that my heart belongs to Brad.

"What can I say, Sam? Do you want to hear all the details? How my heart yearns for his arms to hold me at night. That seeing him with Em ignites this fire so deep and hot, I'm not sure I can hold myself back. I love him, and yes, we've both done shitty things to each other, but I never stopped loving him."

He huffs and back steps to the door. "You disgust me," he

sneers and opens the door. "Go fuck your life up just like your sister."

At first, I'm taken aback by his insults. It's out of character for the Sam I know. But being unable to hold my mouth back at any point in my life, I have the last word before the door clicks shut. "Go to hell."

The door closes and I rush over, flicking the lock. My back rests along the door and my body slides down until my ass hits the floor. "He's wrong. Brad will not hurt me this time around," I murmur, hoping like hell if I repeat it enough times my fear will never come true.

"OH, EM, HELP MOMMY OUT a little."

Em is standing at my legs, grasping for dear life as I try to pack her things for the weekend trip. I've picked up my phone at least five times this morning, ready to cancel on Brad. The thought of meeting his parents after hiding Em's existence doesn't give me the warm fuzzies. Then add on the fact I invited myself. My only hope is, by some off chance, Piper's in town.

"Mama," she whines, and my shoulders slump, looking down at her, eager for me to hold her.

"One minute, okay?" I abandon her bag and sit in the rocker. She climbs onto my lap with my help and we sit there for a minute. Her hands roam over my face and play with my hair. "You're going to meet some people today," I say.

"Yeah," she replies, her standard answer for almost anything I say.

"Your grandparents."

"Papa," she says, and I shake my head. She thinks she's seeing my dad, who doesn't even know anything about Brad, or the fact I'm leaving town for a few days. His life is that barstool at Carolle's Tap.

"New grandparents."

She busies herself with what I can assume is memorizing the features on my face, which makes me believe I'm having a one-way conversation with myself.

"Brad's," I say, and her hands stop on my face, her eyes widen.

"Dada?" My head draws back and she claps her hands like I just announced we were going to have ice cream.

"Dada?" I question, because it's not something we've ever discussed. Not that she can make sense of our unusual situation, being only twenty-two months.

"Dada?" She twists around, her eyes examining every nook and cranny in the room. Not seeing what she wants, she climbs down from my lap and walks out of the room. "Dada," she repeats. "Dada!" Every time she says it, she's more insistent, and I wonder if she's looking for Sam.

She rolls on her stomach and slides down the stairs as I follow her, wondering where she's going. "Em, I need to pack your bag. Dada, or whoever you believe is Dada, isn't here," I say, but she never turns around. Once her little feet hit the bottom of the stairs, she scampers over to the window, drawing back the curtain.

"Dada!" she screams. She peers up at me and out the window again. "Dada!" Flabbergasted by this whole exchange, I kneel down by her at the window, seeing no one except a man walking his dog across the street.

"That's not Dada, baby." My hand smoothes down her unruly hair. I make a mental note to pull it up into pigtails before we leave. No need for Brad's parents to think I'm incapable of grooming their grandchild.

"Dada!" She pounds on the glass, and I grab her hand.

"That's not Dada," I repeat, trying to persuade her back upstairs.

Just as we're passing the front door, the doorbell rings. I glance at the clock on the wall, noticing it's only eight, then back down to my unshowered self. Letting go of Em's hand, I walk to the door and investigate through the peephole. Brad stands there with his hands in his jacket pockets, rocking back and forth on his feet.

"You're early," I say through the door, running a hand through my greasy hair.

"Thought you might need help."

"I'm not ready."

"Yeah, that's why I'm here. Why are we having this conversation through the door?"

"Because I'm not ready."

"Open the door, Taylor."

"No."

"I held your hair back while you threw up Taco Bell in an alley. Open the door." My shoulders slump. He has a point. "Maybe we should discuss the times we'd screw each other in the morning, or how I ventured down—"

I unlock the door and open it up before he can finish. "No need to go down memory lane," I say once we're standing face to face.

"Dada!" Em screams and runs toward him. Brad's barely able to pull his hands out of his pockets to catch her.

"Emerson." He scoops her up and she runs her hands down his scratchy beard.

"I quite enjoyed thinking about those times when you couldn't keep your hands off me," he softly says, and presses his lips to Em's forehead.

"Well, that's probably how we got her," I mention, twisting my mop of hair into a ball behind my head.

"Let's make some more." He chuckles, and a nervous laugh sneaks out, unsure how serious he is.

"You mind filling me in on why she's calling you Dada?" Em's admiring eyes stare up at her dad like he's Santa Clause. She already loves him. Those annoying words Sam spilled out last night float back to the forefront of my mind. Brad will stick around, I'm sure of it.

"I taught it to her." A proud expression splashes across his face and he carries Em into my house.

"When?" I shut the door and flick the lock while trying not to inhale his cologne that makes me dizzy with want.

"We worked on it when I'd pick her up. Who am I, Emerson?" he prompts her.

"Dada," she answers, and he reaches into his pocket to grab a row of Smarties. He unrolls it and hands her a colored sugar disc.

"Good job." She places it on the tongue she's stuck out once she answered.

"She's not a dog," I comment. "It's like you're conducting Pavlov's experiment while I'm at work."

"No, it's not. I don't give her the reward, and then she says it. It's reinforcement. She says Mama and she should say Dada too." He places her on the ground and she scurries over to her toy bin. "And not to that jackass," he whispers only to me, and I roll my eyes because this whole thing is so Brad.

I exhale a deep breath and decide not to fight. I took enough away from him all those years ago.

"Do you mind watching her while I shower?" I begin to back step to the stairs, and he sits with Em on the floor.

"Not at all. Em likes spending time with her Dada." He laughs, tickling her, which entices her laughter, and then he looks back to me with a cocky grin. All I can do is smile back because they are terribly cute together.

"I'll be fast."

"Taylor?" Brad yells, and I stop, looking back over to him.

"You're a knock-out in the morning." One side of his mouth curves up and a rush of heat floods my body. After a deep inhale, I double-time it up the stairs before I run over to him and sprinkle kisses all over his face.

An hour later, we're packed up in Brad's truck and on our way out of Roosevelt.

"Good riddance," I say as we pass the Leaving Roosevelt sign.

"That's not nice," Brad comments, fiddling with the radio.

I glance back at Em staring out the window, holding one of the princess dolls that her Dada gave her. Her eyes are droopy, signaling she's close to falling asleep.

"I hate this town," I whisper, which he should already know. I rambled on enough about it in college. But then again, maybe he wasn't listening.

"I remember," he says on cue, and my heart thaws more toward him. He reaches across the center console and squeezes my leg. "Why did you come back?"

I look over my shoulder, finding Em asleep, so I turn my eyes to Brad, who I find is checking on her in the rearview mirror, too. At this rate, my heart will be leaping out of my chest and into his hands before we hit his parents' house.

"My sister had promised to help me, but that was short-lived. She vanished before I delivered. Actually, the day I went into labor she disappeared. The nurse kept trying to call her, but she never picked up. I delivered Em by myself with a nurse holding my hand."

I hear his quick intake of breath next to me. "I'm sorry. I didn't mean to make you feel sorry for me."

He shakes his head and his eyes focus on the road in front of us. "I wish things would have been different. The thought of you by yourself is hard to swallow."

It had been excruciating at the time. I never thought we'd get through it, but we did. "It was my own doing." I cross my legs and shift them toward the window, because if he tries to console me now, I'm fairly sure my willpower will wane.

"No one deserves to go through that alone. I wish you would have told me."

But I didn't and I can't change that fact, so I don't respond and he seems to drop the topic.

"I told my parents about Emerson. You should be prepared

by knowing that Tanner's parents live next to mine, so they might come by too. It might be awkward at first."

"Were your parents upset that they are just finding out now?" I feel like my lungs are on fire and I can't catch my breath from the anxiety resting in my chest.

"A little. I explained the situation, but I'll run interference if need be."

"Brad, maybe I shouldn't go." I turn my body to face him. I don't do confrontation well, and it sounds like there could be an altercation. The last thing I can deal with is Brad fighting with his parents.

"Don't be silly. They'll forgive and forget." He waves me off. I'm guessing they've forgiven and forgotten his mistakes.

His hand on my thigh pulls me from my thoughts. "Hey, don't worry. I promise my parents are as great as me. Hell, they raised me. They know what a screwup I am, so don't worry. Plus, I'll never let them treat you bad. Not that they would. Fuck, listen to me ramble." He shakes his head as though that will stop his mouth from moving.

"Okay." What else could I say at this point?

"Do you remember Bea from college? Piper's friend?"

The sassy blonde that always made rude comments to me. How could I forget? "Yeah."

"She and Tanner's brother, Dylan, have some screwed and weird thing going on, so they might join us for dinner one night."

"Great." Too bad the sarcasm didn't leave my tone before the word came out.

Brad looks over and smiles. "I gotcha. Don't worry."

No matter how many times he promises it, my level of anxiety continues to rise. I can't help thinking, *what did I sign myself up for?*

eleven

Brad

I F I THOUGHT FACING MY parents after I decided to call off my wedding to Bayli was appalling, walking in with Taylor and Emerson is dreadful. My parents didn't say much when I told them over the phone, which means in the hours since, they could have turned either angry or understanding. You never can tell with them. In the end, they're both usually even-keeled, and give Piper and me the benefit of the doubt.

I drive through downtown, passing Carsen's Steakhouse, and check to see Emerson's head slumped over.

"Is that okay?" I nod my head toward the back of the car and Taylor checks on her.

She shifts back to fix our daughter's head. Her breasts press against my arm and my hand tightens on the steering wheel. It's bad enough she's wearing tight-ass skinny pants that show off every damn curve she's developed after having Emerson, now all I can imagine is her pebbled nipples that always looked like little kisses, begging me to devour them.

Emerson mumbles something and shifts her head to the other side while Taylor settles back into the passenger seat, fastening her seatbelt. I try not to stare at the view of her separated breasts the seatbelt causes. Instead I stare forward, weaving through the backstreets to my parents' house.

"You grew up here?" She stares out the window, admiring the downtown houses. Hearthwood isn't as small as Roosevelt, but believe me, everyone knows everyone. Especially when you call off your engagement and your biggest mistakes are stationed on every news channel. When your best friend makes the Olympics and you don't, it's known.

"Yeah. Down that street is my high school." I take a sharp turn left, detouring us. "I'll show you."

A minute later, I'm parked in the lot of my high school where GO COUGARS is painted on the side of the pool house. All my dreams sprouted from my freshman year in that water, got me a scholarship to Michigan along with Tanner. I always thought we were equal, but if I'm honest with myself, which I rarely ever am, he's always been a faster swimmer than me. His form perfected well before mine did.

"Nice," she says, looking at the sporadic cars in the parking lot.

I do a quick U-turn, suddenly not liking memory lane.

"Yeah. That's where I became the man I am," I joke to dodge any emotions she might be able to sense.

Her hand grips my bicep. "I can't imagine you without these."

She's a damn ego boost, and there was a time I convinced myself the only reason I fell in love with her was because she was gracious with the compliments. Oh, how wrong I was.

Her hand rests on my forearm and I know she's not done with trying to pry me open.

"You know you can talk to me, right? That I'd never judge you." There it is, the real reason I love her. She actually gives a shit about me. Took me too damn long to figure that one out.

"I know." My eyes fixate on the cracks on the road. There's a zillion things I want to tell her, but not when I'm a minute away from my parents' house. I need to armor the façade before going into my childhood home. Eventually, her hand ventures back over to her lap and the despair I don't want anyone to find out about slithers back down.

Silence takes over the car for the rest of the drive. I turn into my parents' neighborhood and Taylor gasps.

"Brad?" she asks, and I should have warned her, but how do I do that when to me it's no big deal? But Taylor has always been hung up on money.

"Relax." Her hand grips the car door handle as she peers out to the houses on the hills. It's not like my family has Bayli's kind of money. I think Taylor would throw up if she saw their mansion.

"I figured, but this is just—" Fear strikes her beautiful blue eyes and I wish I could calm her down from the panic attack she's about to have.

"It's just a house." I try my best to ease her concern, but her body is becoming defensive as she twists and turns like a damn pretzel. She stares back at Emerson and I fear she's developing an escape plan.

I pull into the driveway, and the first thing I notice is the pool, which is covered up for the winter, but I know the hot tub is good to go. Maybe with some convincing, I can get Taylor in there at some point.

We park under the basketball hoop and I take her hands in mine. "My parents are normal, okay? I promise you, whatever you are thinking isn't the case. Like I said, I'm here for you. No one will treat you like less than a princess." I wink and her shoulders relax a little.

"I have to tell you something," she spits out at the same time as the garage door opens. Should have known my mom would be peering out the window, waiting on us.

I look up to find my parents approaching the truck, and then back to her. "Can it wait?"

Her face pales, but she nods, uncertainty occupying her eyes.

"Just be yourself, I know they'll love you." I squeeze her hands, turn off the engine, and climb out.

113

"Brad," my mom says first. There's a light smile on her face, and I relax, realizing she's going to be on my side with this one.

"Hey, Mom." I wrap my arms around her thin frame and lift her feet off the ground.

She smacks my shoulders to place her feet back down, which I do. My dad approaches, holding his hand out to me. He bears that stern face, like the time I got caught drinking at a high school party by the cops. He's not on my side, but he shakes my hand and pulls me into a hug anyway.

"Hey, Dad," I say, and he pats my back but says nothing.

Taylor rounds the back of my car and the air becomes charged with tension. Her eyes concentrate on me, and I smile to ease her apprehension. Her shoulder brushes mine and I swing my arm around her shoulders.

"Mom, Dad, this is Taylor." My mom steps closer to my dad and they each smile. *Good sign.*

"Hi, Taylor," my mom says, and holds her hand out.

"Hi, Mr. and Mrs. Ashby." She's so cute I could kiss her senseless.

"You can call us Chris and Maggie," my mom continues to be the communicator.

"Emerson is sleeping," I say right as a little hand slaps the window.

"Mama," she whines, and Taylor moves out of my hold to open the door. Once Emerson appears, my mom sucks in a quick inhale of breath.

Taylor unbuckles her and sweeps Emerson into her arms. My little girl's eyes observe her new surroundings, gracing me with a small smile before burying her head in Taylor's chest.

"She doesn't wake up well," Taylor excuses, and her hand automatically soothes her back. "It will just take a few minutes."

"Come on, let's go inside." I wave my hand in the air.

My parents lead the way while I wait for Taylor to walk in

front of me. She bites her lip and glances at Emerson clinging to her like a life raft.

By the time we enter the house, my parents are in the kitchen and are laying out a spread of sandwich meats out for us. A highchair sits in the corner and a floor full of toys in the middle of the family room.

"You guys have been busy," I say, and my mom smiles.

"I didn't want you guys to be inconvenienced." Mom's fingers fiddle with a napkin, her eyes fixated on Emerson. "I hope you don't mind, Taylor."

Taylor's eyes widen.

"Not at all. Thank you." They share a smile and I have to think this is a good sign.

Emerson peeks up, but quickly buries her head back into her chest and Taylor sighs. I reach out to Emerson, but she shakes her head. Although a flash of tension runs through me at first, I push it back because she's just a little girl who wants her mommy.

My dad moves to the fridge. "Did you guys want something to drink?"

"I'll take a water, Dad," I answer.

"Taylor?" he asks, and her body relaxes a little more.

"Water would be great, thank you." My dad brings over the waters, opening Taylor's for her since Em's wrapped around her like a koala bear. "Thank you." My dad nods.

"Brad, may I see you in my office?" my dad asks, and I tilt my head. "It will only take a minute."

I glance down at Taylor. If I thought she had fear in her eyes in the car, she's straight up terrified now.

"We'll be fine, Brad. I don't bite," my mom says and moves over to the table, patting the spot across from her for Taylor.

"Will you be okay?"

Taylor visibly swallows, but seeing my mom looking at us, she nods. I guarantee she's lying.

My dad waits for me in the hallway, tapping his fingers on the crown molding. "I'll make it quick," I say, placing my hand on Emerson's back.

I steadily walk to my dad, who turns on his heels once I reach him, and I follow him into his office. The dark mahogany furniture is intimidating. Maybe it's because all of my punishments have started in this office. Just the mere presence of that chair across from his with only a strip of wood between us, makes my heart beat faster.

I shut the door and sit down, not leaning back because this needs to go quick.

"I talked to Rick." He links his hands together. Rick is our lawyer, the same one who swindled the justice system to free me from the idiotic things I've done since I was a teenager.

"I don't want to hear it, Dad. I'm handling it." I place my hand in the air, hoping it will speed up this conversation.

"Just listen. He suggests you file for joint custody. You have no rights, and he guarantees your name isn't on her birth certificate." He leans back in his chair, and I notice his face is starting to bear wrinkles. I'm probably responsible for most of them. The small amount of grey hair sprinkled at his temples shows he's growing older.

"I trust her."

"She withheld the fact that you had a daughter for almost two years. You can't trust her." His lips tense into a straight line. "Your mother, she's beside herself for missing so much time with her granddaughter."

"Is this about Mom or me?" Irritation making my voice sharp. Is he worried more about my wellbeing or hers?

"Both. You have to hold rights to her, Brad. Otherwise, nothing is stopping her from taking your daughter again. You have to see my point this time."

I do, but I won't tell him that. I'm scared shitless about something happening and Emerson disappearing from my life, but everything in my gut tells me to believe in us.

"Since the minute I showed back up in Taylor's life, she's done nothing but accommodate me."

"Your daughter won't even go to you. You're fooling yourself." His nostrils start to flare, which is a telltale sign he's about to lose his temper.

"She just woke up. Give it more than five minutes." I stand, not willing to sit here and listen to his bullshit.

His fist pounds on the desk, startling me. "I can't give you more time. You just never think with your head, Brad."

"You're kidding me, right? It's my life. In case you haven't noticed, I'm all grown up."

"I'll believe it when I have to stop bailing you out."

"You don't have to bail me out. I'm perfectly fine."

"How do you suppose you'll support her or them?"

"I'm looking for a job, okay?"

I tread toward the door and my dad stands, his height similar to mine.

"Brad, Rick's coming tomorrow," he says, and my heart clenches as I hold the doorknob in my hand.

"Tell him not to. I'm not going to fight her for Emerson." I open the door a sliver to free myself.

"You're being ridiculous. Think about what I said."

I slam the door shut again and pin him with my matching eyes.

"No. It's done, Dad. Tell Rick not to waste his time."

My dad stares at me long and hard, contemplating his next step. He's never one to back down.

"Fine, but believe me, you'll regret it."

I don't respond and open the door, leaving the confines of his office. I'm not fifteen anymore, and this isn't about me TP-ing Johnny Carmichael's house. I'm a grown man with a family to support. He'll figure that out soon enough.

Making a beeline right to the kitchen, I can hear Emerson giggling. When I turn the corner, my mom is tickling her feet in the highchair while she gobbles down some of the lunchmeat my mom had out.

"Dada!" Em exclaims, and my mom's mouth hangs open, peering over to me.

"Hey, baby girl," I say, kissing the top of her head before taking the seat next to Taylor.

"She knows?" my mom asks, and Taylor rolls her eyes.

"Hell, yes. I taught her who I was." I grab a roll and start preparing a sandwich, happy to see Taylor already has a plate full of food.

"You'll have to use better language now." My mom raises her eyebrows at me and I nod, agreeing.

My dad follows me in a few minutes later. Hopefully, after he's called off the wolves, namely Rick and his guys, from Taylor. He sits and begins to prepare his own sandwich with little acknowledgement of anyone in the room.

Emerson eats her plate and then wiggles and whines in her highchair. Taylor moves to stand and so does my mom.

"Do you mind?" my mom asks Taylor, and Taylor sits back down with a smile.

"No."

You'd think my mom just won the lottery with the smile plastered to her face. She holds her arms out and Emerson accepts the invitation. At this point, I think she'll go to anyone who will free her from the contraption. If I've learned anything about my daughter these past weeks, it's that she doesn't like restrictions. She probably inherited that from me.

My mom glows as she carries Emerson out of the kitchen. "I'll just take her to the family room." My mom informs Taylor, who looks behind her, seeing the toys by the couch.

"Don't worry. She's already had some poor schmuck here to child safety the place early this morning," my dad mumbles over a mouthful of his turkey sandwich.

"Oh, you didn't need to go to that much trouble," Taylor says, and I smile over at her. She's so sweet.

"Well, we don't want any harm done to her." The kitchen

chair slides along the floor and my dad walks over to the fridge.

"He's moody," I whisper, and she shoots me a nervous smile. Like one does to the dentist right before they're about to shoot you up with Novocain.

"How's Golden child?" I change the subject to Piper, because since she married the star Olympian, she's the number one child.

"Tanner and Piper are coming home for Thanksgiving. The McCains are hosting. Won't you join us, Taylor?" My dad opens up his Orangina on the way back to the table, and I'm wondering what spurred on his niceness in the last minute.

"Oh, I wish I could, but I usually have the meal for my family, and I wouldn't want to disappoint anyone."

"Then I'll probably be over there," I tell my dad, and I watch his chest rise and fall from a big breath.

"We can talk about it later," he says, taking a healthy bite of his sandwich.

"Are your parents in Roosevelt?" my dad asks, and Taylor's shaking hand grabs a hold of her water glass.

"Just my dad. My mom died when I was twelve." She downs a gulp of water while my stomach churns for never having asked her.

"I'm sorry to hear that." My dad sounds genuine.

"Thank you." Taylor's voice is so low I barely recognize it without the chipper tone it usually holds.

Emerson's squeal breaks the silence filling our table. I turn in my seat to find her with a basketball in her hand, throwing it into a small net. My mom claps and Emerson does it again, enticing that squeal once more. My daughter might be the most beautiful little girl in the world, though I'm a bit biased. My mom's eyes meet mine, and all the regrets I've felt after talking with my dad disappear. Happiness shines from her eyes right to my heart and I don't want that taken away from her.

Taylor swivels in her chair and our eyes lock. Hers aren't quite as happy as mine. Actually, there's worry and apprehension in them.

"I'm going over there." She stands and picks up her dish.

I take it from her hands. "I've got it, go."

She doesn't respond, but moves swiftly over to the floor. In a second, Emerson is on her lap and long forgotten is the basketball hoop and ball. My mom gives them a tight smile, but I can see her confusion. I feel the same way. What changed within Taylor in one swish of a basketball net?

twelve

Taylor

I SIT ON THE FLOOR and Em plops down onto my lap, like I knew she would. Watching her so ecstatic and already comfortable with Maggie, makes alarm bells go off inside me. Brad's family has money and with money there's power. They have another think coming if they believe they are going to steal her from me.

Em plays with the blocks between my legs and I sense Maggie's eyes teetering between Em and me. She's my daughter, and the sooner I make that clear, the better.

Brad's mom hands Em one of the blocks that escaped her hands and slides a little closer to us.

"She's very beautiful, Taylor." Her voice is low, almost like she's cautious now.

"Thank you. She has Brad and Piper's eyes."

"Yes, if you are up for it later, I'd love to show you their baby pictures. There's a lot of similarities in Emerson." She leans her back along the sofa, scooting next to me. "You've done a great job with her." She pats my leg and I wish the motherly approval didn't pull that guilt for invading their private play time to the forefront.

"Thank you." Those two words seem to be the only ones in my language currently.

"Would you mind going to lunch tomorrow so we can talk? Give Brad and Chris some alone time with her." She looks down at my hands and I curl my fingers into my palms. "Maybe we could get manicures."

Either the Ashby's are trying to suck up to me or she's just nice; either way, it sounds lovely and so does she. "Sure."

Her eyes express complete surprise, as though she never thought in a million years I would accept her invitation.

"Great. I'm going to call for reservations right now." She stands and waltzes back into the kitchen.

I'm not alone for a minute before Brad plops down shoulder to shoulder with me on the floor and kidnaps Em from between my legs. She laughs and her small hand brushes the fresh stubble of hair along his cheek. I've noticed she does it a lot now, like he's her little security blanket.

Brad jokes that he's going to put all the blocks in the plastic container and she slaps his hand.

"Hey, you've got Daddy's temper." He laughs and peers over at me, his eyes shining with pride.

"That she does," I confirm, and Brad wraps his arm around me.

I stiffen from the affection with his parents only a room away.

"Will you go out with only me tomorrow night?" he whispers, and if I thought my body was stiff a second ago, I was dead wrong. I'm a damn ironing board now.

"What about Em?" My eyes fixate on her, focusing on the small curls at the base of her neck that I refuse to cut off.

"My parents will watch her. They raised me." He's so carefree about the same thought that makes me fearful to a degree I'm not comfortable with.

"I don't know. Can we see how it goes?"

"Why? They are good people, Taylor. You can trust them."

Isn't this the way it always is with Brad? He's impulsive and wants what he wants when he wants it. But he's asking me to leave my daughter with people I didn't meet until today.

"I said maybe."

Em walks back to the basketball hoop and he turns to me, taking my hand in his. My eyes ping from corner to corner. "If we're going to give us a chance, we need to go out just the two of us. Taylor, I want to be with you, free of distractions." Tears threaten to escape, because in all the years I've waited for those words, now it comes with a condition. Being in the house with the people I fear could take my daughter away from me has those walls from two years ago building at a pace faster than I can rationally tear them down.

I nod, mostly because I want him to remove his hands from my face in front of his parents. I'm not used to showing any type of affection in front of parents.

"So, it's settled. Me and you on a date tomorrow night." He winks. "I've been waiting too long to get you alone, Taylor Delaney." My stomach flips, but I press my hand down to calm it down. Brad hasn't proven anything.

The doorbell rings and I jump before Brad's hands tightens around my head. Footsteps move to the door and Brad brings my head to his lips to kiss my forehead. All I want to do is snuggle into his strong chest with his arms safely around me, especially when Bea's voice rings through the foyer.

A second later, she and a guy who resembles Tanner McCain enter the room. She's dressed in a pair of skinny jeans and a long sweater with crazy polka dot socks. Her hair has grown a little longer now, to shoulder length. Her dark-rimmed glasses still adorn her face. She looks exactly the same.

"Taylor." She smiles as though we were friends. "You look great." She sits on the floor right beside me and I wish someone could explain why she's here.

"Hi, I'm Dylan." A hand outstretches in front of me. My eyes follow a sleeve of tattoos up to the same stunning green eyes of his brother. Dylan's different though. Where Tanner always had that boy next door, high school heartthrob look,

Dylan looks a little more dangerous and dark. Suddenly, it all makes sense why they are a couple. Bea always liked challenges.

"Hi. Taylor." I shake his hand and he cracks a smile.

"I know plenty about you." He shoots me a grin similar to what I remember of Tanner, and suddenly, I feel okay with him around.

"I've filled him in on the gory details," Bea says from next to me and that safe feeling vanishes.

"Don't listen to her," Dylan interrupts her. "Bea, come sit next to me." He sits down on the couch and pats the seat next to him. He crosses his ankle over his knee, showing it's not only his arms with tattoos. There's another one snaking out from his jeans.

"Emerson," Brad calls out to our daughter, and she looks his way after staring at Dylan and Bea. She runs over and into my lap, finally figuring out there are strangers in the room.

Brad's hand moves to her back.

"She's already scared of you?" Dylan laughs.

"No, she just has a high sensitivity when assholes enter the room," Brad throws back his own insult.

"Bradley," his mom scolds, joining the party.

"Sorry. Anyway, Emerson this is my good friend, Dylan." She peeks out from my shoulder, curious about who it is. "His friend, Bea." Brad continues and I can't see what she's looking at, but quickly her head turns in the direction of Brad's mom on my other side. Her hand soothes along Em's back just like Brad's did. A pain deepens in my heart that I'll never have that. With my mom gone, her memories fade with each day. There was a time when the smell of lilacs could pull me into the warmth of her embrace. Not anymore though.

"Come on, little girl. I'm a friend of your aunt's." Bea kneels down on the carpet, but Dylan plucks her up by her sweater.

"Don't scare her," Dylan remarks, and Bea's eyes fixate

on Em's back.

"I just want her to like me."

"Then give her time. You're scary to adults; what do you think a child sees?" Dylan shakes his head and Brad laughs as he scoots closer to me. His arm pulls me and Em to him like we're one happy little family. As though he's protecting us from the big bad Bea.

"Are you two, like . . . together again?" Bea asks, disdain clear in her voice. I swallow deep and tighten my arms around Em.

"Sly, Bea," Dylan says to her, but that doesn't move her vision from being fixated on us.

"So?"

"Cut it," Brad says, low and threatening. "You cannot tell Piper, by the way. I've yet to tell her," Brad adds, and I tilt my head at him. Why would he be holding it back from her?

"Piper will be home for Thanksgiving, Bea." Brad's mom interjects, shifting the conversation another way. *Thank you, Maggie.*

"Oh, she told me. I'm so excited." She practically bounces in her seat.

"Don't you have a family of your own?" Brad asks. The warmth of his thigh burns through my jeans.

"So, how is fatherhood for you, Brad?" Dylan dodges Brad's question with one of his own.

"Couldn't be better." Brad holds his arms out for Em, who has decided she could bless them with a peek.

Surprisingly, Em shifts over to him and he hands her the basketball that had fallen when she ran over to me.

She looks out of the corner of her eye, but Brad's mom reaches over and pulls the basketball net over to the middle of the room. Em instantly shifts her way and they begin playing basketball. Should have known she'd feel the gut instinct I did about her. She's warm, loving, and safe like a mother should be.

"Where's your dad?" I whisper to Brad and he shrugs.

"Who cares?"

Those two words tell me the meeting in the office was more than a welcome home celebration. Brad's dad isn't happy, and I can only imagine he's used to having power and isn't going to take it too kindly if Brad challenges him. Which from the tension in the kitchen after they returned, and knowing Brad, I'm positive they're disagreeing over something.

Dylan and Brad carry on about Tanner and how his butterfly position is slipping. The trainers are trying to work with him, but for some reason, he isn't gaining the speed he needs. It all goes over my head, and I don't really want to start a conversation with Bea, so I allow the illusion that I'm with Brad feel real as his fingers trace my shoulder in a steady circle and I watch our daughter with her only grandmother.

THE NEXT MORNING, I QUICKLY shower in my own private bathroom. On top of that, it's attached to a guest bedroom. A big difference from the two-bedroom house I grew up in. I'm drying my hair with one towel and have another wrapped around my body when I'm startled by a deep voice.

"Now, this is a nice morning." Brad and Em are sprawled on my bed with cartoons blaring from the television.

As I step back into the bathroom, the one towel drops from my hand as I make sure the other covers me completely.

"What are you doing here?"

"I live here." He smirks that devilish grin that makes me want to lick him all over.

"In this room?"

"Truthfully, I wish you were staying down the hall in mine." His alluring eyes roam my body and my breathing stops at his obvious approval. Little does he know, the body under this towel is very different from the one he remembers. There are light stretch marks and a little extra cushion now.

I move over to my bag in the corner and try to grab my clothes as discreetly as possible.

"Aren't you going to respond?" he asks, and if I could find my voice, I'd say something. Hopefully, something snarky.

"Leave?" I bundle my clothes in my hands and tiptoe past the television.

"Mama." Em crawls to the edge with her arms extended, but I can't take her and conceal my flesh at the same time.

"Hold on, baby. I'll be right back." I kiss the top of her head and she sits down contently.

"Mommy should sit on the bed with us," Brad chimes in, and I narrow my eyes.

"Sit." Em pats the spot next to her.

"In a second, baby. I have to get dressed."

"Sit!" Her voice raises and I shake my head.

I step away toward the serenity of the bathroom.

"You're going to disappoint our daughter," he adds, that grin still plastered on his face.

"Brad," I warn with as stern of a voice as I can muster.

"Did you think about tonight?" I hear him moving off the bed and my heart beats out of my chest. Unable to not allow him to kill me with his affection, I wait, and two seconds later, those strong hands land on my shoulders. The scent of his cologne wafts around me. "I dreamed about you last night."

"I don't know, Brad," I answer his first question, but he seems to be over that one already.

"I would love to do the things I was doing to you last night, tonight." His breath tickles my damp skin and my center heats with a burning passion.

"Brad." This time, any authority in my voice wanes with my weakness for Brad, leaving that 'breathless take me now' tone. The one Brad can always pull out of me because my body will never stop craving his.

His arms round my shoulders and travel painfully slow

down the length of my exposed arms. "Please, one night." My skin pricks from his breath hitting the most sensitive spot of my neck.

I twist around and his hands find my hips. Glancing over at Em, whose eyes are pinned on the cartoon, I allow myself to sink into all of him. His crisp cologne and the pouty bottom lip I used to nibble on. The contours of his muscles that I'd memorized are still present. Lastly, his eyes that continually tell me what he's feeling. Right now, love is shining from them. Honest love. There's no way I can refuse him this date, and since Maggie seems so nice, I trust her as much as I can.

"Okay," I softly agree, and a wide smile spreads across his face.

"You just made my day." He leans forward, but I catch Em looking at us from the corner of my eye. I draw back, and then my bedroom door opens.

We have no time to prepare before Maggie steps in the room. "Girls?" she asks. Em jumps off the bed and runs over to her. Maggie picks her up and automatically covers Em's eyes when she finds Brad and me so close.

"I'll just take her downstairs, if that's okay?" Maggie backpedals toward the door while my face blazes with heat.

"Thanks, Mom," Brad says, his eyes locked with mine the entire time.

My breathing hesitates, trying to catch up to everything going on around me. Brad's always been so consuming to me, but I need to remember that little girl is my number-one priority now.

The door shuts and my tense shoulders relax slightly once it's only the two of us. "How embarrassing." I sigh, breaking away from him and sitting on the edge of the bed.

Brad searches out the remote and clicks off the "Olivia" cartoon. "My mom doesn't care." The bed dips with his weight and my skin prickles with goose bumps when his hand lands on my knee.

"I was standing in a towel with our daughter on the bed. I look like a horrible mother." My face lands in my hands and I shake my head at who I'm becoming.

A bellowing laugh rises out of his throat. "No, you don't. It's not like I had you pinned to the bed naked and was grinding into you."

That thought only heats my cheeks more.

"You just don't get it. Here I am in your parents' house with my daughter, who I've kept secret for two years. I'm already being judged, and you sneaking into my room this morning only makes me look like some dime-store whore."

Unable to sit any longer, I stand and pace the floor.

"Dime-store whore? Is there such a thing?" Brad laughs again, leaning back on the bed. His Henley rises up, showing his abs, which haven't diminished over the years.

"Cover yourself up," I mumble, ignoring his question to me about the whore.

He glances down and shakes his head. "Why? Is it turning you on?" Of course, he doesn't move even a millimeter.

"No." Not getting anywhere in the same room, I disappear into the bathroom, but a second later, he's standing in the doorway, arms stretched over his head, holding on to the doorframe, that bare piece of skin on display once again.

"Well, does it?" he asks. Refusing to look, I concentrate on my make-up bag. "It's okay. I mean, you're standing in a towel in front of me. Do you want to see more of my skin? Better yet, how about a touch?" His arms fall and he steps into the room, making the steamy bathroom confining.

"I have to get ready, so bye." My hands land on his shoulders, twisting him around and pushing him out the bathroom. I shut the door and flick the lock.

He knocks softly. "We're still on for tonight, right?" he asks through the door.

Say no, say no, say no.

"Yes. Now leave me alone to get ready."

"Taylor?"

"What?" I sigh.

"You look more edible than a King Ice Cream Cone."

I cover my mouth to hide the laugh ready to squeak out.

"Thank you," I say, using every ounce of self-control I have not to let him know how much that absurdity warms my heart.

We'd been on a few dates already, and it was the first real warm day after a long winter. He was sitting on the edge of the wall at the Student Center with Tanner and a few guys on the swim team. I walked by, not wanting to interrupt his guy time. He was chomping down on a huge ice cream cone, laughing and carrying on. Brad was a guy's guy. Never alone and usually throwing a Frisbee or football around campus with his friends.

I tried to act as though I hadn't heard his laugh fifty feet away, and I definitely didn't want him to know how much my body wanted to veer his way. So, I acted like the details of my friend Vivian's Art History class were the most enthralling thing I'd ever heard.

"Hey, it's Taylor," Tanner said to him. Disappointment washed over me that it was his best friend who noticed me first.

To make matters worse, Vivian stopped and looked over at the group. What the hell was she doing? Having no choice, I glanced over, giving Brad a little wave and big smile. Then I tugged on Vivian's shirt to keep her going.

Vivian seemed almost frozen in her tracks. "That's Greg Mendes." Her mouth was practically hanging open. Vivian was a quiet girl in my sorority, and I think that's why we had become friends. She usually calms me down.

I waved my hand in front of her face. "Do you want me to introduce you?" I wasn't best buds with the guy, but I'd met him a few times at a party. He was kind of timid too.

"Taylor." Brad's voice had come from right behind me

and my heartbeat sped up. Then her eyes were glued to Brad. "Hey, I'm Brad." His hand bypassed me to reach Vivian.

She shook it without saying anything, so I turned around and practically choked on my saliva. Brad's tongue snaked out to lick some ice cream about to drip down the waffle cone.

"This is Vivian." I pointed toward my mute friend, wishing I could pry my eyes off his mouth, but the way he ate an ice cream cone was heating me up fast.

"Hi," Vivian squeaked out.

Brad nodded. "Do you mind if I steal Taylor away for a second?"

"No, go ahead. I should get going." Vivian began to walk away, but Brad grabbed her arm.

"Stay. I only have a few minutes before practice, and I don't want Taylor walking by herself." Vivian stopped and nodded. "Here." He turned to his friends. "Jackasses, come over and keep this girl company." He pointed down to Vivian, whose poor cheeks were bright red.

"It's really okay." She tried to fight it, but when Greg was the first one to saunter over, she quickly stopped arguing.

Brad looked back and forth between them, puzzled, but grabbed my hand and led me to a secluded area on the side of the building. He pinned me to the brick wall and tossed his ice cream cone in the trashcan.

"That's a waste," I said, using any kind of distraction I could find away from my racing heart and sweaty palms.

"Nah, it was a sad replacement for you." Without warning, his lips crashed down on mine, kidnapping every one of my senses with his light cologne, his clean face, and his calloused palms along my cheeks.

His tongue didn't wait patiently to slide in, but was determined, seeking mine out. My whole body ignited with want from that one kiss. I rose to my tiptoes, just as urgent as he was for more, as our mouths collided together unable to fully quench what we wanted.

Finally, after a blissful few minutes, Brad's hands loosened on my head and my heels rocked back down. He laid is forehead to mine and stared into my eyes while we both caught our breath.

"You're so much more edible than a King Cone," he whispered.

He won me over in that moment on the side of the Student Center building. I knew then he had the ability to break my heart, which he succeeded in doing.

thirteen

Brad

I'M SLOWLY WINNING HER OVER, I think as I click her bedroom door shut. She's remembering how good we were together. There's no way she'll be able to deny our chemistry any longer after we talk tonight over dinner and I take her dancing. Taylor's always loved to dance, and it was the first thing that popped into my head when she agreed to our date.

I round the corner of the staircase and enter the kitchen, finding my little girl's grubby hands picking up pancake. My mom's at the stove, while my dad sits a few seats away from his granddaughter reading the paper.

"Dada!" Em holds up a hand full of pancake, and I watch the syrup drip down her arm to the sleeve of her sweater.

"Hey, baby girl." I grab a napkin on my way over and quickly wipe the sticky crap off her.

My mom glances over her shoulder. "Are you hungry?" she asks, and I crinkle my eyebrows, making her laugh. "Yeah, dumb question."

The rustling of the newspaper reminds me that my dad is still sitting there, keeping his distance from Emerson. My anger is about to hit the limit on that topic. This isn't the dad I grew up with. Not the one who coached my t-ball and played Barbies with Piper.

Emerson is completely content with her spoon, trying to pick up the pancake and make it to her mouth. She's entertaining herself.

"You still up for watching Emerson tonight?" I ask, and my dad peers over the rim of his reading glasses at me, but doesn't answer.

"Of course. We can't wait to have some time with her," my mom says over her shoulder, but my dad's judgmental eyes continue to bore into mine.

"Great. I have to make a few phone calls." I stand, but my dad's hand grabs my wrist on the table.

I look down and back to him. "Rick is coming by this afternoon." He lowers his voice so my mom doesn't hear him. He's lost his marbles if he thinks I'll even entertain this idea.

"Have a nice meeting. I'm taking my daughter out for the day." I pull back my wrist from his hold and leave the room.

"Dada!" Em yells, and I turn around, holding my finger up. "I'll be right back, baby girl." Her bottom lips quivers and she drops her spoon.

My mom rushes over, dropping a plate full of pancakes on the table before sitting down to distract her. She waves me on, letting me know she's got it covered, and I watch my dad turn the page of his newspaper. *What a jackass.*

I pick up my phone, praying I can get this favor in on such short notice.

Two rings, she answers and I release a breath. "What would Brad Ashby want with me?" That high-pitched voice hijacks me back to the days of high school.

"Hey, Audrey, how have you been?"

"Let's see. I'm eight months pregnant, and can barely fit behind my desk. My husband knows jack shit and disappoints me every day. So, all in all, I'm tired."

"Eight months, that's great. When are you due?"

"Cut the bullshit, Ashby. What do you want?"

Audrey swam with Piper in high school, and she's one of

the only ones who returned home after college. Lucky for me tonight, she now runs Washington Court Athletic Club.

"I was just checking in with you." I'm thankful we're not in person, because she'd see me nibbling on my bottom lip.

"Did I mention, I'm temperamental? *What do you want?*"

I laugh, but when the line remains silent, I figure I better start talking.

"I need to use the pool tonight."

"Nuh-uh. Last time, you had some sort of an orgy and I almost got fired."

"It wasn't an orgy. It was a party, and I've apologized for my friend's poor judgment how many times? Not to mention, that was like four years ago." The Thanksgiving weekend back together party got a little out of control. "Plus, if I remember, you snuck off to the locker room."

"You have me mistaken with someone else. Are you training again?"

If only.

"No, and I don't want to go into specifics, but it's just me and another person coming in, but I want it after hours. Only us."

"You sure come with a lot of demands. Hold on." I hear the shuffling of paper as I pace back and forth in my parents' foyer.

"Eight. That's the best I can do." The clicking of keys now replaces the sounds in the background.

"Great. Thanks, Audrey."

"Ashby, I'll be here to let you in, and then you'll lock up. Don't fuck this up." I can just imagine her getting up on those tiptoes, all five feet of her trying to intimidate me.

"Thanks. Boy or girl?" I stop her before she hangs up on me.

"Boy." I hear excitement and happiness in her voice.

"That's great. I have a daughter myself."

"You? Have a daughter?"

"Yep." I'm proud to tell people I'm a father of an amazing girl, whose mother did an outstanding job of raising her.

"I had no idea. It's a scary thought though, you as a father." She laughs. "Eight o'clock, Ashby. Don't be late."

"I won't."

The line goes dead at the same time Taylor walks down the stairs.

She still has the capacity to take my breath away. Her hair is pulled back in a ponytail again, and she's wearing a pair of skinny pants and a sweater. She's beautiful, and it hurts me that she's not solely mine yet.

"You look gorgeous," I say when she reaches the last step.

"Thank you." She blushes, making me want to see her flushed like that after I've made love to her.

The urge to kiss her is so strong, but I keep my distance, not wanting to ruin anything before we start.

My phone alerts me of a text message, so I pull it out, finding Cayden's name.

"Emerson is in the kitchen eating. I'll be right in." She smiles and walks by me.

I watch her ass sway and I'm barely holding on right now. Needing a distraction from her body and desire for it, I read the text message.

Cayden: Can you meet Monday morning

Me: Yeah. Meet me at Creadle's Aquatic Center. You have a car, right?

Cayden: Yes, I'll see you there.

Me: Great. See you then.

I tuck my phone in my pocket, thinking about how I'm going to help Cayden. I just hope I have enough tricks up my sleeve for him to stay on the team. I was always fortunate to be on the upper scale of the team and didn't have to worry about cuts.

My mom and Taylor are laughing at Emerson when I enter the room. My dad's newspaper is abandoned on the table. I glance down at it and my mom must sense my aggravation because she shoots me a small smile. She's struggling with my dad, too.

"When are you guys heading out?" I ask, taking the seat next to Taylor and filling my plate with pancakes and bacon.

"Our appointments are at ten-thirty. What are you doing?" my mom asks, leaning back in her chair with her hand wrapped around her cup of coffee. She blows on it before taking a hesitant sip.

"I'm taking Em to the mall. Maybe ride the carousel." Instinctively, I look over at Taylor to see what she thinks. She smiles, and her approval does nothing but light me up inside.

"You and Piper loved that carousel when you were little," my mom gushes and glances over at Emerson. "She'll love it, too."

"I hope so."

It's odd the insecurity that lives inside of me when it comes to Emerson. I'm the cocky guy who never second-guesses his decisions, but with her, I never think I'm good enough. Every memory we make needs to be perfect. The last thing I could handle is to disappoint her somehow.

A warm hand covers mine on the table. My eyes follow the hand to find Taylor looking at me. "She will. She's never been on one."

A burst of fireworks explode in my stomach that I finally get to experience a first in my little girl's life. "A first?" I question, and she nods, a smile gracing her lips.

"Yes. Take a picture for me?"

I give her hand a tight squeeze. "Yeah."

My voice cracks from the emotional roller coaster that little girl puts me through every day. I glance at the clock, mostly because this is getting a little too sappy for me.

"Well, I better get going." I move over to her highchair.

"Us too," my mom says, standing up and piling up the plates. I admire the fact that Taylor is helping her. She's more comfortable than she was yesterday.

"Why don't you ask your father to go with you?"

"Because he doesn't seem to care for Emerson at all. He hasn't even talked to her."

"You're being silly. He has."

I shake my head and my mom's eyes scrunch in confusion.

"Chris!" she screams, and I roll my eyes. Taylor comes alongside me, that jasmine scent wafting up to my nostrils.

My dad walks in the room and looks around at all of us standing together.

"Yeah?"

"Brad is going to the mall with Emerson. I thought you'd want to go." My mom quickly loads the dishes in the dishwasher.

A sour look contorts his face. "I have someone coming over. I had asked Brad to stay."

"Emerson has a nap schedule I have to adhere to. I'm leaving now."

I sidestep him and walk off to the foyer to grab her shoes and my own. Taylor follows, probably assuming I need some help dressing my daughter, which I don't. Then again, my dad doesn't make a warm companion at this moment either. She could be fleeing his presence.

My parents' hushed voices carry through the high ceilings of their house. As always, my mom works her magic and my dad comes in a few minutes later with his jacket on.

"I'll go."

"Don't do me any favors," I sneer. Taylor busies herself putting her boots on, probably trying to ignore the animosity in the room.

"Ready, Taylor?" My mom walks around the corner with her purse swung over her arm, bearing an exaggerated smile.

"Yes," Taylor answers, rounding Emerson up in her arms to kiss her temple.

"Bye," Emerson says.

"Bye. Have fun." One more kiss and Taylor steps back.

"What about my kiss?" I ask, and she rolls her eyes, but we both know she wants to kiss me. "That's okay. I'll cash in tonight."

"Don't count your chickens—"

"Never." I lean in closer, happy to hear my parents talking amongst themselves in the hallway. "I'm fairly certain they will hatch tonight." I wink and her cheeks flush.

"Always arrogant." She turns to walk away.

"You love it." She can act annoyed by my high self-esteem, but I'm positive, it's a characteristic she fell in love with.

"We'll be back around two or three. I'll text you," my mom says to my dad, and they hug and kiss good-bye.

"Enjoy your time," my dad responds, and you'd never think he's been acting like a dick for the last two days from his charming voice.

Twenty minutes later, my dad patiently waits at the back of my truck for me to unhook Emerson from her car seat.

I buckle her in the stroller, shoving the damn diaper bag in the bottom. Mission One is to find a manlier diaper bag than one with flowers.

My dad hasn't spoken since we left the house, and I'm not spending a rare day alone with my daughter with his crabby ass.

"We can separate if you'd like. I know Mom made you come."

He opens the door to the mall for me. "No, I'm fine. Are you looking for something here?"

"I'm taking Emerson on the carousel, and then I might buy a few things for her."

He nods. "You know I'm just protecting you and your rights." He's never been good at quiet. Constantly wants others to see his points.

"I get that, but don't you see I'm trying to make something with Taylor. You were all for me seeking her out and telling her how much I love her before you found out about Emerson, so I don't understand."

Emerson is awfully quiet, so I peek into the stroller to find her already asleep. She's so peaceful and beautiful with her princess doll tucked under her arm.

"She hid her from you. You aren't that hard to find, Brad."

I keep the stroller moving so as not to wake her up, and before I realize it, we're in sync with all the mall walkers.

"You don't need to worry about that. It's my job to forgive her, not yours."

"Don't get me wrong. I'm positive you did something horrible for the breakup, but to hide your kid? It's inexcusable."

Unable to hear the venom in my dad's voice in regards to Taylor anymore, I confess, "I cheated on her. Right after I didn't make the cut, before I went to see Dr. Freeman, she caught me with someone else."

"Cheating doesn't mean you have the person's baby secretly." His voice might have toned down the anger some, but he's looking for answers I don't have.

"No, but having a drug-addicted sister and alcoholic father does. I'm talking with her about it tonight, but I understand already. She was worried about the situation she'd be putting her child in, and I'm not sure I blame her. I was a different person then."

"That you were." He lowers his voice, and I wonder if he finally understands Taylor's reasoning.

"Still, I don't see the harm in having papers drawn up, making sure you have the rights to her."

"Because I want both of them, and the way you're suggesting only gets me Emerson."

He nods, seeming appeased by my answers. Maybe he's figuring out I'm not the train wreck douche I once was.

"Just keep your options open." He clasps me on the shoulder, the first sign of affection since I arrived.

"I know what I'm doing, Dad. Trust me." I stop us in front of the bathrooms, so he can see the determination in my eyes.

"It's hard for me to do. You're my son and it's my job to protect you, but I'll try."

I nod a few times.

"Glad that's cleared up. Now, I have to run into the bathroom. Watch her for me?" My head dips down to make sure she's asleep.

"Yeah." My dad sits on the bench, pushing the stroller back and forth.

"Thanks. I'll be right back." I jog into the hallway where the bathrooms are located.

On my way out, I text Taylor quickly to make sure she's still sane with my mom. I'm sure a spa day with my mom isn't what she thought she'd be doing this weekend. Talk about uncomfortable.

Me: Your nails all pretty for tonight?

Taylor: Just my toes. Your mom is doing too much. She's offering to have me get a massage too.

Me: Tell her that's my job.

Taylor: Not yet it isn't. Crap, I think I just saw the masseuse.

Me: I'm not there, so you didn't.

Taylor: He's six-two, short brown hair, bulging biceps, strong hands. I think I'm going to accept the offer.

Me: You better be describing me.

Taylor: I guess you'll have to wait to find out. ;-)

Me: Don't give me that damn wink face.

Taylor: Oh, surely you can handle a man's hands on me.

Me: Not unless they're mine.

Taylor: LOL . . . you always were the jealous type.

Me: So were you, Thunder Taylor.

In college, Taylor made a hundred percent sure the girls knew who I belonged to. There's something oddly appealing when a girl stakes her claim on you.

Taylor: Time for hands. See you later.

Me: No massage. I mean it.

Taylor: ;)

Damn her, she always gets a rise out of me. I stop in my tracks when I find my dad playing peekaboo with the stroller. The tension that's been knotted in my shoulders all morning loosens watching my dad's first interaction with her. He smiles and Emerson's feet kick from excitement. That's the dad I remember.

I show my face and my dad quickly straightens his back on the bench, handing her a toy as if he's completely enthralled with her.

"She woke up, huh?"

"Dada!" She claps, putting her hands over her face toward my dad, but he doesn't engage with her.

"Go ahead, I won't tell anyone you actually like your granddaughter."

His wide eyes meet mine. "Of course I like her."

"You don't act like it."

He stands and hands Emerson her juice cup.

"I'm just being cautious. You and your mom just jump into the deep end. What if Taylor runs again? Try testing the waters occasionally."

We walk toward the carousel and I shake my head at his line of thinking.

"What fun is that?" I ask him. I might have lived my life a little on the crazy and spontaneous side, but it's a hell of a lot more fun than playing it safe.

Piper and my dad are more similar in that they dip their toes in and then painfully and slowly walk down the stairs into the water. I do a cannonball, not knowing if the water is cold as fuck or warm as pie. I prefer my method much more.

"Just be careful, Brad." He slaps my back, and the reason for his crankiness clicks into place. My dad's worried about me, and that's why he's being this tough-assed guy who wants to take Taylor to court.

"I will." I smile, because when it comes to Taylor, there's no being careful. I'm in it to win it, and I'm positive I'm about to win the jackpot.

With our heart to heart behind us, the atmosphere becomes free of the earlier tension and we move on to enjoy the day with Emerson.

fourteen

Taylor

MY FEET GET THE SHIT beat out of them with Brad's mom seated to my right. As hard as the massage on my feet feels, it's equally enjoyable. Kind of like my love for Brad. There's no use in fighting us anymore, because my body refuses to listen to the warnings my brain is sending out. If only I can find a way to forgive him for cheating.

"So, Taylor." Maggie's voice pulls me from the usual ring of drama my mind races through.

I turn to find a welcome and warm smile. Seriously, this woman is a saint.

"Can you tell me how you and Brad met?"

My teeth clench. Oh shit, that's not really a story you tell the mother. Couldn't we talk about Em instead?

"At a fraternity party."

Her smile only widens as she waits for more information, and my stomach churns. Surely, I can put our first encounter in a more innocent way than it really was.

"I spilled my drink on him." My cheeks flame at the memory of that night.

I wss on my third cup of "juice," and my friends were on the dance floor. Staggering, I attempted to make my way from the kitchen to the makeshift dance floor. But I failed when a brick wall of a man stepped in my way. My head flew forward, my blonde strands obstructing my view, and before I realized it. "What the fuck?" someone spat out in a deep male voice. The guy right in front of me.

I brushed away my hair, quickly noticing my empty cup spinning on the floor.

"Oh, my God, I'm so sorry." My hand moved to touch his T-shirt, but he back stepped and my hand fell to my side. I sobered up quickly and straightened my back to find Brad Ashby.

Our college was mid-size, but everyone knew the athletes. At least, in my circle they did. Brad Ashby's reputation preceded him. He'd been lip-locked with most of the sorority circle, but still he didn't disgust me. I was fresh off quarterback Jake Michaels; recently breaking up after finding him with some redhead with his pants around his ankles.

The animosity between Jake and Brad was just as well-known around campus as the disgusting egg concoction in the cafeteria.

"Taylor, right?" Brad clarified, and for some reason, the fact that he knew my name electrified every nerve in my body.

"Yeah." Our eyes locked, his filled with mischief and mine with a little tipsy desire.

"Help me clean up?" He tilted his head to the staircase, and I glanced back at my friends on the dance floor, wrapped around each other, grinding with all the football players. Jake was right in the middle with two of my friends on either side. Some friends.

I looked back at Brad with that goofy smirk that screamed sex appeal. "I did cause the mess," I flirted, and he rested his hand on the small of my back, leading me toward the staircase.

We reached the bottom stair when his sister, Piper, stepped in front of us. She was feisty and a little on the mean side to the sorority girls.

"I want to go home." She crossed her arms, glancing over

at me like I was a piece of trash.

"Go. I'll be okay." Brad put his hand on her shoulder and pushed her out of the way.

"I'm your DD tonight, remember?" She ignored my existence, not that I was going to argue with her.

"Taylor's got me." His hand grazed along my arm until it was clasped in mine, igniting shivers up and down my back. The feeling of safety should not have surrounded me in that moment, but it did.

"Um, she just spilled her drink on you." She points to his wet T-shirt. "She can't drive you home."

If matters couldn't get worse, Tanner McCain, Brad's best friend sauntered over.

"I got him." He rested his hand on Piper's shoulder, but she stepped to the side, letting it fall off. Tanner's eyes drooped and he took a big breath.

"Both of you go. I'll be fine." Brad dragged me up a few steps and then swiveled around so fast, I became dizzy. "Not together, though."

Both their checks heated with a pink flush and Tanner looked over to Piper, who was trying to act indifferent by not meeting his gaze, but anyone could figure out there was something going on there.

"Coach said if you get in trouble again, he's taking you out of meets." Piper hollered over the music, coming up a step to meet us. This was not what I was expecting when I agreed to help him 'clean his shirt.'

"Give it a damn rest. You're not our mom." Then he pulled me up a few more steps and stopped on the landing.

"Suit yourself. We're out." Tanner screamed, and his hand led Piper away, just like Brad had done to me moments before. Something was going on there.

"Hey, Michaels!" Brad yelled, and the whole dance floor looked up at us. "Taylor's actually found a real man." He dipped me and crushed his lips to mine.

His tongue didn't wait for me to allow him in; instead, it swept into my mouth, as though he was claiming me. My hand snaked around the back of his head, the light-brown strands tickling my skin. In all the chaos around us, he slowed and his lips merged with mine. Quickly, I was lost in Brad Ashby, until he swung me upright. The music had lessened and there was no carrying on in the party. Everyone's eyes were locked on us, with a very angry Jake in the middle. He looked at me with complete disgust, but I didn't give a shit.

"Fuck, Brad!" Tanner stomped up the stairs, two other guys from the swim team following. "Let's go." He grabbed Brad by the arm, dragged him down the stairs, but before they could get too far away, Brad linked hands with mine.

"She's coming." He smiled up to me, and every fiber in my body said, Stay put. This guy is trouble. *But I went anyway.*

"Whatever," Tanner said.

We reached the bottom of the staircase and I heard the rustling of people, some chanting, "Fight." Tanner pushed Brad's back, making him stumble forward through the door.

Quickly, we were on the porch with party goers who didn't know a fight was brewing.

"Give it a break, Jake. You're done with her." The painful words came from one of Brad's friends who was at the door. I suspected he was keeping the football team back until we could escape in the red Jeep parked out front.

Brad ducked in, never letting go of my hand the entire way. Tanner flew into the passenger seat, and when I found time to absorb everything, I discovered Piper in the driver's seat.

"Go, Piper." She pressed on the gas and drove down the road. "Thanks, guys!" Tanner yelled to his friends, hanging out the window. They each raise their hand in a wave. "Fuck off, Jake."

Tanner sat down in his seat, grabbing his seatbelt.

"Why do you have to start shit?" Tanner's green eyes lit up from the streetlights whizzing by. They centered on me for a

second before switching to Brad.

He shrugged. "He's a jackass." He disregarded Tanner and turned to me. "What did you ever see in him anyway?"

I focused on my lap, but his hand let go of mine and moved to my thigh. A rush of electricity shot up my leg with his touch. "I have no idea." That was the truth, but I was shallow and my friends thought so highly of me because I was dating Jake Michaels. I was fairly sure it would be horrible if I admitted that right then.

"He's a complete douche," Piper chimed in from the front, and I watched Tanner's arm sling across the back of her seat. Piper scooted toward the window as though his touch was disgusting, which I believed was the exact opposite of what she felt.

"Well, girls can make mistakes," I half stuck up for myself.

"Are we dropping you off, Taylor?" She changed the subject, and I was thankful.

I inched forward. "Sure, I live at Alpha—"

Brad tugged me back, his head in the crook of my neck. "Come home with me." His hot breath caused goose bumps to scatter across my skin.

"I don't know," I said, enjoying the warmth of his body so near.

His mouth covered my earlobe, sucking it into his mouth. His teeth began to nibble on my neck and my breathing hitched. "Please," he begged.

"Okay." Any willpower I had left vanished in that moment. Not that the numerous cups of "juice" didn't help the cause.

"Perfect," he said, and leaned back to his side. "She's coming to our place."

Piper made a grunting sound and the Jeep started going faster.

"Can I stay at your place tonight?" Tanner asked, and Piper tried to act indifferent, narrowing her eyes at him.

"Fine. Wendy went back home anyway." She never looked

at him, because I'm fairly certain she'd be smiling. How could Tanner McCain not affect her?

"Great," Brad said, moving over to me again. His fingers grazed my cheek, resting in the strands of my hair. "We'll be alone."

I swallowed a big gulp right before he kissed me again. This time, his mechanics were slow and gradual until I was a complete puddle in the cloth seats.

We parted ways with Piper and Tanner as they got off on the floor below ours. Once the elevator doors shut, Brad's hand ventured south to my ass, in turn, pulling me toward him more. He dragged me down the hallway, his hand warm in mine.

You'd think he was completely sober by the way the key flawlessly fit in the lock and clicked open. He waited for me to enter first, and as the door closed, he had me pressed against the wall, my wrists pinned with one hand above my head. His finger traveled down the dip between my breasts. My tight shirt didn't leave much to the imagination.

"You sure, Taylor?" he asked, and in that moment, I couldn't imagine doing anything else.

"Yes," was my last word before Brad Ashby was all I felt, saw, and heard around me.

"Thank God." His fingers manipulated the button of my jeans and the sound of the zipper bounced off the empty apartment walls. I gasped for air when his hand snaked down my pants and his mouth cast small kisses to my neck.

"Oh, I can image Brad's reaction." Maggie's voice cools me from the memory.

I touch my hot cheek. "Yeah, he took it well, though." A smile snakes across my lips as I think about his smirk that night.

"You're very beautiful, so I imagine he did."

I nod, unable to form a coherent sentence. The recollection of our first time together only makes me yearn for his touch.

I concentrate on the woman polishing my toes, but still, my body is a hum of electricity.

"You know, fear can make people do things outside of themselves." She continues to talk, and I really don't want to have a heart-to-heart right now, especially with Maggie.

"Uh-huh," I say, nodding my head.

"Did Brad tell you about Bayli?"

Hearing the name is like a million little needles pricking my skin at once.

"I know about her, yes."

Her hand rests on my arm, and I really wish her pedicurist would ask her to stop fidgeting because I'm not good with affection and this woman seems to thrive on it.

"I knew she wasn't the one for him. Brad is charismatic."

If that's what you want to call it.

"He's quick with his decisions and actions. Never fully thinking things through before acting on his wants." She smiles and I wonder why those are good qualities. "I'm very similar to him."

Gotcha.

"He can be rash," I add, even though it's a quality I admire in him. Being with Brad made me spontaneous, which I enjoyed.

"But usually he knows what he's doing. Things always seem to work out for him. But when he didn't get a shot at the Olympics, it took him down a long road of depression."

"Maggie," I interrupt her because I witnessed it and I tried to heal him. She stops talking, so I take my opportunity to intervene. "I tried to help him, to pull him up from the trenches, but he couldn't be saved. You're right, things always work out for Brad, and when they didn't, he spun a world of heartbreak in his path. I'm not sure what you know about why we broke up, and it's really not my business to tell you, but know this, you don't have to sell me on your son. I'm still very much in love him. It's trust that's keeping us apart right now."

"Tayl—"

"Just please let me finish." She nods. "I apologize for keeping Em away from you these years. I was wrong to do that. My family comes from a life of addiction and a long line of hurting the ones you love to gain what you want. When Brad fell into drugs, drinking, and depression, I tried to pick him back up, but he wouldn't meet me halfway. I got more confused. Suddenly, that love and belief I always had in him waned, and I saw my baby's life being one of feeling lost and unloved by her father. That's why I left him without telling him about my pregnancy."

She nods, a tear slowly falling from her.

"It wasn't my intention to make you cry."

She shakes her head, wiping the tears from her eyes.

"You love him. You love him for him." Her voice trembles, and I'm confused she's taking that from my confession.

Her hand ventures back over, clasping mine. "The best thing in the world is when you discover someone loves your child for who they are."

"Um, Maggie, love isn't enough." I'm trying to slowly bring her back down from the love bubble she's floating on.

"Yes, it is. I can see he hurt you quite a bit, but you're here with him, willing to help him, and that speaks to how much you love him."

She claps her hands and the two women doing our toes stare, intrigued by the crazy lady next to me.

"We aren't back together," I clarify before she pulls her feet from the woman's hands and starts dancing in the middle of the salon.

"Yet, honey. Yet."

"Maybe never," again, I correct her.

"Oh, sweetie. You love him too much to let him go completely. He's your one."

"Um, I can't promise you that, Maggie. Em comes first."

Her hand squeezes mine. "I know, and I'm sure that's the

same for Brad too, but more comes from love than hate, darling. And you love him."

She smiles wide, as if I just told her we were getting married. But her excitement is contagious and a stir of hope spurs inside of me that maybe love will heal Brad and me. If only the vision of that girl would erase from my memory.

fifteen

Brad

TAYLOR ROUNDS THE BACK OF my truck and I rush ahead to open the door for her. With a gentle smile, she climbs in. I circle around to my side while excitement builds inside of me. Now that I finally have Taylor alone, I'm as giddy as a kid on Christmas morning. Alone to convince her the love we shared back in college never diminished. It's time that we nurture the ember that still burns between us.

"Where are we going?" she asks once I'm comfortable in my seat with the key in the ignition.

"First, we're going to talk. Then, we're going to have fun." The truck engine turns over and I back out of my parents' driveway.

"Oh, fun. I forget what that is when it doesn't involve a two-year-old."

"I'm going to dig up that old Taylor. The one who isn't worried about bedtimes and vegetables." I glance over and we share a smile. It's only been weeks and I think about those things, I can't imagine two years.

"You'll have to dig deep." She leans back and crosses her legs, getting comfortable in the cloth seats.

"Don't worry." I stop at a light and take the opportunity to smell her perfume. "You remember how good I am with my hands, right?"

She sucks in a deep breath, and I love the fact that I can still get to her.

"Play fair," she warns. Acting as though I didn't just make the hairs on the back of her neck stand on end, she straightens her back.

"Always." I wink. A horn honks behind us and I quickly move my eyes back to the road.

"Not really." She makes me regret the way I treated her. I despise myself for what I did to her two years ago. "Sorry," she rushes out, when the truck grows silent. She continues to worry about hurting my feelings. Shows again, she's too good of a person to be with me.

"Don't be." I drive up the long drive to Trudle's Arboretum. Every tree and bush are lit up with white Christmas lights lining our drive down the winding path.

"It's so beautiful." Taylor peers out the window like a kid at Disney World.

"They've already decorated for Christmas and have an amazing tree exhibit. Each one decorated in a different theme."

"Is the theme different every year?"

"Yeah. This year is decades. Each tree is done up in a specific era."

"That's so cool." Her hands plaster to the window on either side of her face. "I've never heard of this place."

"It's more of a local thing, but sometimes a television station comes out to film for a story." I park next to the few other cars in the lot. "Let's go."

Taylor practically skips to the entrance, tugging on my hand. I think the swimming I have planned after this might seem dull compared to the enthusiasm buzzing off her here.

I barely reach the door to open it for her. I pay and we follow the path out to the different trees.

"Oh my God, this is so cool." Her hand pulls at my arm.

"If I'd known it only took a few trees to excite you, I'd

have brought you here sooner."

She playfully swats at my arm, but I quickly wrap around her shoulders and snuggle her in closer. We pass by the 1920's tree and stop to admire it.

"I was hoping we'd talk while we look, but I'm worried it'll ruin your time here." I'm hopeful we can delay the impending 'I fucked up, please forgive me' conversation.

She stops on the cobblestone pathway and meets my eyes. "Okay."

Guess my hopes for a reprieve aren't viable.

"Do you want me to just state my case, or do you want to ask a question?" I wish I wasn't about to hyperventilate with the thought of dredging up our past.

Our footsteps proceed to the next tree, and I reach for her hand to stay connected in this moment.

"You aren't on the stand, Brad. I've forgiven you already. Tell me what you want." Her eyes don't meet mine, though.

"After the Olympics fell through for me, and Tanner left for Colorado, I didn't know who I was. It was as though I was in someone else's body—someone who'd lost their dream. Ever since I was young, I imagined myself standing on that pedestal claiming the gold. So, I started using the drugs as a way to escape the sense of imprisonment I felt. When I pushed you away, it was because you saw me as the person I thought I was until I was just another college swimmer with no future. So, in a way, I purposely sabotaged us just to show you the piece of shit you were with."

"Brad," she sighs, and I can see she wants to argue with me about this, but she can't. And she shouldn't.

"The girl though . . . I'm sorry." I shake my head as though I have an image of her in my head. I couldn't pick her out of a lineup, but I could conjure up the hurt in Taylor's eyes that night.

"How come you never fought for me?" Her voice is shallow and a bit hesitant, which only makes me hate myself more.

I grip her hand tighter, stopping us in front of the next tree.

"God, Taylor." I run my hand down my face. "I honestly thought you were better off without me. I had nothing to offer you. No future, no dreams, no will to live."

The recollection of that time is still hazy. I've never been able to recover every minute of the time right after Taylor left me. "I locked myself in my apartment," I confess, mostly because it's what I remember. The drapes drawn shut and reruns of *Seinfeld* over and over again. The only time I left was at night when I would sneak off and buy my next mind-numbing drug.

"Piper finally got through to me. She and a couple guys waited for me to leave one night and staged an intervention. I went straight home where I went through counseling and eventually started graduate school."

I stop us, holding her cheeks in my chilled hands. Her pure and honest eyes search mine for the sincerity she fears I won't give her. "Even after I cleaned myself up, and thought maybe I could live a life without swimming, I'd convinced myself you were better off without me."

Her eyes close and a tear falls down her rosy cheek. "Brad, I never thought that."

My hands drop to my sides and I snatch her hand up to lead us away. For some reason, walking makes this heart-to-heart easier. Maybe because it hides the hurt in her eyes.

"Lately, I think to myself, thank God you never came looking for me. What a douche of a father I would have been."

"Don't say that," she argues, like always. I think I used her confidence in me as a crutch when we were in college. Like if Taylor truly believed I was a good person, then I was. When in truth, I was an asshole who did unthinkable things to make my dream come true.

"Don't argue, Taylor. It's the truth. I was a class A douchebag in college, because if I was half a man—half the man I believe I am today—I'd had never cheated on you. And I sure as shit would have chased after you."

She's silent, signaling that she's relenting on the fact I'm speaking the truth.

I lead her over to the park bench and wait for her to sit. She lets go of my hand, slides onto the bench, and tucks her hands under her legs. I squat down in front of her, resting my hands on her jean-clad thighs, and her legs, which are bouncing with nerves slow down.

"I'm sorry, Taylor. I know those two words aren't enough, but I guarantee you, I'll prove my worth if you give me the chance. I'll show you that you are the only woman I've ever loved—past, present, and future." I stare directly in her tear-filled eyes, practically crossing my fingers and toes in hope she believes me.

Her head slowly nods, but she says nothing. The silence is deafening until a round of high school kids on a double date cross our path. They carry on with one another, the guys definitely showing off for their dates. I wait for them to pass, giving Taylor time to process what I've said.

After they've turned the corner, I inch closer, my hands sliding around her waist until they rest on the small of her back. My head falls into her lap and I hug her tightly until her hands have no choice but to thread through my dark hair. I lay there for several minutes, loving the way her fingers outline patterns across my scalp.

"Okay."

I pick up my head and her hands fall away. I miss them already. "Yeah?" I question to double-check I heard her right.

A shy smile crosses her lips. "If you forgive me for not telling you about Em, how can I not forgive you for cheating on me? So, okay, let's give us an honest try."

"I forgive you," I rush out fast before she changes her mind.

I spring up to my feet and pluck her up from the bench. Wrapping my arms around her, I lift her feet off the ground and twirl us around. As I slow down, her toes return to the concrete path and my hand moves along her cheek into her hair.

"You just made me the happiest man." I bend down and my lips lightly brush hers. After I test the waters, and discover she's just as eager as I am for the kiss, I press firmer. Her fingers hook in my belt loops and she draws me closer. Unable to pull myself away from her, my tongue slides in, needing to taste her again. She doesn't hesitate, but smashes her lips harder to mine, our mouths returning to a dance we'd mastered years ago. When we finally break away, my chest aches as I catch my breath. Her lips match her pink cheeks now, but for an entirely different reason.

"God, I missed you," I murmur, and a small laugh escapes her.

"Me too," she says, and nothing in this world will ever feel more right than Taylor Delaney in my arms.

"Now, do you want to look at some trees?"

"That'd be nice." Her hands clench my jacket, not letting go of me yet, and I revel in the smell of jasmine as her hair tickles my nostrils.

Finally, after a long hug, my hand travels down the length of her arm until her hand is tucked inside mine. We walk by a few trees, Taylor's eyes light up with intrigue for each one. Granting every tree equal attention, she reads the plaques describing who decorated them. She even points out the highlights for me.

"You always were the best tutor." I smile down at her as her finger runs along the glass case enthralled about the 1960s tree.

"You weren't my best student." She raises her eyebrows, and instantly, that moment in the library flashes to mind.

She points her finger in my face, the light above shining on her new pink nail polish. "Don't even say it." Her face turns a shade of pink. She's remembering the time I snuck her in the study room on the false pretense I needed help in Organic

Chemistry.

"What? I really was struggling." I counter from numerous arguments we had about this incident before that I had a B in the class already, but snuck her in there just to screw her.

"Uh-huh. What about the fact you snuck that poor freshman a twenty to make sure we weren't interrupted? That kid always gave me the creeps after that when I would ask for a study room. Like he was ready to pounce on me." She shakes her head and leans into me a little more. Oh, how easy our relationship always was.

"I would have kicked his ass."

She looks up, a smile creasing her lips. "I know you would have. My protector." She wraps her arm around my waist and pulls me closer. Damn she feels good.

"Always," I promise her. I'll never fail her again.

We finally arrive at this decade's tree, and my jaw could hit the floor. There in all its glory is Tanner's fucking face on the top of the tree. The star he is in this town.

"What the fuck?" I murmur, stepping closer to check my eyes aren't deceiving me.

Written on the damn sheet of paper, Tanner McCain, Olympian gold Medalist hopeful. "They decorated a tree for him?" Taylor's voice is as surprised as my wide eyes.

"Glory boy," I remind her.

"Obviously." She reads over the sheet of paper describing the tree while I bypass the bio of my best friend turned town hopeful. I notice this time she fails to recite any highlights; although, I could probably say them verbatim. Even I'm positive Tanner will claim a medal in one of the races next year.

Without even really noticing, I back step to the bench and sit down. I'm lost in that tunnel of doubt, believing I'll ever be as happy as I was when my dream was reachable. I would watch the Olympics and picture myself on that stand with the American flag descending down. I'd be on that platform with Tanner right next to me. We'd do it together. For a while, I blamed him for leaving me behind to pursue his own career, but I quickly got over that, because what can I say? My best friend is pretty fucking awesome. He never throws it in my face; instead, he tries to make sure I'm on the straight and narrow.

Taylor sits down and her hand heats my thigh. "I know it must be hard."

My hand drags down my face, sliding back to my neck and I give it a quick crack. "It's like a constant reminder. The thing is, I'm happy for him. I truly am, but my happiness for him doesn't diminish the despair I feel for my own failed dreams."

"I understand that."

"I just wish the pain of it all would go away. I thought when I went back to get my master's in business, I'd graduate with a newfound dream, but I hated being tied to a desk job. When I rushed into an engagement with Bayli, I thought I'd live for her, but,"—I look over at her and tighten my hand on hers—"she wasn't you."

"That she isn't." We share a smile.

"Sometimes I feel like the hotshot from high school, who turned into a piece of crap, swearing at the players who had what it took to play."

"No." She shakes her head. "You'll find your place, Brad. I promise." This time, her hand tightens around mine. "You will."

Our eyes lock, and I know no one has ever believed in me or guided me like she does. I stand up, unwilling to ruin our date with my bullshit 'feel sorry for me' crap. She dealt with enough of that in college. "Let's go." I hold my hand out for her, and she tilts her head at me, curious as to what I'm up to. "It's about time we leave this seriousness behind and have some fun, don't you think?"

Her delicate hand slides into mine and she stands. "Absolutely."

I'm texting Audrey as we walk up to the neighborhood

bar, Breaker's. It's one of a few in this city, but it has a dance floor, so I'm hoping Taylor will want to make use of it. The thought of her body pressed against mine as I lead us around the floor arouses something in me that's been dead for a while.

Me: I'm sorry, Audrey, I changed plans for the date. Hope I didn't ruin your night.

Audrey: It's okay. I'm here working anyway. Don't be a stranger.

Me: I won't. Thanks again.

I tuck my phone in my pocket and find Taylor waiting at the front doors for me. There's something in her eyes. She's worried about what I'm doing, who I'm texting.

"Everything okay?" she asks as she places her hand on the pool cue shaped handle.

"Yeah. I had another thing planned, so I cancelled it." I reach for the door handle at the same time her hand drops.

"Oh, we can go do that. I don't care what we do."

"No, I'd much prefer my hands on you, even if it's on a dance floor in front of forty people."

"Me too."

I pull the heavy wooden door open and Taylor sneaks under my arm to enter the bar.

The lights are dim over booths and tables with a square-shaped bar smack in the middle of the room. In the back are the pool tables I played at when I'd return from college for the holidays. At the exact moment I remember the late nights Tanner and I would have here when we'd be home, my eyes scan the room, finding a few faces that graduated years after me. It hurts that I'm the old man now.

"This is a nice place." Taylor checks out the crowded dance floor where people are jumping around to some eighties song.

"Come on." I lay my hand on the small of her back,

leading her to the side where I spot an empty booth.

Once we're snuggled in, Taylor eyes the deals in the plastic holder.

"Oh, margaritas are on special."

My eyes search out the waitress.

"And they have Heineken, Brad. Is that still your favorite?" She continues to read the specials insert.

I stop looking to give her my attention. *Slow down, Brad,* I tell myself.

"Yeah, they are. What about you? You always loved Seven Up and Raspberry Vodka."

"I don't keep hard liquor in the house, so I've turned into a wino, but I think tonight—"

The waitress comes over, wiping the sweat from her forehead.

"What can I get you?"

I release a breath of relief that I don't recognize her. "I'll have a Heineken and she'll have a Seven Up and Raspberry Absolute." She jots it down, nods, and walks away.

The two of us sit there, Taylor fiddling with the plastic holder and my hands glued to the side of the bench. All of a sudden, it's awkward between us.

"So . . . ," I say, and she giggles the most soothing and relaxing laugh.

"Mind if I come over?" I nod to the place next to her on the bench.

"And be one of those couples?" Her nose crinkles, but I stand and slide next to her.

My arm swings around her shoulders. She pretends to scoot away, but I keep sideling up to her until she's blocked against the wall.

"There's no running away from me," I whisper, and her hand lands on my chest.

"I think I've realized that. Brad,"—she presses her fingers to my lips—"don't hurt us." Tears brim her eyes. She's putting herself on the line for us and she wants me to know this is my final chance.

I hold up two fingers, even if I was never a Boy Scout. "I promise." I mean those two words more than anything. Hurting them is not an option this time around. "May I kiss you now?"

"You may." Her finger drops from my lips and my mouth descends on hers, shielding her body with mine.

I softly press my lips to hers, sliding my tongue through her parted ones for a taste. My hands mold to her cheeks while her fingers fist my shirt, making my breath hitch. Like she's always done, Taylor makes me forget where I am or what I'm doing with one kiss. We're lip-locked in a passionate kiss that causes me to want more of her.

I draw the kiss to a close and rest my forehead against hers. "I've missed you," I say.

"Oh, honey, I've missed you too," another voice, not Taylor's, says from across the table.

My head jerks up and Taylor quickly straightens so her back is pressed to the back of the booth. I grab Taylor's hand in mine to protect her, as though this girl won't still try to eat her alive.

"Bayli."

sixteen

Taylor

"SO, THIS IS HER." HER beady little eyes look me over like I'm scum under this bar table. "I don't see the competition, honey."

Brad's hand clamps on to me as though he's afraid I'm about to bolt. This girl wants to play, we'll play.

"You didn't tell me your . . . ex was so polite."

His head swings to mine, and then a slow smirk develops as he realizes, I'll play her game.

"Did he finally find you in that trailer park?"

I ignore the scab she's picking off of my wound. "I'm surprised someone of your status would be here. Trying to find yourself a new guy to manipulate?"

A fake laugh escapes her throat and her jaw cocks to the side. "Oh, honey, that's the difference between us. I don't have to look for men. They wait in lines for me."

I withdraw my hand from Brad's and wrap it around his neck. I inch up and kiss his cheek. "Neither do I." The satisfaction that the guy we have in common left her for me is too grand to hide. Especially with her grandiose mean-girl attitude.

"I wouldn't call him much of a man. I heard he's on the unemployment line." She cocks her head to the side, as though she gets some sick happiness knowing she got Brad fired.

"It's a good thing we're not together then," Brad speaks up for the first time since saying her name. He must have been dumbfounded.

"Yeah. You know I really shouldn't be with a has-been. Oh, wait . . ." She begins to slide out of the booth. "I mean, a never-was."

She stands and I choke on the little bit of saliva in my mouth.

Her hands slide over her stomach at the same time the waitress brings our drinks to the table. I reach for mine immediately, downing half of it in one gulp.

"Bayli?" Brad asks her, his voice quivering, exemplifying the emotions flowing through my veins.

She looks down. "Didn't I tell you? You're going to be a dad." Her hands pat her stomach and half my drink sprays across the table as my heart plunges to my stomach.

The only part I love is that Brad looks down at me, like we're a couple and he needs me there to support him if this really is the case. That or the fact he doesn't understand why all these women are hiding kids from him.

"Are you serious?" he asks her, his hand turning cold in mine.

She laughs, releasing a conniving and scary noise. Bile surges up my throat. "No. See, I always knew you were a loser, so I had a back-up." She holds her hand up in the air. "You just saved me from having to hide the fact that you would have been raising a kid that wasn't yours."

Brad's hand slides from mine and he moves out of the booth, towering over Bayli. His eyes bear down on her taunting ones. "Your parents tried to sue me for the cost of the wedding. Your dad got me fired from my job. And you were already knocked up with someone else's kid. You're sick."

I watch the show in front of me, wishing Brad and I could have one drama-free night.

Bayli shrugs her shoulders. "You left me two days before

the wedding. Fuck yourself, Brad. Go take your trash,"—her eyes veer to mine and then back to his—"and start a new life in loserville."

Brad's head falls back and a hollow laugh flows out of him. "Your originality in trying to be a bitch needs a lot more work." He digs into his pocket, pulling out his wallet. "I'd give you this twenty to find class, but,"—his eyes slowly look her up and down—"obviously, there are some things money can't buy." He tosses the twenty on the table and holds his hand out for me.

"Excuse us. I'm going to take my beautiful girlfriend home and screw her until she's hoarse from screaming my name. Good luck with the whole baby thing." His eyes fixate on mine until I clutch my purse and grab his hand. He tugs me out so fast, I fall into his arms. "You wonder what the competition is?" He snakes his arm around my waist, snuggling me nice and close to him. "There isn't one, because Taylor is so out of your league, you'll never even skim the surface of where she is. Oh, I should introduce you two."

"That's okay." Bayli narrows her eyes at us and twists to walk away.

"This is Taylor, the love of my life. Taylor, this is my ex, Bitchy Boob-job Bayli."

With a cough, I conceal my laughter, which is begging to escape.

"Grow up, Brad." She stalks off toward the dance floor and ends up with a few girls, who I assume are her friends.

"You first," Brad calls out, but she doesn't hear him. With the fact that none of her friends turned around, it's obvious she didn't tell them she just saw her ex with another girl.

"Let's find another bar, shall we?" Brad turns to me and I nod. He grabs his jacket from the booth and leads me across the dance floor.

I feel her eyes on me, and I honestly worry that the baby in her belly could very well be Brad's. I'm surprised he didn't second-guess it at all. Especially when I do the math in my head.

The cold air burns my face when we step outside, but the chill expands my lungs to suck in much-needed oxygen after what just happened.

Brad's quiet on the way to his truck, and he opens the door for me. I climb in and patiently wait for him to get in. His key is in the ignition when I lay my hand over his.

"Brad?"

"It's not mine, Taylor," he answers the unasked question.

"How can you be sure?"

The idea of him having another kid out there is like a knife to the chest, but it's not a deal-breaker for us to get back together. Then again, after what I had to endure in that bar in the last five minutes, I can't really imagine a lifetime of it.

"I didn't sleep with Bayli in the last two months before our wedding date."

His head hangs like he's ashamed while I want to jump up and down in my seat like it's my twenty-first birthday and I'm about to walk into my first bar.

Calming myself down, I try to act concerned since he's so upset about it.

"Why?"

He remains silent for a few seconds. "I knew I shouldn't marry her, but you know, I always wait until last minute to confess to anything. I made excuses about business trips and having to stay at my apartment, said I was sore from the gym, anything to get me out of it."

I want to laugh, and now I get the part where he said he was going to go home and screw me. It was twisting the corkscrew into Bayli more.

"Oh." I try to sympathize, while my insides are bursting with joy.

"There's another reason." He gives me his attention, and I suck in my lips to keep them straight.

"Oh."

"I kept envisioning you, and it felt wrong. I said your name once, and I started making excuses after that. Believe me, Bayli knows exactly why she lost out to you."

Unable to hold back my enthusiasm that Brad really was thinking about me, I climb over his center console and straddle him in his seat.

His hands seem unsure of where to go, so he pins one on the gear shift and the other on the door handle.

"Relax." I kiss his forehead and he instantly eases more into his seat.

"Forget her," I say, kissing his nose.

"She had some truths in her digs."

My hands move up to hold his chiseled jaw, the dimple in his right cheek not showing because of his frown. "There was no truth to what she said, Brad. She never saw what's in here." My hand slowly moves down to cover his heart. "She never saw what I see every time I'm with you. You're working on finding your way; don't let her ruin that progress." I move my hand back up to his cheek because the minute that dimple appears, my lips are smashing on his. "Remember that sweet girl, who's asleep, waiting for her mommy and daddy to come home? She knows her daddy, and you know what she thinks of him?"

"What?" His unenthusiastic response shows how unconvinced he is.

"He's the bravest, strongest man, who loves her. So, I think you have at least four women, who believe in you." I hold up my fingers. "Em, Piper, your mom, and me."

"You believe in me?" The honesty pouring from those caramel eyes could undo me and my pants.

"So much, Brad. So much."

The dimple makes an appearance, and unable to control myself, I crash my lips to his. His hand lands on the back of my head, pulling me into the kiss, and I grind my center against his crotch. He matches my rhythm and our teeth collide as we're unable to quench our thirst for one another.

"God, Taylor, I want you so bad." He tugs my hair, spurring my lust on, so I capture his words with my mouth as I dive in to kiss him deeper.

His hands glide down my sides until he cups my ass, pressing me into him. Moans and groans escape from both of us. Abruptly, I'm pushed away as he holds my head in his hands.

"Not here. Not now," he says, and I sit back as much is humanly possible with a steering wheel pressed into my back. His right hand stays on my cheek in a tender caress. "The first time we're together again, will not be in my truck."

"We could fool around," I say seductively, and he sucks in a big breath.

"How about I take you home and properly feel you up in my parents' basement?" He winks and my body melts.

"Sounds good. I may even let you venture south." I raise my eyebrows.

"Me too." His eyes veer down to his crotch, so I reach down and rub the hardness with my palm.

"How fast can you drive?" I give him a chaste kiss on the lips and move back over to my side.

"I know back roads." He starts up the truck and I buckle myself in. He cranks on the defroster to high, to be able to see out of the fogged up windows.

I lick my lips as he looks at me while backing out of the parking spot.

"Temptress," he murmurs with a sly smile.

A warm buzz strums through my body with the thought of being lip-locked with Brad in the basement of his parents' house.

Brad parks the truck under his basketball hoop and I wonder if Em or another kid will play on it one day. Will Brad and I really defy the chances and live happily ever after? I'm not sure how long I'm off in la-la land, but Brad's hand moves across my face and I blink to come back to the present.

"I made record time here." He glances at his watch before escaping the truck. He jogs over to my side and opens the door, holding his hand out for me.

"Yes, you did. And your hands didn't veer over the console once." I lean closer. "That was a little disappointing."

His chuckles echo through the still, dark night. "I hate to disappoint you. Let me escort you in." He guides me up his sidewalk to his front door, stopping on the cement stoop like he's not about to come in with me. "I had a great time, Taylor."

I roll back on my heels, my eyes fluttering up to the sky. "Me too."

"Could I kiss you?" He steps forward, but I hold my hand up in the air.

"On one condition." He stops, tilting his head in intrigue. "It's on your basement couch."

"Deal, baby." The term baby only spurs more warmth in my heart for him. He used to call me that more than my actual name, and I've longed for it again.

He inserts his key into the lock, and I eagerly wait behind him, my stomach fluttering to be with him again. We quietly step into the foyer, each toeing off our shoes. The house is quiet and I'm thankful Chris and Maggie accomplished getting Em to sleep. We both look upstairs to my room where she should be nestled in the Pack 'N Play. We look at each other, and I'm fairly sure we're contemplating ditching our other plans to check on her.

"No," I mouth, and Brad's lips purse because he doesn't like my answer. I shake my head again and he smiles, waving his hand in the air.

We tiptoe toward the basement door, and right as we're there, Brad's hand molds to my hip and he flips me around so my back presses to the wall. The hand snakes up my body and his thumb brushes my cheek.

His lips slowly move over mine, and I suck in a breath and

let it go slowly, knowing that we're together. I melt into the gentle touch of his lips, sinking in the familiarity of him and us. His other hand slowly rises and his thumb brushes across my nipple, making me want to drag him down the stairs myself.

"Dada!" Em screams, and Brad flies off my body like I'm a live grenade.

"Emerson," he croaks out and moves behind the island in the kitchen, shielding his arousal from her.

I stifle a laugh and his pleading eyes fly to mine to handle the situation.

"Em." I bend down and hold my arms out to her.

Her eyes are red and sunken as she shuffles over in her pajamas.

"I'm sorry, guys." Maggie rounds the corner in a nice matching plaid pajama set. Her hair still looking perfect, but her make-up is scrubbed off.

"It's okay."

I scoop Em up and Maggie looks over at Brad with a confused look.

I watch him adjust himself once more, and then he tentatively slides into view.

"Did she not want to go down?" he asks his mom, hiding his body behind mine.

His hand reaches out to his daughter and he smooths out the back of her hair.

"She fell asleep, but then woke up about forty-minutes ago, and we've been trying to get her back down ever since."

"I'm sorry, Maggie. I've got it. Go get some sleep."

"Did you guys have fun?" she asks, opening the fridge and grabbing a bottle of water.

"We did, thank you for watching her."

Maggie moves to the hallway and we follow. Brad holds his hands out to Em, his predicament obviously calmed down now. Kids can put out the fire of arousal faster than a bucket of water to a match.

"Baby girl, it's sleepy time," he tells her as she nuzzles her head in the nook of his neck.

"Anytime." Maggie stops at the bottom of the stairs and places her hand on my shoulder. "Chris and I had a lot of fun with her."

"Thank you."

She walks up the stairs and I hear her bedroom door shut. We follow and Brad places Em on the bed. Instead of rolling over to sleep, she sits up and stares at the television.

"Peppa!"

"No, it's bedtime," I say, but she shakes her head.

"Peppa!"

"That damn British show." Brad rolls his eyes.

"Peppa!"

I look at Brad, exhausted, and he chuckles.

"Do you want me to take her to my room for the night?"

He's so sweet and I love the fact he's willing to do that for me.

"Why don't you stay with us for a while?" I'm not even sure why I'm okay with all three of us in the same bed, but I'm not ready to be away from him.

"Are you sure?"

"Yeah."

"Thanks."

He grabs the remote for the television and clicks on the On Demand feature to find *Peppa Pig*.

Em snuggles up in the crook of his arm and laughs when the pig family is introduced.

"Peppa," she says in a much calmer voice.

I smile at them together. It's truly magical how close they've become in such a short time.

"I'm going to get ready for bed." I sneak into the bathroom to change and wash my face.

Things between Brad and me are moving so fast, I can barely see a straight line now. But the scariest part is I'm not sure I want to. I've yearned for this life since I walked out on him, and I'm going to fight to keep it. I scrub my face and dry it with a towel, planning how I'll tell Brad exactly my thoughts on our future. How I don't see my future without him in it.

I open the bathroom door, and there, in that bed, is my dream come to reality. Em's arm is thrown over her daddy's stomach. His arm is above his head with his eyes closed. I move over and pry the remote from Brad's lifeless hands. Clicking off the television, I grab the extra blanket and put it over each of them. I nestle into my side and reach my arm across Em to Brad's stomach. His hand comes down and he links his fingers with mine.

"Good night."

"Good night, Tay," he mumbles, and nothing has sounded better than those three words.

SLAP

Slap

"Mama!"

My head shakes and my eyes blink a few times before I realize it's Em smacking me in the face.

"No." I grab her wrist when she's coming down on me again.

I sit up and see Brad's asleep.

"Shhh." I hold my finger up to my lips.

"Shhh," she mimics me.

I pick her up, and luckily, she stays quiet in my arms until the door is shut behind us.

Knowing my time is precious to get her downstairs if my point of having Brad sleep in is successful, I rush down the stairs. We are the first ones up, and when I check on the clock, I see why. It's six o'clock in the morning. Even for Em it's early.

I set her down on the floor and she instantly walks over to the new toys. I'm winding my head around to free the crick in my neck from the way I slept when the back door opens and shuts quietly.

I push my fingers through my hair to look presentable when Chris rounds the corner from the garage. He's all decked out in running gear. He breezes by us, until Em squeals.

"Pa!" she says, and I'm impressed she's nailed down all these names so fast.

He swivels around in shock.

"Emerson," he responds, and a smile hijacks his serious face. He bends down as she runs over to him. "I thought you'd sleep in after the night you had."

She doesn't allow him to hold her for very long before she wiggles out of his hold and moves back over to her toys.

Chris looks up and sees it's me with her, not his son. He nods. "Taylor."

"Hi." I wave my hand in the air like an idiot.

Awkwardness fills every square inch of this man's home. The one I entered in with full will. Stupid decision really.

He toes out of his running shoes and enters the room.

Oh, God.

My stomach knots thinking about what he wants to talk about.

"Brad and Maggie still asleep?" He sits in the armchair, his arms resting on his thighs. In this position, he resembles Brad. I see that same dimple in his right cheek as he smiles over at Em.

"Yes."

"I'm surprised Maggie is still sleeping. Then again, she's not used to chasing after a two-year-old." I take it as a dig, but when I look up at him, he's not being bitter, just stating a fact. My guilt for keeping her away from these people who would love her misinterpreted his tone.

"She's tiring."

"I imagine it's been hard with you doing it all by yourself."

"It is what it is." I shrug, not really wanting to have this conversation, especially with him.

"I think I owe you an apology, Taylor." He slides down and rests his back along the chair. Em rushes over and hands him a toy onion from her shopping cart.

"No, Chris, I'm sure you don't."

"Yes." He nods his head. "See this whole thing scares me on multiple levels. The fact that you kept her from Brad and us for two years terrifies me. The thought that you might do it again does too. It's the reason I was standoffish at first. I didn't want to get too close, then have her stripped away."

"I'm not going to take her anywhere, Chris. You have my word."

He nods, but his furrowed brow shows he's not completely convinced.

"Maggie already loves her, so I hope not."

"You don't have to worry about it."

"Thank you, but I still will. Second, it's Brad. He's made a lot of mistakes in his life and he's still finding his way to where he belongs. To me, it seems he fits in with you and Em, of course."

My heart swells at hearing that someone outside of us sees the rare connection Brad and I have.

"But if you hurt my son, I worry he'll never recover. He's quickly finding out that when you're a husband and a father, all the needs of your family come before yours. That everything you do is for them, not yourself. That's a hard thing for Brad. I'm not sure I've ever met anyone as selfish as my son." He shrugs, like what can he do about it now?

"So, I guess what I'm asking you, Taylor, is to please protect my family because the control of their hearts is slowly turning in your hands. It scared me when you first walked through that door because I don't know you very well." I nod, unsure if I should argue back. This man, who has made me nervous every second this weekend, is now being so open with me. "I'd like to change that though." He smiles and there's that matching dimple of Brad's.

My shoulders relax. "I'd like that, too."

"Roosevelt isn't that far from us," he reminds me. "If you and Brad are going to give this an honest try, you'll need some time without Emerson. Let Maggie and I get to know our granddaughter."

I look over at Em, going back and forth between two bins to hand Chris and me food. How can I take her away from this family, who has accepted us both with no conditions or qualms?

"Thank you, Chris. I'd like that, too."

His hands smack his legs. "Good. I'm glad you woke your mommy up so early so I could talk with her." He lays down on his stomach and Em climbs on his back.

I laugh at her riding him like a pony. "Go, Pa!" she exclaims when a much younger version with just as big of a heart barrels down the stairs, his eyes searching for his family.

Our eyes lock on one another as he stops in the hallway, finding us. A slow and easy smile comes over his face and all my worries fade. He sees his dad on the floor, and his stature tenses.

He closes the distance and comes alongside me, kissing my temple. His jean-clad legs rub along my old pajama pants. "How did you sleep?" I ask him, finding his dad's eyes glance over a few times.

"The best I've had in two years." He winks.

A scorching warm bolt hits my heart, telling me that my love for this man overflows it.

seventeen

Brad

TAYLOR KICKED ME OUT OF her house last night. She raised a good point on the fact that Emerson shouldn't see us sleeping together because it might confuse her, but at the same time, if things go right, it's exactly where we'll end up. Shouldn't my daughter know there will be a day I'll be there when she wakes up? Not wanting to cause any ruffles, I left after thoroughly kissing her, which hopefully resulted in her regretting her decision the minute my taillights faded into the dark.

Honestly, I was closer to the pool this morning when I woke up, so to me it worked out, but damn did I miss her . . . both of them.

Shivers run up my spine when I enter the aquatic center. The Michigan air only becoming colder every day.

"Hey, Brad." Amanda waves at me while clicking away on the computer.

"Good morning, Amanda," I nod, bypassing the desk to a waiting Cayden.

He stands to greet me, his hand extended and a huge smile on his face. Those dark-brown eyes filled with determination remind me of Greg. If I didn't know any better and it was a few years ago, I would have confused the two.

"Thank you so much, Brad." He appears eager, unable

to wait for me to walk the next five steps before closing the distance.

I shake his hand. "No problem. I just hope I can help."

I secretly pray my work-outs with Tanner over the years will keep this kid on the team. We made up crazy shit, but something worked since both of us earned scholarships to Michigan and Tanner a spot on the Olympic team.

"I'm sure you can." He rushes to catch up to me at the locker room doors. "Greg would rave about you and how much you helped him shave time off his laps. I know it was some sign from him when you showed up that day at practice."

I mindlessly go over to the lockers, Cayden on my heels the entire time. "What does Coach say needs help?" It's easier to disregard memories of Greg because I've never handled my guilt very well. The fact that a good friend of mine died and I had no idea won't stop eating away at me.

I grab the back of my shirt and pull it off my body as I toe out of my shoes.

Cayden starts stripping off the layers of warmth the Michigan weather warrants. "He said I need to shave time off all strokes if I have a chance to make the cut. He moved it up to right after Thanksgiving weekend, so that only gives me a week now."

"Fuck." I grab my cap and goggles from my bag and sit on the bench until he's finished. "That's not a lot of time, Cayden." My last intention is to make this endeavor seem hopeless, but since I haven't seen him swim yet, I truly don't know what we're up against. Greg was a good swimmer though, so I'm hoping the skill is in the genes.

He bites his lip, looking at me as though he's already been cut. "Is this whole thing useless?" He locks up his locker and stands there in front of me like he's staring at his dog that just got run over. Shit, who am I to doubt his dream?

"Hell no." I jump up and slap him on the back. "You have to believe that you have this up until that last touch of the wall.

Half the battle is in here." I press my finger into his chest. "You have to believe in yourself because you're the only one who can set the drive that leads you to success."

He stands there like a lump on a stick. No enthusiasm. I guess he isn't Greg's double, because that man led our pep talks before meets. "Come on, get psyched up." My shoulders rise and fall fast as the buzz of excitement fills my body. I shake out my arms and legs.

Cayden tries to mimic me, but I'm not sure he's feeling it, so I stop looking like a moron in front of him.

"Do you want this?" I ask the question I'm not sure he's asked himself. He's acting like a six-year-old on the t-ball field because his parents signed him up. At some point, you have to find your own love of the game to keep going.

"Yeah."

"Yeah," I mimic his meager answer. "I didn't ask you if you'd like beer. Do you want to make the team?"

No answer. Instead, he sits down on the bench and his head falls into his hands. "I do, but I'm scared."

My excitement falters. I sit down on the opposite bench and wait for him to give me more information. When I don't ask any more questions, his eyes peer up at me. "I'm scared I'll be a failure. That I won't be what Greg was and I'll disappoint my whole family."

I nod, understanding the pressure of other's expectations. That pressure might be the reason I've fucked up majority decisions in my life. "Let's say Greg was with us, would you want to make the team?"

His eyes widen and he nods as frantically as a bobblehead. "Yeah."

"Then that's it. I hate to say this, but Greg has to be an afterthought. Believe me, he's watching and he wants you to succeed in whatever you want to do. You aren't going to disappoint him if you lose your spot on the team, but you will if you don't try and be honest with yourself."

Shit, I'm surprised by myself. I'm usually not the one spouting advice, but rather I'm on Cayden's side of this conversation.

He nods, but his eyes are shifting everywhere but at me.

"So, let's get out there before we lose our lane time." I stand, positioning my cap and goggles on my head.

"Okay."

"All right, I'm going to need more excitement. Maybe you need some music to pump you up. I'm going to send over a playlist for you that is mandatory for you to play on your drive here. Got it?" I eye him and he nods. He'll agree to anything right now. I'm familiar with the desperate shoes he's in.

We enter the pool area and the chlorine smell generates a fast pulse in my veins.

Wes is sitting at the table, his foot bouncing a mile a minute while he jots something down on the paper. "Hey, Wes," I say and he startles.

"Shit, you scared the crap out of me."

"It's quiet in the morning." I inspect the pool area, noticing not one person in the lanes. I thought for sure it'd be packed. "Where the hell is everyone?"

He shakes his head, his eyes closing briefly. "Not here." He glances at Cayden. "You're from Michigan, right?"

"Yeah, Cayden Mendes." The polite kid holds out his hand.

"Brad told me about you. Good luck, man. Coach Kass is hell."

We laugh, all well aware of Coach Kass's intolerant to anything that jeopardizes his team's standings.

"Hey, Cayden, why don't you go dip in and warm up a little. I'll be right there."

"Sure." He moves to walk away, but turns back. "It's nice to meet you, Wes."

Wes glances up from his papers, and from what I can see, there's a bunch of numbers scribbled on a spreadsheet. I've seen the look of panic on many faces during my internship at Lincoln, and Wes is baring a similar expression right now. Something is wrong with Creadle's Aquatic's future.

"You too, Cayden." He smiles and most would believe everything to be all right. Hell, I would have, if he didn't appear so stressed out with the piece of paper in front of his face.

I watch Cayden move to the pool, and once he's out of earshot, I sit on the chair next to the table, pretending to reposition my goggles.

"What's going on?" My eyes gaze down and then back to him.

He flips over the sheet, leans back in the chair, and crosses his arms over his chest. Should have known he wouldn't make this easy. He has pride, and I get that.

"Nothing. Just going over some stuff. So, you think this kid's got a chance to make the team?" Wes had been recruited with a scholarship just like me, so we're not completely familiar with the 'your position is on the line' crap like Cayden's facing, but that doesn't mean there wasn't any pressure to hold our spot.

"I've never seen him swim."

Wes's eyebrows scrunch together.

"You're kidding me?"

"No, he asked me for help and I agreed. His brother was one of my teammates. He passed away."

"I gotcha. Maybe I'll head over and look in on you guys in a little bit. See how you're doing."

I stand to leave him to his secret paperwork. "That would be great. I'm kind of helping him with shit Tanner and I did all our life."

"It worked for both of you, so I'm sure it will for him."

"Yeah. I better get going." I walk away, but back step to him. "Wes." He flips the paper back over and practically throws himself on top of it. "If you ever want help with the business paperwork, just ask."

He shakes his head vehemently. "No, no. Everything's fine, Brad. But thank you."

"Okay, just thought I'd mention it. You've done so much for me." I try to spin it so he doesn't feel bad or embarrassed. They taught us at Lincoln that was half the battle in fixing people's business.

"Thanks," he says and stares at me until I leave.

I walk on the dry tiled floor, bare of any puddles due to the fact that no one has been here since last night. Not a good sign. It's a rarity to not have your feet get sloshed on your way to the lane. I only remember experiencing it in the early dark mornings Coach Kass would make me come in before everyone else to penalize me because I made a bonehead decision. I didn't mind though because there's something serene about knowing your body is the first one to break through the water, though.

Cayden is moving back and forth across the pool with little wake from his feet, his arms gliding well, but there's something odd with his form. Continuing to watch him, I analyze each stroke until I discover his hiccup. It's so minor I see how it's been missed all these years.

I blow the whistle and slide into the water in the lane next to him. The warm water swarms my body and I'm quickly back in my element. Cayden stops at the wall and lifts his goggles. His chest heaves, his lungs fighting for a breath, and I'm worried that, if he's this winded from a few laps, he'll never make the butterfly.

"Endurance is your friend," I remind him of a phrase he's heard before. If you aren't in the pool, you should be at the gym or out on a run. Your lungs have to get the work-out they deserve to keep you going in the pool.

"I've been working on that."

"If you don't, you'll be out for sure. You just have to beat the other guys." Cayden nods, and I'm not sure this kid will ever argue back with me. "I think I see something you need to adjust. So, we're going to perfect that today."

"Okay."

I move into his lane, helping him get into form to show him exactly where his issue lies. Cayden is very responsive, which is nice and makes the training easier for both of us.

For the next hour, we repeat his freestyle. Each time, he's shaving a little more off his time. The only problem is I don't know who the slowest and fastest guys currently are on his team, which is information I'll need to know in order to figure out if he'll be ready by next week. Wes never comes over, and it's probably for the best. Cayden appears to get intimidated quickly, which isn't going to benefit him.

We're walking back to the locker room when I spot my swim lesson coming in. Damn, Quinn the nanny. She eyes me and Cayden in our spandex shorts, her eyes zooming in on the crotches.

"Brad." She stops us at the sign-in table. "Ava, has been begging for you all day."

"That's great." I ruffle Ava's hair and she beams up at me. "I'll be with you in a second."

"I'm Quinn." She holds her hand out to Cayden, twirling a strand of her fire-engine red hair around her finger.

"Oh, uh . . . I'm Cayden." He eyes me, a smirk teasing the corner of his lips. He likes what he sees, and if I was nineteen, I would too.

"Are you an instructor, too?" Her eyes light up, and I fear if he said yes, I'd be replaced. Which wouldn't be bad, except it doesn't bode well to have an open spot on your schedule.

"No, I'm a student at Michigan." Cayden's honestly amazes me. I'm not sure the kid has any game.

"Cayden's on the swim team up at Michigan. I'm just training him, but he doesn't need much help because he's so exceptional. You know those natural athletes." I shrug and her eyes drink him up like he's her breakfast latte.

"Oh." She steps closer and fear strikes Cayden's eyes. I push my hands down in the air to signal him behind her back to calm down. "So, Cayden, do you have a girlfriend at Michigan?" Her nipples have to be touching his wet chest right now, and I'm half tempted to cover Ava's eyes from seeing an NC-17 rated 'Nanny Goes After Super–stud' episode.

He swallows hard, his eyes fixated on her tits. "Um . . . no."

"Oh." She steps back and her tongue snakes across her lips. "Maybe I'll see you around here sometime." She grabs Ava's hand and moves across the floor to the bench. "We'll wait over here, Brad," she calls over her shoulder, giving Cayden one last examination.

I clasp him on the shoulder. "Looks like you have an admirer." I toss my head in Quinn's parting direction.

"Man, I've never had a girl come on to me like that before." He shakes his head while his eyes keep trying to sneak peeks at her.

"Not all are as forward as Quinn." I change the conversation to what matters in Cayden's life. "So, I need you to get me the times for your competition. Does Coach still post it as an incentive?"

"Yeah, I'm usually at the bottom."

"Not for long. I promise. Bring that in tomorrow. Same time. If you can squeeze some time in after practice today, try to get into the groove with the position of your arm. The faster your body figures out the new movement, the better off we'll be."

He smiles, but still has that panicked look splashed across his face. "Okay."

"Hey, relax. We'll get you there," I assure him, and I think by me saying it, he's starting to believe it.

"Thanks, Brad."

I wave off his gratitude.

"I'm happy to do it." Truth is, it feels good to help someone. Reminds me of when Tanner and I would beat our records practicing and how much we'd celebrate. Usually by moving over to the diving boards and doing some crazy dive that could have seriously injured us. "Now, go and don't think too much about it. Just get done whatever you need to."

"Okay." He shoots one more look at Quinn, his eyes studying her up and down, and then nods his head her way. Maybe I was wrong. Maybe the kid does have game.

Cayden leaves and Cami barrels though the side door, skipping to something streaming through her beats. She waves enthusiastically.

"Hey, I need to talk to you." Her finger jabs my shoulder and intrigue sets in me. She spots Quinn on the bench. "Later, after lessons. But did you really think you could hide it from me?"

I hold up my hands while slowly backing away from her toward the lesson pool. "I've never hidden anything."

"Omitting is lying, Brad." She shakes her head and rushes into the office.

I turn on my heels to start my lessons for the day.

Four hours later, my body is a prune, not that I care much. I've grown used to the wrinkles on my fingers and the bottom of my feet. Cami's in the office reading on her e-reader with her feet kicked up on the table.

"So?" I throw myself in the other office chair, exhausted and ready to go home. "What do you want to talk about?"

She holds her finger in the air. Her face transforms into five different reactions and feelings before she gasps. Her hand covers her heart and she sets the e-reader down on the table.

"Man, that was a good one."

I nod, wanting to get this powwow started so I can get out of here.

"Okay." She shakes her head as though that's going to clear whatever has taken over her thoughts.

"Yeah." I'm quickly losing my patience.

"You are Emerson's dad?" Her finger points at me again as though she's accusing me of something I didn't already know.

"Yeah." I can't stop the smile from overtaking my face. "I

am."

"Good. I'm glad. You seem like a good guy, but I must warn you, if you hurt her, I'll gut you." All five feet of her stalks over to me. "Got it?" She flashes her sternest and most intimidating look.

I sit in the office chair, my hands in my lap. "I won't."

"Okay. I've heard things about you, but you seem like a good guy."

"Thank you. I am."

The whole conversation is very cordial and Cami should realize she couldn't intimidate a fly.

"Good. I'm glad we had this talk. You may go." She waves her hand in the air like I'm her servant, one who's being dismissed for the day.

I jump to my feet and she springs back. "Nice talk." I raise my eyebrows.

"Don't think I don't mean it. I have a hot temper, Ashby. You just haven't seen it yet," she screams out the door before it shuts.

I get to my locker and reach for my phone. It sucks not being able to text or talk to Taylor all day. After three consecutive days with her, it's a rough change. Seeing a text from her on my phone, my stomach stirs with excitement.

Taylor: Dinner at six?

Me: Why, Ms. Delaney, are you asking me to come over?

Unsure if I'll get an answer since she should be at work, I put it on the shelf and grab my things for a shower. My phone beeps.

Taylor: I am. Maybe you could bring the sparkling grape juice?

Me: I'll pick some up along with a stop in the pharmaceutical aisle.

Taylor: Not yet . . . patience.

Me: You know I'm not a saint. I like what I want when I want it.

Taylor: I know.

Me: You don't care that I've been whacking off to memories of us from two years ago every night.

Taylor: I think it's cute.

Me: It's not cute. It's painful.

Taylor: Soon. :) See you at six.

Me: I'll be there. :)

While the warm water streams down on me in the shower, I think about Taylor and me. How will I ever get us back to where we were? I'm an inpatient person, but one thing is for sure, I'd wait forever for her. A life with her and Emerson is what I yearn for more than anything. The thought feels right, like it's where I belong, but I can't disregard Taylor's apprehension.

Fifteen minutes later, I'm walking out of the Aquatic Center and I spot a man in a suit sitting on the stool by Amanda's desk.

"Hey, Amanda." I stop, leaning forward as though I'm looking over a schedule. "Who's this?"

The guy glances up from his phone and I see a big folder peeking out of his briefcase.

"A Mitchel Henderson," she whispers. "From some firm." She slides the business card in front of me and I smile over at the guy to appease him. It works and he concentrates on his phone again.

I check out the card and mentally process the name Grager and Grager, Inc. Business Consultant. I shake my head, because if Wes would rather pay someone to tell him how to run his business, what can I do? But a guy who is busy on Facebook or some other shit before he has to meet with you isn't going to save your company. I think Wes is a smart enough guy to realize that, at least I hope he is.

At the exact moment I lean back from the counter, Wes walks out of the locker room in a nice pair of slacks and a button down shirt. All of his tattoos are hidden except the few on his hands. I hate to see him portraying to be someone he's not. If anything, it tells me he's desperate and the Aquatic Center is in worse shape than I thought earlier today. His eyes meet mine and then zoom in on Mitchel Henderson, aka the douche who will make you lose your company faster.

"Wes," I call out, circling around the receptionist desk. "Can I steal you for one second?"

Wes holds up his hand to stop me. "Not right now, Brad. I have an appointment. I'm sure this can wait until tomorrow." He beelines it to Mitchel, not giving me the opportunity to respond.

"Okay." I back up and watch the two of them shuffle through the locker room doors.

"Has he ever been here before?" I ask Amanda, and she shakes her head.

"I've never seen him before."

"Good. That's a good thing."

eighteen

Taylor

"SEE YOU, GUYS." I WAVE to my shift replacements and walk out the hospital doors.

My mind races with everything I need to do before Brad comes over tonight. Get the groceries for dinner and pick Em up. Clean up a little and hope maybe he'll stay for a movie afterwards. I'm so distracted, I don't notice Sam standing by my car until I reach the bumper.

Dark circles line his eyes and his clothes are untucked and dirty, like he hasn't been taking care of himself.

"Sam." I draw back in surprise. He leans on his truck door with his hands tucked in his pockets.

"Taylor," he says my name with such distain I wonder why he's bothered to come see me.

"Is something going on?" I fiddle with my keys.

"I miss you. I miss Em."

My heart breaks for Sam being stuck in the middle of all this.

"I'm sorry, Sam, but for Em, I have to give this a chance. I wish there was room for both of you, but clearly neither one of you will be the bigger person." I place my purse on my trunk since I'm guessing we'll be here for a while.

"He cheated on you. Got engaged to someone else. I don't get why he can waltz into town, and bam, you love him again." Sam approaches me and there's hurt mixed with something else in his eyes. Oh, God, he's still hopeful for a chance.

"I've forgiven him. This is my decision, Sam. I understand you're upset and I've apologized so many times for what I allowed to happen. I should have never leaned on you as much as I did. But my heart has always been with Brad. I've never stopped loving him, and that's why it's so easy for me to forgive him." Obviously, my gentle nudges aren't working and it's time to be a more direct.

He takes off his hat to thread his finger through his hair. "I don't get how such a smart girl can make so many mistakes."

Now he's stepping over the line, and I'm not going to allow him to knock me down. "You don't have to get it, Sam. It's none of your business." My voice rises because I'm mentally exhausted from this conversation. "Listen, I would love for you to be a part of our lives, but as an uncle to Em. A friend to me. I'll toe the line with Brad on the subject, if you really think you can handle being around him, because it's all three of us, or none. You have to make that choice." I grab my purse, swinging it over my shoulder.

"That's not a choice. I can't be around you as a happy family while my life falls apart," he argues, and I take a deep breath. "So, I'm leaving town."

"What? Where are you going?"

"My uncle suffered a heart attack, so I'm going up north to manage his farm." He stares down at the ground, kicking a loose rock with his foot. "I wanted to make sure there wasn't a chance for us."

I'm happy for Sam because this is what he needs, to get out of Roosevelt and start a new life. "I think that's actually a good thing." I step closer, placing my hand on his arm. "You can get out of here and all the shit that comes with this town."

"Well, I'd rather stay, but if I don't have you and Em then

I'm going. If April ever comes back will you contact me, I'd like to file divorce papers."

A tight smile crosses my lips. Sam might not see his departure as a good thing, but it is. "Of course."

He places his John Deere hat back on his head, straightening the bill. "I am happy for you, Tay, if Brad's what you want. I just don't want to see you or Em hurt." He stands straight, signaling an end to our conversation.

"Thank you, Sam. I can't thank you enough for all the help you've given me over the years. Keep in touch, let me know the new address, I'll send pictures of Em if you'd like." I need this to end amicably. Sam's friendship is important to me if he can handle not being anything more.

"I'd like that. I'll text you once I'm settled up there." He steps closer, his arms awkwardly wrapping around me.

My hands pat his back and sadness washes over me that he's moving, but happiness quickly takes its place. He's going where he needs to, far away from my sister.

"Sounds good. Bye Sam."

"Bye Taylor."

I slide past him and unlock my car.

He does the same, rounding the front of his truck to the driver's side. As I pull away, I say goodbye to a part of my past that I'll never forget.

Two hours later, I'm in the kitchen, waiting for Brad to show up. Em is playing with the princess dolls he bought her and I'm preparing the casserole for dinner. The doorbell rings and Em screams.

"Dada!"

She runs to the door, now associating the doorbell with Brad, since he's the only one who comes around lately. God knows my dad doesn't show up for a visit. The only time I see him is during the holidays or when I stop by Carolle's Tap to make sure he's still occupying his worn-out stool.

I open the door and there's my knight with a fist full of

flowers and a bottle of sparkling kiddie wine.

"How are my girls?" he asks, coming into the house. Bending down, he envelops Em in a hug and kisses her cheek. "I missed you," he whispers, and anyone could hear the honesty and heartfelt sincerity in his voice.

"Miss you," Em responds and grabs his hand.

"Hold on, baby girl. Mommy needs a hug." He lets go of our daughter's hand and stands, wrapping his arms around my waist.

His lips grace my neck and shivers run up my spine. "I'm always prepared just in case the mere sight of me has you stripping your clothes off," he softly says in my ear before his hand gives my ass a concealed tight squeeze.

I push him away, finding his usual smirk.

"No!" Em stomps her foot and pushes at my legs. Brad and I share a look of confusion, and I'm wondering where her outburst is coming from.

"What?" I ask her, and she stomps as she pushes me again.

"Emerson, don't push Mommy," Brad disciplines, bending down to her level.

"My Dada," she says and crawls into his arms. Suddenly, it's all very clear. Em doesn't want to share her daddy, which will bring a whole new slew of problems in our world.

"I am your Dada, but I love Mommy too," Brad tells her, but she's already shut down. Her arms are tight around his neck, and as much as I find this as a new obstacle, it's cute that she's become so attached to him.

"Just let it go for now." I grab the flowers and wine from his hands, and walk into the kitchen. "Dinner's ready," I holler over my shoulder and begin shuffling the food to the table.

Brad walks in with her in his arms and places her in her high chair. Just like that, she's back to her usual self, singing and tapping on her tray.

"Food," she says, and I pull her plate from the fridge where I had it to cool off and place it on her tray.

"Do you need any help?" Brad asks, his eyes watching every move I make around the kitchen.

"Nope. You can sit there and admire."

He leans back in his chair, his long legs stretched out in front of him. "Gladly," he says, his eyes burning with pure lust.

"Not too long though. You'll be taking your little stash home with you." I move my finger back and forth as though I'm reprimanding him, which doesn't faze him. Not much does though.

"So, I trained Cayden today." He starts the conversation about our day, and I haven't decided if I'm going to tell him about Sam waiting by my car after my shift.

"How did you like it?" I ask, bringing our plates over to the table.

"Looks delicious, Taylor." He inhales the scent and closes his eyes. I'm by no means a great cook, but I've learned a few things over the years, especially during my little obsession with cooking shows last year. He picks up his fork. "I really liked it." He bites his lip as though he doesn't want to reveal how much.

"That's great. Do you think he'll make the team?"

"I don't know. The problem is he's slower than he should be. It'll take work, and I wish I had a lot longer than one week, especially with Thanksgiving this week, but I'll give it everything I have. I really want him to make it." His eyes focus on his plate of enchilada casserole. "But, man, it was nice to feel useful. I mean, I was able to pinpoint that when his right shoulder rotated it was changing his body . . ."

Brad continues and his excitement over his day thrills me. I don't like hearing how he usually doesn't feel useful, but I'm going to keep it my secret that he's starting to find his place— where he needs to be in life and a second love after competing. I sit there enthralled in a conversation I know nothing about. Cayden's arm and his knocking only milliseconds off his time, but Brad's sparkling eyes are what I'm enamored with.

"I just hope he makes it." He releases a breath after talking for minutes straight.

I place my hand on his and he looks up at me. "I know. Just take it one day at a time."

"Yeah." He dishes up a fork full and tastes my meal. "Amazing." Then he shovels another bite into his mouth. I watch Em do the same thing, busy with her fork and plate, picking up the kernels of corn one at a time.

"What else?"

He swallows a bite and places his fork down. "I wanted to ask you, how long have you known Wes?"

"From high school."

"And Cami?"

"She was my sister's best friend, so most of my life."

"She cornered me today and tried to intimidate me if I hurt you." He rolls his eyes and I laugh.

"She didn't?"

"She did. But I assured her I won't hurt either of you." He looks over at Em and my heart swells a little more.

"I know."

"But I think the business is struggling."

"No, really?" That would be horrible. I don't know where Wes got the money to open Creadle's Aquatic after he came home from college, but it's been a success.

"How stubborn of a guy is he?"

I purse my lips, thinking. Truth is, I don't know Wes that well other than the date we went on and his fights with Cami. "Stubborn." I remember him and Cami fighting over my sister once. Or the time they broke up. "But I think he comes around after a while. Why?"

"I told him I'd help him by looking through some things for the business, but there was a consultant there when I left. I'm worried for him, but I'm not going to butt my nose where it doesn't belong."

I forgot how kindhearted Brad is. A lot of people only see

a cocky, arrogant guy, who goes after whatever he wants with the same fierce competitiveness he used against his opponents in the water. But deep down, he cares. I witnessed him buying a meal for a homeless man on campus on more than one occasion. I waited for him on the bench in the pool house while he helped his teammates with a hiccup after practice.

He practically ran the fundraising for the swim team, but I guess those things can be clouded when the same person spouts off his mouth and starts fights for no reason at all sometimes. After graduation, I can imagine the people who knew him best even doubted him.

"You're so sweet," I say, sipping my Diet Coke.

"Don't tell anyone." He rolls those heart-melting eyes.

"Never, I don't want any competition," I joke back, liking this dynamic between us.

"Ah, baby, there's no competition." He leans over with his lips puckered at me.

I glance to Em and quickly lean in and give him a chaste kiss.

"Too short."

"Later," I mumble, forking my food.

"I'm holding you to that."

We walk down the stairs with an exhausted Em fast asleep in her crib. My feet touch the cold tile floor and two warm arms surround me. He draws me back to his chest, his mouth already at the nape of my neck. After sliding my hair to the side to give him better access to my skin, his hands venture up my ribcage.

There's nothing better than when the one you love can't wait a second more to have you. I twist in his arms, and his strong hands descend to grip my ass.

"Mr. Ashby, you need to calm down." I step backward toward the couch with him chest to chest with me. Unable to keep the pace he's dictating for us, I fall to the couch and he doesn't stop until he's lying on top of me. "No movie tonight?" I smile and he shakes his head.

His brown eyes burn with so much desire, I fear I can't put out the fire in them, especially since I'm not ready to sleep with him yet as our daughter sleeps upstairs. God, he makes it hard though. His lips linger over my collarbone and his magical hands touch every inch of me except where I need him to, and that only fuels my body to a frenzy of uncontrolled need.

"We should stop." My voice breaks because I'm already panting and he hasn't even kissed me yet.

"Nuh-uh." He slides down the length of my body, his fingers grazing past the cups of my bra. I suck in another breath.

"Uh-huh," I say, my fingers digging deep into the dark strands of his hair.

He lifts his head from between my legs, his right hand covering my jean-clad center. "One of us is coming tonight." He flicks the button of my jeans and my breath catches in my throat.

"She's upstairs." My excuse sounds weak with the whimpered moan as his thumb massages my clit. Even with the barrier of my panties, I'm soaked.

"She's asleep, Tay. Just keep your screams down." He winks, teasing me about my uncontrollable mouth.

He hooks his fingers onto each side of my jeans and I lift my ass to help him slide them down my legs. "One leg over." His hand guides my leg so it hangs off the back of the couch. "Other down. Have you forgotten the drill?" The sly grin on his face says he's enjoying bringing me to the brink. Then again, he always did, but usually that made him too horny and he was in me instantly. There's no way I'm remembering our first night on the couch with Em upstairs.

My fight is weak and I lose the battle with myself. My back arches begging for more as his tongue sucks my nub into his hot waiting mouth. He pushes my hips back down and moves one finger inside of me. "Stay down, baby," he whispers, but his words sound like I'm in a tunnel.

He inserts another finger and I'm writhing underneath his

touch as a burst of ecstasy travel through me. Minutes later, his hair is wrapped tight around my fingers and I'm grinding his face to my core.

"Brad," I sigh, my body slowly coming down from the explosions he manipulated out of my body.

His thumb leaves me and circles around my clit in a slow soothing motion as my body sinks into the couch to catch my breath. He slides back up my body, his hardness straining his jeans against my naked bottom half.

He kisses me lightly on the lips and draws back with a smile on his face. "I told you one of us would be coming."

My hand slides into his pocket, searching for a condom. Maybe I'm making too much out of this whole special moment the second time around.

"Whatcha doing, babe?" He leans away from me and I dig into another pocket, coming up empty-handed.

"Where is it?"

"Where's what?"

"The condom. You said you brought them."

A devilish grin emerges on his face.

"I don't have them. We're not going to have sex with our daughter upstairs. I'm not the old Brad, remember?" Although he seems casual and okay with the fact that I still may think of him that way, the hurt in his eyes isn't hard to miss, especially when you know Brad as well as I do.

"I know, but usually when you go down on me, it only makes you hotter." He sits back and I crawl up on my knees, not allowing the space to separate us after this pivotal moment.

He takes my hand and places it between his legs. The hard bulge is visible, but I rub it up and down a little because I'm not a selfish person; I'm a giver. "Believe me, babe, I'm hot, ready to combust, so I really need you to stop doing that." He picks up my hand and places it on my bare leg.

"Nuh-uh." I shake my head and bite my lower lip.

"No, Taylor. I did not do that for you to reciprocate." He

shakes his head and actually pretends to watch the television.

"I know." I scoot closer, my hands fiddling with his belt buckle. "I want to, too." I shoot him my best seductive look, and he inhales a deep breath.

"Are you sure?"

I nod instantly. "Yes. Let me." I act like I'm asking permission. He always enjoyed that school-girl thing when I'd act all innocent.

"Don't do the school girl," he begs, because we both know it will only escalate the situation.

I lean forward as both my legs straddle his hips. "Don't worry, I'll save the real temptress until we're completely alone."

He wiggles under me and I can only imagine he's growing harder by the second.

"Let me give you some relief." I slide down off his lap, my knees hitting the floor while my fingers manipulate his pants to free him.

Once my hands are wrapped around his girth and my mouth rests just above the tip, I look through my eyelashes, and his eyes could be a laser they're burning so strong.

A little while later, it's his hands clenching my head.

nineteen

Brad

"GREAT PRACTICE, CAYDEN. YOU'RE GETTING into the groove now." I slap him on the back while he makes his way to the locker room.

I'm impressed because he really is improving on his time. From the list he gave me of the other guy's times, he's got a chance.

Cayden walks through the locker room and I turn toward the office, noticing I have fifteen minutes before my first lesson. Wes's head is in his hands as he studies a paper in front of him. He scribbles and then crosses it out and scribbles again. It's gut-wrenching witnessing him so distraught. This place could be amazing, especially since it's not too far from the affluent cities in the area. The problem is, he doesn't want to ask for help, and I respect that. But by not asking, he's going to be left with nothing. Believe me, I'm a prime example of having too much pride.

I walk through the glass door and he tries to shuffle the papers. He spins around in his chair with a fake-ass grin plastered on his face.

"What are you doing?" I scoot up on the table by the window.

"Just some paperwork. When's your next appointment?"

203

He rests his ankle on his knee, and internally I debate if I should say something. Wes seems like a cool guy, and I think we have a kinship in a way that both of our dreams didn't pan out. He found his place, but he needs help to continue.

"Who's Mitchel?" I ask.

"A friend."

"Bullshit." I widen my eyes and wait for him to be honest with me and himself.

"Just stay out of it, Brad."

I jump off the table and break the distance between us. Sliding into a chair across from him, I lean my elbows on my thighs.

"I can't. See, I have a daughter to take care of and a girl who I'm hoping will one day be my wife. This is my place of employment, so I have to care."

"Don't worry, you're getting paid."

I wish I could honestly believe that, but from what I've witnessed the past two days, I fear one day I'll arrive to a set of locked doors.

"I get the pride thing. I'm not one to share a lot, but I think I can help you."

He leans back and stares up at the ceiling for a moment before his eyes land on me. Even before he agrees, I see in his eyes, he's relented.

"Here." He hands me the papers he was scrutinizing.

The first thing I notice is red everywhere. One line has black and that's swim lessons. So at least those are making him some money, meaning I get paid way too little.

"What did Mitchel think you should do?"

He's quiet for a minute, but when I look up from the paper, he sighs.

"Fire you." He shrugs with a smile on his face, indicating that isn't going to happen.

"Interesting, since I'm your best instructor." I shrug like I really mean that.

"Jeez, Brad, this stays between us. Cami knows nothing, and she can't. Do you understand me? She'd freak out." I can see the gears moving on overdrive in his head.

"Don't worry. This is between us. Do you have your taxes from last year? I need all your profit/loss reports since you opened. I'll go through them all tonight, and then we can talk."

"You'd do that? I have no way of paying you, Brad."

I wave my hand in the air. "I'm doing this because you're a friend and went out on a limb to help me."

For the first time in two days, his shoulders relax slightly.

"Thanks, man."

"Of course, there is one favor I might ask in return." He cocks his head to the side.

"What?"

"Do you babysit?" A smile creeps on his face. "I want to take Taylor away for the night, but we have Emerson and there's no way she'll let just anyone watch her."

"Sam?"

"Fuck off."

He laughs and holds out his hand.

"Deal."

"I'll grab everything before I leave and we can talk tomorrow?"

"Sounds good. Thank you."

"No problem." My eyes study the sheet of the paper in front of me, and I wonder if this is even fixable.

Someone knocks on the window and Wes waves at them.

"Your lesson is here," he tells me, and I hand the paper back to him where he turns it over on top of another pile.

"All right. Don't worry, we'll figure this out."

Later that afternoon, I'm sitting at my apartment surrounded by Dylan's boxes, trying to make heads or tails where this business went downhill. I gave Taylor the lowdown, and as much as I don't want to be away from her and Emerson tonight, especially with Taylor being off today, I want to make sure this has my full attention. She understood, of course. It doesn't stop me from trying to finish early and surprise her.

Dylan walks in and stops, holding the door open. "Whoa, call the police. There's been an invader."

"Funny. Where's your latch on?" I drop the pen and sit back in my chair.

"She's packing. We leave Saturday." He drops his computer bag on the back of a chair before sitting down in the one across from me.

"What's that?" He nods toward the strewn papers on the table and my open computer.

"That Aquatic Center I go to, I'm looking at their profit and loss statements. They're struggling badly, and I can't figure out why. They were doing great their first year." I stare down at all the red, shaking my head.

"Hmm . . . and you say business isn't for you."

I'd like to knock his cocky smirk off his face.

"I'm doing it as a favor."

"You might be doing it as a favor, but I think you're enjoying it, hence the reason you're here." He stands and ventures into the kitchen.

"What do you mean?"

"I mean, you've been completely occupied with Taylor and Emerson, and haven't shown your face around here. I have no idea what you're going to do about rent. Honestly, you should just move in with her or down there. But this guy asks you to help him, and here you are willing to spend time away from them to do it. I just find it all interesting, that's all." He cracks open a beer, holding one up for me.

I shake my head and he places it back in the fridge.

"I won't be able to concentrate over there, but I'm trying to finish up so I can surprise them."

He comes back over and sits down, oblivious to the fact I just told him I want to finish.

"What's the deal with you guys? Are you one happy little

family now?"

"Taylor and I are together, but I'm not about to move in with her. We have to consider Emerson."

"They coming to Thanksgiving?" he asks, and my head falls back.

"Shit. My mom called me today, asking me about coming. I think I might stay at Taylor's. She usually has her family and a few friends over."

"Why don't we all go on down to Mayberry?"

"It's Roosevelt, idiot," I clarify and he narrows his eyes.

"I know, but the town is like fucking Mayberry. I dated this girl down there once. Not sure where I met her." He looks up at the ceiling, still coming up empty. "Anyway, I picked her up and they say there's only one cop. It's creepy."

"Whatever. Mayberry had two cops by the way."

"Look at you knowing trivia shit." He downs the rest of his beer. "Let me know if you need any help. I'm in for the night."

"Okay. See you."

His bedroom door shuts and I focus back on the paperwork.

Two hours later, I'm in my truck on my way to surprise my girls. Thank goodness for that A in Accounting. But even with me being able to pinpoint where all their money is going, the mystery to fix it is still running through my head. The only person I know who could tell me how they'd be able to profit without spending an arm and a leg would be Tanner.

I dial him up on my car's Bluetooth, fully expecting my sister to answer his phone, which seems to be the norm nowadays. Not that he has a ton of time between practicing and the endorsements which are starting to come in for him. It's not a secret that he's the up-and-coming, and I guarantee after the Olympics next year, his face will be everywhere, including a Wheaties box.

"I'm seriously going to beat your ass." My sister, Piper, answers the phone. I've been meaning to call her. "I've given you space to call me and announce that I'm an aunt. So, expect an ass kicking come Thursday."

"I'm sorry. I've had some shit going on and I thought it would be a good surprise."

"What, were you going to have her wear a sign when I walk in the door, saying, 'You're my aunt'. You can tell Taylor I'm thoroughly pissed at her, too." I can hear Tanner urging her to calm down in the background. Then there's some muffled voices and what I assume is a tug of war over the phone.

"Go take a bath, baby," Tanner says. "What's up?" I can just imagine him on the couch with his legs up on the coffee table and remote in hand. He's so different to me. He takes everything in stride, nothing truly excites him. Well, with the exception of my sister.

Piper yells in the background.

"Yeah, I'll tell him." He gets back on the phone. "She says she fully expects to spend all Thanksgiving vacation with Emerson." I guess my mom talked to her in detail. "You should have called her."

"I'm busy. Plus, she never was a big fan of Taylor's."

"Still, I shouldn't be talking to you either, because you left me on the receiving end of her wrath."

I release a breath, turning onto the highway. "Sorry. I'll take you out for a drink this weekend."

"And Piper." He laughs and I can hear the humor in his voice.

"And Piper."

"Good. So, what's going on?"

"I have a daughter."

"So I hear." I thought this would get some reaction out of him. "I thought you might have one out there somewhere, but never did I think it would be Taylor's."

"Hardy har. We can chat about all the crap going on with that when you get home, but I've been swimming down at Creadle's Aquatic Center."

"Is it new? I've never heard of it."

"It's about twenty minutes from me. Anyway, I started teaching swim lessons there. Oh, shit, I forgot to tell you, Greg Mendes died."

"What?" Tanner's voice sounds surprised and more alert.

"So, I went to see Coach and Greg's brother came out and asked me if I'd train him. Greg died in a car accident last year, right after he'd graduated."

"Oh, man. I'm sorry to hear that. Why didn't we know anything about it?"

"I don't know." I shake my head, thinking about how we both should have been at his funeral. "Maybe they didn't have a funeral or visitation."

"We need to get the guys together." When Tanner says guys, he means the swim team. We've all spread out like a spider web across the United States, but at one time, we were one tight group.

"Definitely. Maybe once you become a gold medalist you can rent some island for all of us to party on."

"Whatever. That island would be for me to screw your sister every which way but missionary."

"You asshole. That shit isn't funny when you're actually with her. Damn, now I'm having visuals." I hammer my hand against the steering wheel like that can dislodge the images from my brain.

Tanner just laughs in the background. "Seriously though, I'll have to send something to his parents. I feel horrible."

"Well, I have two favors, and one might help you with that. The first is come to the center with me on Friday to help me train his brother, Cayden."

"Done."

I expected nothing less when it comes to Tanner. He's always willing to help anyone.

"Second, I'm trying to come up with some ideas on how the center can capitalize their profits. I need to brainstorm because they are in desperate need."

"You'd be more the man for that than me. Shit, I'm a dumb-ass swimmer. You're the one with the master's degree." He has a point, not sure what made me think he has any expertise in this.

"They could do more lessons, but instructors aren't cheap." I begin the brainstorming process myself.

"I'm guessing you're not. Are they charging enough?"

"They seem to be doing well with the swim lessons, but it's mostly lane reservations. I met Cayden there Monday and no one else was there."

"What about parties? Does it have anything for children?"

A light bulb goes off in my head. "See, you're just good at these things."

He chuckles. "I don't know about that, but we can talk at Thanksgiving."

I bite my lip. "I'm not sure. I might spend it with Taylor and Emerson. I'm going to see if we can do both. I'm on my way to talk to her now."

"Are you two together?" I hear the apprehension in his voice. Tanner's the only one who knew I had cheated on her right after it happened. Then my sister found out after they got together, and she cornered me before my wedding to Bayli.

"Yeah." A smile slowly forms on my lips with the elation that we are in fact a couple again.

"That's great. So, you're really trying to make it work?"

"Yeah." My smile grows wider, especially as I pull off the highway and come that much closer to her house.

"I'm happy for you." I can hear he's genuine. Isn't that the kicker in our relationship? He's always wanting what's best for me, and I'm consistently envious of everything he has.

I pass the Welcome to Roosevelt sign and my body itches to see them both.

"I gotta go. When do you get in?"

"Not until Thursday morning."

"Practice?"

"Yeah." He's always short with his answers in regards to his swimming. I know him well enough to know it's because of me. "Hey, do me a favor? Call her. Talk to her, okay?" I should have known the sister conversation wasn't at rest. "Try to do it before we leave. She was really upset you hadn't told her."

"Okay." I nod although he can't see me. The guilt trip he's laying on me works and I regret not calling Piper right off. "I'll call her."

"Thanks. See you Thursday."

"Bye."

We hang up at the same moment I pull into Taylor's driveway. A breath of relief escapes my throat when I spot her car up ahead and the light in the kitchen glowing. I get out of the truck and move around the house toward the front door.

A loud crashing sound emanates from inside. Taylor screams and I run the last few steps. With my hand on the knob and shoulder against her door, I push, ready to go in. The door doesn't budge, and I continue to throw my body into it until the lock eventually busts, easier than I expected; easier than it should.

I stumble into the room. Taylor's hand is on the door, and she's peering down at me. Across the room, an older, heavyweight man is staring over at me.

"I heard a crash and you yelled." My eyes inspect the room, finding a broken snow globe in pieces all over the floor.

"Who the hell is this kid?" the guy asks, and all the light bulbs go off in my head.

"Dad." Yep, that's what I thought. "This is Brad. Brad, this is my dad, Dean."

I stand up straighter, looking Taylor over quickly to make sure she's okay. Once I'm satisfied that nothing happened to her, I walk across the room—stepping over the shattered glass, water, and glitter—to reach her father.

"It's a pleasure, Mr. Delaney."

He laughs and stares down at my hand. "Brad? As in the dad?" His eyes are bloodshot and there's a stain of liquid down the front of his shirt.

"Dad." Taylor sighs behind me, moving into the kitchen.

"That's me, sir." My hand continues to hang between our bodies.

He lays his hand in mine, gripping as hard as I will the day Emerson brings a guy home.

"Why are you here now?"

"Just let it go, Dad. We're working things out." Taylor comes into the room with a broom and I release Dean's hand to help her.

"Working what out? God, Taylor, you make the worst decisions." He moves over to the couch and Taylor doesn't grant him a response.

"Where's Emerson?" I ask her as we bend down to clean up the mess.

"She's asleep. It's been a long couple of days for her. Thanks for surprising me." She smiles and I can't stop myself from matching it.

"What did I walk in on?"

"Apparently, his tab is due and he doesn't get paid until tomorrow. So, he has some time to spend with his daughter."

"What about the snow globe?"

"We got into a fight about my sister. He thinks we should be involving the police to find her. I don't. Same old, same old. He'll forget once he can get back to Carolle's."

"I'm leaving," Dean says as he gets up from the couch, weaving over to get his coat.

"You don't have a car. Sleep on the couch." Taylor stands and I finish cleaning up the mess while she handles him.

What a crappy hand Taylor got dealt as far as her family is concerned.

"No. I want my own bed. I'll walk." His hand reaches for the knob and he misses.

"Dad, you live five miles away." She looks back at me with panic in her eyes.

"I'll drive you, sir." I rise to my feet and move to the door.

"Stop calling me sir. Actually, you call me nothing because you are a piece of shit, leaving my daughter with a baby." I look over at Taylor and she holds her hands in the air.

"I told you, Dad, I never told Brad about Em."

"Lies. All you, your mother, and your sister do is lie." He yanks the door open and stumbles down the stairs.

"I'll be right back. Text me his address." I kiss her on the cheek and jog down the steps to catch up to Dean Delaney, aka the town drunk.

I'm able to loosely guide Dean to my truck, and Taylor's text shows up on my phone as soon I'm situated in my seat. I enter the address into my GPS.

"Fancy car." He shakes his head back and forth a few times.

I ignore his comment and the fact his seatbelt isn't fastened. Backing out of the driveway, I spot Taylor's silhouette in the window. I flash my lights at her.

"Why did you come back?" Dean asks once I drive down the road a bit. There goes the hope of a quiet ride to his house.

"I love your daughter." I refrain from using 'sir' since somehow it offends him, and since he didn't inform me what to call him in exchange, I figure nothing is the option.

"Where were you two years ago?"

"In a bad spot." Wish I could say, 'much like you are now', but I'm not going to offend what I hope is my future father-in-law.

"Huh," he mumbles and looks out the window. "So you edged Sam out?" he asks, and I study the GPS, noticing we still have three minutes before we're due to arrive at our destination.

"With all due respect, they're my family, not his." I give him my most politically correct answer.

"I might not be a fan of you, but I hate him. To go from one of my daughters to the next is sick in my book. The fact he tried to get with Taylor disgusts me."

I'm not sure what to say, so I don't say anything.

"Not that you're much better."

Okay, I'll take the hit. Isn't that what one does when the father of the girl they love insults him? I can take this abuse up to a point, and I cross my fingers he doesn't go over that limit.

"I'm trying to make amends." I turn down what should be his street, and I pray this ride will be over shortly.

"Good luck. She holds a grudge. You see how she treats me. She won't even look for her sister. Of course, her mother did no wrong, so her gravesite is always the prettiest one in the cemetery."

Just hearing the fact that Taylor keeps up her mother's plot tears at my heart. She's been so independent and alone all these years. I hate myself for not coming to find her sooner.

"I'm hoping she'll forgive me." I pull along the curb of a small ranch house and get out before he can argue anything further. Hopefully, this is the end of my first encounter with him.

He opens the truck door and almost falls out, but catches himself. I begin to escort him up the sidewalk, but he swats his hands at me.

"Leave me the fuck alone."

Abiding with his wishes, I stop in the middle of the path, double-checking he makes it inside. He fiddles in his pocket for what seems like hours until he retrieves his keys.

Once he's in the doorway, he turns back toward me.

"You can tell Taylor I'm not coming to Thanksgiving unless her sister is there."

I nod, and he slams the door shut.

I jog over to my truck, turn the key in the ignition, and gun it back to my girl's house. After a night with that asshole, she'll need to be assured of the amazing person she is.

twenty

Taylor

THE MONITOR IS QUIET, SHOWING how tired Em was. I pace back and forth in front of the window, waiting for Brad's truck's headlights to appear out of the darkness.

My stomach rumbles with nausea because Brad witnessed my dad and his nastiness toward me. Carolle's Tap finally kicked him out of the bar, and a half hour into his visit, I was ready to pay his tab. Unfortunately, that would mean I'd break the promise I made a year ago—I'd never again pay for his or my sister's vices with my hard-earned money. My daughter deserves that money, not them.

Finally, before I leave a worn-out path on the carpet, Brad's truck slowly pulls into the driveway. I open the door, my feet bouncing on the wet cement. Brad turns the corner of my house with an emerging smile for me.

"Hey, get inside. This is nasty." He glances at the snow-covered streets and the constant trickling of snow falling from the sky.

"It's beautiful. I love snow before the holidays. It's after that it can go away."

Brad reaches me faster than I expected, and with one swoop, he scoops me up into his arms, leaving me no choice but to lock my legs around his waist.

"It's my time now," he says, walking us up the stairs and through the door. Without letting me go, he shuts the door, and carries me to the couch.

"So, you finished early?"

"I did." His lips cast small kisses along my neck while his hands explore my body.

"Brad." I sigh, because after my dad's visit and everything with Sam, I need to be reassured I'm not the villain they make me out to be. For some reason, Brad's always brought me a feeling of worth, acting as though without me, he'd be lost. I need that ego boost right now.

"Taylor." He stops kissing and stares into my eyes. Long and hard, we connect, and although there's no need for words, he speaks. "I know you might not want to hear this right now, and maybe it's too soon . . ."

My heart slams against my chest while I wait for the words.

"I love you." His hands tighten on my cheeks, his nervousness apparent.

My hands slide up his arms until they hold his hands to my skin. "I love you, too."

His whole body slumps, as though he's relieved he's not alone.

Our eyes lock a little longer. I'd like to think we're exchanging unspoken promises to one another. He's healed me, and I can say without a doubt, I completely forgive him for the past.

He crashes his lips down on mine, and as always, he hijacks all thoughts of anything that doesn't pertain to him. Our bodies grind, my legs easing open for him to slide between, needing the relief from the fire he's fueling within me with his body.

"Take me upstairs," I whisper when he breaks our kiss and veers down to my jawline.

"Taylor, we said we'd wait."

How does he have the willpower to fight this?

His hands slide around to my back and lock my hips down as he pushes his hardness into my center.

"Please," I beg, and he looks up at me. His eyes are pools of the lust we're feeling at the moment. He rocks into me one more time as his eyes fix on to my lips.

"I don't want to take advantage." He lays back down on top of me, pressing small kisses to my forehead, nose, and cheeks.

I grasp his head, holding it inches above my own. "I need to feel wanted right now, and you're the only one who can do that. I'm asking you, Brad, make love to me."

His eyelids close briefly, and I fear he's about to deny my request, topping my list of utter disasters for the night. But my heart pitter-patters when he stands, and holds his hand out to me. I grip it, and he helps me up, then picks me up in his arms bridal style.

"Your wish will always be my command."

I smile, wrapping my arms around him, teasing him with kisses to his neck and earlobe as he carries me up the stairs to my bedroom.

Once we step inside, he lays me on the bed. While he shuts the door quietly, I turn on the second monitor in my room. I know Em is down the hall, but surely parents have sex with kids in the house.

His shoulders rise when the door clicks shut, not that she can climb out of her crib yet.

"That's loud," he says and stops at the end of my bed. My eyes fixate on him from the plush mattress, watching him flick the button on his jeans. The zipper slowly lowers, granting me a peek at his blue boxer briefs.

"You have something, right?" I ask, certain we aren't taking any chances for another Em.

"Yeah." He snakes his hand into his pocket, retrieving the condom. A release a breath, happy I'll be getting my wish granted tonight.

He smiles, twirls it in his hand and tosses it on the bed next to me.

"Come closer," I urge, but he shakes his head, preparing to tease me.

His jeans drop to the floor at the same time he strips his shirt off. Good God, he's an Adonis. I thought I remembered what he looked like, but my memory didn't do him justice. My mouth waters seeing the rippled muscles down his stomach.

He crawls up the bed toward me, my pulse quickening with every dip of the mattress. His legs straddle mine and his fingers dig into the sides of my yoga pants. My breathing completely stops. He scoots down the bed, sliding my panties and pants down my legs at the same time.

I deny the impulse to cross my legs and conceal myself from his eyes. I'm not the girl he remembers with slim hips and a flat stomach. There's more to love now, and I'm scared he won't like that.

Once he throws my pants to the floor, his hands glide up my sides, pushing my shirt along with them. Soon we're skin to skin and his hands are exploring each new curve of my body.

His hands venture around my chest and he unhooks my bra with too much finesse. The straps fall to my arms and his fingers glide them down the rest of the way, leaving me completely naked for his viewing.

With the lights on and no blanket to cover myself, I stay still, secretly sucking in my stomach as much as possible.

His eyes are bright with fire like a flare gun shooting off in midnight sky. "You're gorgeous." My body aches for his expert touch. "I've missed looking at you." Each inch of my skin prickles with shivers as his eyes travel across it.

"I'm not the same."

"No, you're not." Still, his eyes travel my stomach, hips, and thighs. Leaving a wake of scorching heat behind. "So much better." His tongue snakes out of his mouth and licks his lips like he's about to feast on me. Please do.

The lust in his eyes intensifies my arousal even more, if that's possible. At the moment, I crave the feeling of him inside me.

I bend forward, climbing to my knees and crawl toward him. We meet in the middle of the bed, both on our knees. Our mouths collide and my breasts crush against his hard chest. My hands slide under the waistband of his boxers, yanking them down to his knees. "I need you." I break the kiss, my mouth paying homage to every contoured muscle.

He flips over, placing me on top of him, wiggling out of his boxers the rest of the way. I reach for the condom and his thumbs gently circle my nipples, and they peak harder from his touch.

Remembering he enjoyed it when I put the condom on, I rip it open. My fingers stroke down his ripped stomach and a tormented groan escapes his throat. Hearing his elation to my touch only shoots a blaze of fire to my center. I unroll the condom over his long length and his hands knead my breasts without abandonment.

Rising up, I hover over him, his hands sliding down to rest on my hips. With his guidance, I sink down on top of him.

"Jesus," he mumbles.

The moan that erupts out of me stems from nothing short of sweet, sweet bliss. I haven't been with anyone since him, and I had one thing right these past years, my vibrators are no comparison.

I rock my hips and his strong fingers dig into my flesh, keeping me in place. Damn if he still doesn't possess the moves to set me off.

His eyes lock on mine, and the amount of love brimming from his eyes brings my old self out. I'm the woman he loves, and he doesn't seem to mind the extra pounds. With the newfound confidence, I lean my hands back on his legs, giving him the full view of us together. He moves his hand off my hip and onto my clit, only enticing a deep rumbling roar from my throat. As he rubs circles, I clench harder to keep the ecstasy at bay, but the firmer he presses, the more my body soars. My toes curl as my fingernails dig into the hard muscles of his thighs. He doesn't relent on me, and I shudder, having no more control of the hysteria whirling through my veins.

"Brad . . ." Brad flips us again, his hand quickly covering my mouth. Just as fast as he left me, he's back inside me, moving at a frantic pace. A minute later, he stills inside me, and falls on top of me.

The tidal waves slow to ripples, and Brad removes his hand from my mouth. "Still loud." He smiles down to me, a bead of sweat falling to my chest.

"I guess so."

He slides off me, getting up from the bed. While he's in the bathroom, I lift the covers and sneak under. Not taking long, he returns to the room, confused as to why I'm now hiding.

"Taylor, we need to talk." He walks around to the other side. "Can I join you?" he asks, the corner of the comforter in his hand.

"Yes," I answer, surprised and happy he asked permission.

He smiles and moves onto the bed, quickly breaking any distance between us. Leaning on one hand, he stares down at me. After a long of stretch of time, his hand reaches for mine and pulls the sheet out of my grip.

"You are beautiful, and I don't like it that you think differently."

I roll my eyes because this should not be part of the afterglow talk. Sitting up, I slide to sit up, taking the comforter with me. "It's just Em changed my body."

"She did."

"Thank you for noticing." My reply is snippy, not that I'd want him to lie.

"Did I not get aroused? Do you have any idea how hard it was for me to hold out until you had your orgasm? Listen to me,

Taylor, because we aren't going to rehash this conversation."

I nod, worried about what he might say.

"You're gorgeous, smokin' hot, and I'll always want to be inside you. So, I want this whole 'hiding your body and shifty eyes when naked' to stop. Got it?"

I laugh, unable to take him seriously. His hand cups my cheek and his eyes dim. "I'm serious, baby. If you're insecure, I'm not doing my job."

The corners of my lips curve up at the sweet things he says.

"I'll try."

"Let's start here." He pulls the comforter from my hands and they reach to grab a hold of it like someone's taking my life vest in the middle of the ocean.

I lay in front of him naked. "There we go."

A few minutes later, I'm snuggled into his arms and my hand is tracing the small patch of hair on his chest.

"Tell me about your sister," he says, and I think about all the stories. The problem is, I don't want to rehash anything that has to do with my dysfunctional family. His family seems perfect, and mine is all types of crazies.

"In high school, she started using. One time on heroine and it was over, she was hooked. Somehow she graduated, and then weaved in and out of our lives for the next four years. When I went to college, I thought she had cleaned herself up. She married Sam and I assumed things were looking up for her. But she used him. See, Sam's family owns a ranch on the outskirts of town and he was supposed to be the heir to it. April, my sister, ruined that for him. She convinced him to steal money, and now he works for his younger brother. It's a whole sordid mess, and it only confirms my sister is a tornado. When she leaves, the people who love her are left to rebuild their life."

"I'm sorry." His fingers thread through my hair, soothing me.

"She's been gone for two years, and I stopped looking for

her after three months. I went to crazy lengths to find her. I even took Em on drives through the worst of neighborhoods. I should have never done that, but I was desperate to find and fix her." I rest my chin on his chest, the tears teetering in my eyes. "It took me a long time to realize I can't fix people." There's so much truth in that sentence, and it doesn't only pertain to my sister, but also Brad.

"You don't have to fix me. I did it myself." His thumb swipes the tear which escapes my eye, and his lips press to my forehead.

"I know. Anyway, I'm done with her. Sam will occasionally search the streets of downtown Detroit. He can't seem to let it go. My dad thinks I should contact the FBI or something. He doesn't understand; the last thing she wants is to be found." My head heavy with emotion, I lay it on his shoulder.

"You have to deal with so much crap, Taylor. I promise you, I'll be right next to you from this point on, okay?"

I nod, not wanting this conversation to ruin our night. Rising to my knees, the urge is too great to keep it from him.

"Brad, you have to know, I've forgiven you. I'm not harboring any more feelings about the past. It's over and done. We're making a clean and fresh start, so you have to stop feeling guilty. It's over."

His eyes shift to the windows, the wind howling outside. "I need to seal that tomorrow. Actually, there's a lot I need to do around here."

"Brad, don't deflect." He looks at me with guilt ridden eyes. His past still eats away at him.

"I can't, Taylor. I can't help but obsess over how things could be different." He sits up, his elbows resting on his knees, his chin on his knuckles. "I would have been in that delivery room with you. In the car while you searched for your sister. Paying your dad's damn bar tab. You wouldn't have gone through this alone if I'd only just kept my shit together."

"They were mistakes, and look how far we've come. It's

time for us to enjoy it, and that's not going to happen if we both harbor guilt."

He nods, and maybe all he needs is happy times to enjoy. Although I see him finding his place in life with training Cayden, maybe he hasn't noticed it yet. So, I sit back, deciding to patient. Over time, we'll get where we need to be.

He peeks up at me, his teeth biting his lower lip. "You are the most amazing girlfriend, you know that?"

I smile and wave in the air to jokingly toss off the compliment.

"You're too good to me." He takes my head in his hands again, and soon I'm on my back with him on top of me.

"We're good for each other."

"That we are."

twenty-one

Brad

MY GUT CLENCHES AS I stare over at Taylor curled in the fetal position fast asleep, but at some point, I need to fulfill my promises. It's a no brainer I'd rather wake up with her and my daughter this morning, but I promised Cayden, and we're on our last day before Thanksgiving.

I jot down a quick note and place it on the coffee maker for her to find when she wakes up.

I'm training with Cayden and need to talk to Wes. I know you work today, so Em and I will be waiting for you tonight. Love you, Brad.

I lock the bottom lock before I sneak out the back door to make sure nothing happens to my girls. On the way to the Aquatic Center, my phone rings. Shit, my mom.

I press okay on my car's Bluetooth.

"Hey, Mom," I answer, dread washing over me because I've yet to return her call.

"Hey. You never called me back."

"You know it's only six in the morning, right?" I dodge the question I'm sure she's going to ask me.

"Don't try to divert. What's going on for Thanksgiving?"

"I have to talk to Taylor, but I'm hoping we can do both."

"That would be great. The McCains were so upset that

they missed this weekend. They'd like everyone to be together." Her voice fills with happiness.

"I'll see, Mom, but I can't promise. Obviously, I'll be wherever they are." I leave Roosevelt and hop on the highway toward Creadle's.

"Obviously, but I hope you can at least come Friday or Saturday then. Piper will want to see Emerson."

I roll my eyes because I love my mom and I know she wants to be with her granddaughter, but I don't need more guilt in my life.

"Yes, I get the point. Listen, I'm almost at the pool house, so I'll call you once I talk to her." My finger hovers over the end call button, waiting for her to say her good-byes.

"Okay. Love you, honey."

"Love you too." I press the button and my music flickers back on. I remember that I never sent Cayden a playlist. Shit.

I roll into the parking lot—again, no other cars are in the lot except for Wes's Camaro and Amanda's Honda. Not even a swim lesson this morning. Pulling my bag out of the back I rack my brain on what we can do to drum up some business. This facility is top-notch, one most well-trained athletes could get their workouts completed in. We just need to get them through the door.

Cayden's car pulls in right after me, and I wait for him by Amanda's desk.

"Hey, Amanda, how many lane reservations do we have today?" I pry for information I'm hoping she'll give me.

She clicks away on her computer with no hesitation. "We have one blocked off at ten besides the swim team at four."

"How long does that go for?"

"Swim team meets are for three hours usually. Split up between two age levels."

I think back to when I was truly training. The three of us, Tanner, Piper, and myself were shuttled from school to the pool every day until we hit high school. We need more teams or to rent out the facility. But all that will have to wait until tomorrow because Cayden's walking through the doors. He's dragging ass today, but that's a good thing because you only find your drive once you think you have nothing left to give. One thing though is he doesn't have a damn coat.

"Where's your damn coat?"

He shakes his head. "I forgot it." The kid really is exhausted. Michigan winter and not wearing a coat equal getting sick.

"Hey, man, I'm sorry, I forgot to send you the playlist."

"I made one myself." He pulls his iPhone out of his pocket, handing it over to me.

I examine the songs he picked on the way to the locker room. I'm impressed and surprised at some, but I can't dictate what will psych him up for a swim. Once we are in the locker room, I hand it back to him.

"Good choices."

A smile encompasses his face as though he's proud of himself because I like it. Someone needs to tell him I'm nobody one day and he shouldn't wait for my approval.

"I'll meet you out there. I need to talk to Wes. Get in the water, start with the butterfly today. It's your slowest time."

"Okay," he says, scrambling out of his clothes.

Shrugging my laptop bag over my shoulder, I leave Cayden to pump himself up and search out the second thing to complete today.

Wes is in the office, writing the lesson schedule on the white board under each instructor's name. I'm just thankful he's not sitting in front of his damn financials with his head buried in his hands.

"Hey. Do you have time after Cayden?" I walk in, dropping my bag on the desk.

"Yeah, but let's do it away from here. I can't take the chance with Cami, and she's sneaky."

I smile and shake my head in understanding. "Gotcha. I'll be done in about two hours."

"Sounds good." I move toward the door again. "Brad?" he calls out and I stop. "How bad?"

He turns around, the dark circles only drooping lower now. "Fixable." I shoot him an honest answer. He nods and turns his attention back to the board.

Two hours later, Cayden and I are walking back from the lane, where he had a killer workout. I stop him outside the office. Wes is already wrapped in his coat, ready for our talk. Man, he's anxious, but I would be too if my place was in jeopardy.

"So, do your parents still live in Chesterfield?" I ask Cayden. Although it's impressive how far he's come in three days, we need every day we can. Chesterfield is only forty-five minutes away.

"Yeah."

"Good, I need you to come tomorrow morning. We'll get another workout in, and then you can have the night off. But Friday, Saturday, and Sunday you need to do two workouts, one in the morning and one at night. You can come here, I'll arrange it with Wes, but if you want to make the team, there's no excuses." I feel like a father, or a nicer version of Coach Kass, and it gives me the creeps.

"Great. There's nothing by us except for the YMCA, and it doesn't have the space."

"Sure. I'll leave your name with Amanda for the night swims, but in the morning, I'll be here. Friday and Saturday, I'm bringing Tanner with me so he can, hopefully, help us out on anything I've missed."

He nods a few times with a dazed and confused look in his eyes. "Hey, don't worry. You got this." I pat him on the back as though it's game day.

"I hope so."

His eyes shift to the tile floor and he inhales a deep breath, releasing it in a slow stream. I don't say anything else because he has to find his own reasons for pushing himself to the limits.

"Can I come back tonight? I'll be on my way back to Chesterfield."

"Yeah, no problem. Have Amanda put you on the schedule on your way out."

"Thanks." Cayden walks toward the locker room.

"Cayden!" I yell, and he turns his attention back to me. I scramble into the office, grabbing my coat from the back of the chair. I toss it to him and he catches. "Take my coat. We can't afford you to get sick."

He smiles. "Are you sure?"

"Yeah. I have another one in the car."

"Thanks."

"You're welcome."

Cayden disappears into the locker room, and I don't have to enter the office because Wes is already waiting by my side.

"Here." He hands me my laptop bag.

"Okay. Let's go." I'm thankful I didn't get in the water with Cayden today, so there's no further delay. Wes might have had a slight panic attack if so.

"I'll drive and you can talk." He breezes by me with a wave of his cologne as my trail to follow. Eager beaver he is.

We leave the Aquatic Center and he drives us to a small diner closer to my apartment. Probably as far away from Roosevelt as he can get. From what Taylor says, the gossip circle is alive and fierce there.

A middle-aged hostess, unenthusiastic about her job, leads us to a circle booth in the back. She drops the menus on the table, murmurs something about our waitress, and walks away.

"Who said customer service is dead?" I joke, and Wes shoots me a tight smile. This is not going to be any fun, so I decide we better cut to the chase; otherwise, Wes might end up breathing into a paper bag.

"All right." I open my bag, pulling out the paperwork he gave me plus my computer. While it's firing up, the waitress, whose attitude matches the hostess, finally moseys on over.

Wes orders coffee and I order an egg white omelet and fruit. Now that I have a girlfriend, I need to make sure I don't gain a gut, even though she'd love me anyway.

The spreadsheet I formed for him shows up on the screen, and Wes leans in to get a better view.

"You're making a good profit on your swimming lessons. I think the real issue is the lane reservations."

"We've been slow."

"Non-existent, really. Early morning swim lanes should be booked on a consistent basis. What I'm thinking is maybe you do a membership of sorts. A promotion to get people through the door. Plus, there's advertising. Are you doing any of that?" Wes gives me a blank stare. He's trying to process way too much information at once.

"Can I be frank with you?" He sits back, taking the cup of coffee in his hands. I nod. "I opened Creadle's with a payoff I received. While in college, I injured my shoulder in a car accident. Not horrible, but enough that it ruined my opportunity to advance in swimming. It was another college kid. His parents paid me a substantial amount of money not to make a big deal of it. The kid was rich, his dad some politician or some shit. They didn't want the media to get involved, so they showed up in my hospital room with a check. Enough to get me a loan approved on Creadle's, but if I lose the center, it's over. There's nothing left for me." He sips his coffee, staring down at the dark liquid.

"I said this is fixable." I try to put his mind at ease, but from the pensive expression on his face, it isn't working.

"I can't afford to spend any money on advertising. There's nothing in the bank account. My accountant said my instructors will get paid, but then it's gone. My loan payment is due at month's end, and I don't have the money." He slides the coffee mug on the table and it splashes over the rim.

"Then we have to be inventive. I'm telling you, Wes, you're sitting on a gold mine. I did some research, and there's nothing like Creadle's around here. Do you know how far parents will drive their kids to be trained the way you do? Not to mention, you're an hour from the University. Pool time there isn't easy to get." I know there's a way we can bring it back.

"Would you be interested in more investors?" I bite my lip, because it would be a hard sell for my dad, but I think I can make it happen as long as I'd have some say in how the business is run.

His cheeks fill with air and he studies the stained ceiling while he blows it out. "That's a hard one. I'm not exactly easy to work with."

I pin my eyes on him while the waitress drops my omelet down without a word. Leaving it on the edge of the table, I sit back on the sticky vinyl and wait for him to realize what I'm asking.

The wires click and he tilts his head at me. "You'd want in? Where would you get the money?"

"I might be able to find you an investor, but I'm sure a stipulation would be that I'd help manage. I'm not positive I can even get the money, but if I could, would you be open to it? A business partnership." He nods, but his face pales. "Okay, let's just look at what I think the future can look like if we do a few things."

For the next three hours, Wes and I sit in that corner booth, brainstorming and talking through ideas about how to jive the business and bring the center to its full potential. Between the two of us, there are a lot of connections with our college buddies, and I think we could accomplish a lot with little money.

Wes finally orders a cheeseburger, and it's good to see I've calmed him enough to eat.

"The first thing we need to do is build the swim teams for all ages. Then I have an idea about advertising, but I don't want to say anything until I can fully commit to it."

"Brad, you can't do this all for free." Wes slides out of the booth since we have no choice but to return to the center for lessons.

"I'm not going to." I pack up my bag and quickly meet him at the end of the booth. "You'll pay me for my time or consider my offer. I'll give you until after this weekend to decide."

Again, he shakes his head and releases a sigh. I don't envy his situation, but I'm not putting everything I have into his company and not reaping any rewards. For once in two years, I'm enjoying where my life is heading—things with Taylor and now this role of helping Wes and mixing business with swimming. If Wes decides he doesn't want me involved in Creadle's, I'll figure something out, but I'm thinking it would only be competition for him.

twenty-two

Taylor

I BUNDLE EM UP IN her warmest coat and boots. The snow has started to come down in droves lately, which means winter is here to stay. We get in the car with hardly any time to spare, because I don't want to be late for her swim lesson, even though I'm sure I'll get a pass from the instructor.

My old Jetta's tires slide down the industrial park streets toward the Aquatic Center. The snow falls like rain, melting into water drops on my windshield. Maybe a cancelation of swimming should have been in order, but the idea of seeing Brad is worth taking my chances in a winter weather warning.

I pull up to the center, and park alongside Brad's truck. I'm thinking we'll have to take that home tonight. Home repeats in my head. The word so easily came to mind while thinking of the three of us. I have thought about us living together more than once, but never did I see the reality of the foolish thought that plagued my dreams.

Em and I reach the lobby and I brush off the snow covering her hat and jacket before doing the same for me.

"Snow," Em says, as she tries to pick up a piece of white fluff before it melts on the carpeted floor. "Snowman?" she asks and points outside.

"Maybe tomorrow we can make one at our house." I hold

233

her hand and we walk toward Katie, the receptionist. Thoughts of Em and Brad outside playing tomorrow brings a smile to my lips. She's finally getting to the age where she can handle the wet snow for a little while.

"Hi, Katie," I say and drop Em's hand now that we're a safe distance from the door. She wanders over to the cascading waterfall she loves so much.

"What a night, huh?" She clicks away on her computer to check us in.

"It's horrible out there. Be careful when you leave. There's an advisory until ten tonight." I unzip my coat, shedding the layers due to the humidity from the pool area seeping into the lobby.

"Dada!" Em screams, and my head lifts to search out Brad, half expecting him to be coming out to pick up his girl, but I don't see anyone.

She starts running toward the locker rooms. "Em!" I yell to stop her, but her footsteps continue. "I'll be right back," I say to Katie.

"No, you're good. Go ahead," Katie tells me, so I pick up our bags and jog after her.

At the last minute, she detours from the doors and dodges left behind a pillar.

"Dada!" she yells.

Catching my breath, I see Brad in his jacket and ski cap facing the wall. My eyes roam down to see two sets of feet, and if I'd inspected further, I would have noticed the red hair sooner.

My stomach drops to the floor at the same point Em hits his legs. "Dada!" He finally turns around, and I exhale all the tension that just gripped me with pain.

"Hi." He looks at Em and then to me.

"Oh, my God, you look just like him." My eyes focus on the indent in his chin and his mysterious eyes. His hand reaches up and slides off his skull cap. His dark hair is neatly styled just like Greg's.

"I'm sorry, do I know you?"

The girl steps up to his side, taking his hand in hers to show some sort of claim.

"Oh." I break from the fog. "I'm Taylor Delaney, Brad's girlfriend." Em comes to my side, turning shy that the man in Daddy's jacket isn't Dada. I pick her up in my arms. "This is his daughter, Emerson." He smiles, appeased by my answer. "I knew your brother. I'm sorry." The words cannot do much at this point I know, but what else do you say?

That was a lesson I learned after my mom died. Sorry might not help you, but it makes the others feel useful, because in all honesty, a casserole won't diminish the pain. If anything, it gives you extra time to address it.

"Thank you. He talks about you both a lot." Cayden's hand hangs in the air, and I quickly grab a hold of it.

I'm sure my cheeks are flushing as red as the girl's hair. "Oh, I'm sorry. Is this your girlfriend?"

The girl's eyes narrow at me and Em.

"Um . . ." He hesitates and I figure maybe I should mind my own business. She hits his arm. "We're new." He's honest, which makes me like him even more. Greg was similar in his mannerisms with the girls. Never a promise, but he never used them either. A true gentleman, unlike Brad—the old Brad that is.

"Is she fixated on that waterfall again?" Speaking of, Brad barrels down the hall from the men's locker room in his swim trunks and sandals.

I bite my lip, thinking back to last night and how I really hope there's a repeat tonight. He finds us in the corner, cocking his head at first in confusion as to what we're doing until he catches sight of Cayden and the redhead, who I've yet to be introduced to.

"Dada!" Em turns around and wiggles her body to be freed from my grip. I set her down and her little feet can't go fast enough. Brad continues walking, scooping her up in his arms on his way to me.

"You are late for your swim lesson," he tells her, tapping his finger on her nose. She giggles, doing the same to him.

"I'm pretty sure you aren't going to penalize her," I say, and those perfect, white teeth shine my way.

"I can't show favoritism." His hand casually slides along my back and he gives me a small kiss. "So you met Cayden?" The redhead clears her throat. "And Quinn," he adds, but his voice loses the happy inflection.

"Yes, Em was confused because he is wearing your jacket." I raise my eyebrows to say maybe me too.

He chuckles and shakes his head. "No faith." I'm glad there's no hurt in his eyes for the fact that maybe initially it scared me, but I think anyone would have the same reaction.

I snuggle into his chest, and Em places her hand on my cheek. "He's wearing your jacket and he had a ski cap on, what was I to think?"

Cayden and Quinn stand there, probably wondering what they are witnessing.

"I get ya. Cayden forgot his jacket this morning, so I loaned him the one you bought me." He does remember, there goes that pitter-patter in my heart. Brad must notice the lovey-dovey gleam in my eyes. "No faith." He shakes his head with his usual smirk in place.

"Yeah, sorry for the confusion, Taylor." Cayden's eyes convey his remorse, and I wave it off. "Quinn was going to sit and watch me swim today."

Brad clears his throat, which is usually a sign he might not agree with something. "Just make sure there's no distractions. This might be a dumb question, but where's Ava?"

Quinn laughs and touches Cayden's arm. He doesn't pull her in, but he doesn't move either. "Her parents picked her up. I'm off now." She smiles brightly and pushes out her chest a little.

"Oh," I speak out loud, when really that should have been an internal thought. "You're the nanny?" My mouth needs to shut.

"How did you know?" she asks.

"Oh, um . . ."

"We need to get going. She's going to have like fifteen minutes in the water. Remember to work on the butterfly for the majority of the time. Shorter breaths. The last half hour, work on your endurance only, not form."

A twinge of arousal zings at my center from witnessing Brad being so authoritative.

"Got it. Have a good class, Emerson." Cayden gives her a small wave.

Brad wraps his hand around mine, tugging me a little down the hall.

"It was nice meeting you both," I holler, twisting in Brad's hold as he pulls me through the family locker room doors.

Once we're secure on the opposite side of the doors, Brad quickly undresses Em and shoves everything in the locker.

"I was talking," I say.

"You were about to get me in trouble. The conversation we had about the obsessed nanny was between us. Plus, I don't want Cayden to think she's the athlete groupie type. I think being with her boosts his self-esteem."

He snatches my purse from my arms and throws it in the locker as I stand there awestruck at how caring my boyfriend is.

Unable to resist, I wrap my arms around his neck and kiss him all over his face. "You're such a sweetie. I love you."

He laughs, his hands latching around my waist. "Don't tell anyone."

"I'm going to tell everyone." I dislodge from his hold and run to catch Em before she escapes through the doors to the pool. "Em, did you know your Dada is a great guy?"

"Dada, love." She tilts her head and dreamily stares over

at her dad. There goes that pitter-patter again.

His large arms shelter around us and pull us to his strong chest. "I love you both." He kisses the tops of our heads and steals Em from my arms. "Time for swim, little one."

I watch my two favorite people break through the doors with tears threatening to fall. Happy tears.

Twenty minutes later, Em is screaming because her swim lesson is over. Either that or the fact that Tyler, Brad's next swim lesson, is currently where she wants to be—in her Dada's arms.

I shuffle her away, because it's obvious Brad can't concentrate with his daughter screaming his name. Cami bounces out of the office to save the day, and I'm grateful to see her.

"Why is Em so upset?" She pouts her lips at Em, but that doesn't deter her tears. She holds the office door open for us. "Come in."

I walk in with Em in my arms. Wes is at his desk, working on some spreadsheet. "Hey, Wes." My voice sounds as exhausted as my legs feel. He swivels around in his chair.

"How are you?" His usual smile has lost some of its luster, and I can't help but recollect what Brad told me about the business.

I plaster on my biggest and widest smile, covering up the fact that he shared it with me. His grin turns down, and I realize I laid my act on too thick, giving away the fact I know.

"Cami, why don't you take Em on the slide?" He reaches over and presses the button for the small children's waterslide to start up.

"What a great idea." She strips off her top and shorts, leaving her in a cute boy shorts swimsuit combo that shows off her amazing flat abs. Man, what children do to your body.

She swoops Em up from my arms. "Waterslide time, baby." She twirls the two of them, gearing up the excitement of the event. Cami is full of energy. Em's frown turns into a smile, and soon they're out the door.

Wes stares at me for a minute, holding his hand out to the vacant chair at a nearby desk. I slither over, sliding into the chair, wishing I would have refused Cami's invitation into the office.

"So, he told you?" His lips purse. "Should have assumed."

He leans back in the chair, his hands locked behind his head.

"I'm sorry, Wes, but know that I wouldn't tell anyone."

"Especially not Cami."

"No." I raise my finger in the air. "Although, I do think you should discuss it with her."

His eyes stare into mine like I'm boring him with my long-winded stories, not thrilled in the least with my opinion on the matter.

"Or not," I add.

"I need to ask you a few questions because I've only known Brad for six months or so. He seems like a good guy, but he approached me about something today."

This topic peaks my interest. The only thing I know is that Brad is helping him figure out a business plan that will keep the center running.

"What do you think about that?" I'm vague, hoping to find out information I haven't been trusted with yet.

"Can I trust him?"

That's a loaded question that I just answered myself, even though my mind zoomed into Crazyville only an hour ago when thinking he was in the corner with some hot redhead.

"I do." I'm confident in my answer, and in all truth, he can. Brad might have cheated on me and he might have done some shitty things in his past, but deep down, he's a good guy.

"I know about senior year in college with Tanner McCain."

Doesn't everyone? It made Sports Center.

"He's clean, Wes. He just needs a chance to prove himself. What exactly did he ask you?"

He tilts his head to the side. "So, you don't know?"

I shake my head, and he mimics me, chuckling lightly to himself.

"He asked me for a cut of the business. That he'd find us an investor, but he wants a part."

So, he really is finding his place. The tears shouldn't be ready to tumble out of my eyes, but I can't stop them. He's not only finding happiness with Em and me, but also in his career. He's struggled for so long.

"Are you crying?" Wes springs up, grabs a tissue, and hands it to me. "Why?"

I wipe my eyes. "I'm just happy." He wouldn't understand if I told him.

"You don't have to cry, Tay. I'll do it. Not like I have much choice anyway. Plus, he's got some good ideas, and he's a damn Einstein with business plans."

I smile like a proud mother at my boyfriend's mad skills in the business world. He always tries to portray himself as the dumb jock, but a few conversations with him and people realize differently.

"Yeah, he's perfect."

"Oh, damn, your opinion means nothing. You're fucking in love with him." He shakes his head, but his grin says he's happy for me.

"So, are you going to bring him into the business?" I choke out the question past the tears streaming down my face. Everything is falling into place.

"Most likely. We just need to agree to a few things."

I clap my hands, unable to hold back the excitement buzzing through me. Wes gives me the stern, fatherly look, and I sulk back into my chair. "I mean, that's cool."

"Get out, Tay. Go admire your man, because he's about to call it a night. All his other lessons cancelled due to the weather."

I stand from my chair and close the distance to him. Bending over, I kiss his cheek. "You won't regret taking a chance on him."

He flashes a genuine grin at me. "Neither will you. He's crazy about you both."

As I walk out of his office, I inhale the deepest breath I can muster in the humidity-filled space.

twenty-three

Brad

"SHE'S BEING STUBBORN AGAIN," I yell into the kitchen where Taylor is finishing preparing some trifle dessert thing to take over to my parents.

"You can only blame yourself," she calls back, and I hear a bowl crash to the floor.

Once I wrangle Emerson into her coat after five attempts, I rise to my feet to investigate the commotion.

Taylor is sitting on the floor with chocolate pudding at her feet. "Tay," I sigh, taking a seat next to her.

I swipe a finger full off her arm, placing it in my mouth. "It's awesome."

"It's ruined." She sobs into her hands, and I wrap my arm around her shoulders, persuading her reluctant body to move to mine.

"I told you, my mom doesn't expect you to bring anything."

Taylor was more than happy to go to my family's house for Thanksgiving when I asked her last night. Maybe because her dad's a jackass, her sister a druggie, and who the hell gives a shit about Sam. That elation that came over me when she accepted was short-lived when I was sent out in a snowstorm for supplies to make this trifle, which turned into this fiasco that has ruined my entire Thanksgiving morning.

"You don't show up empty handed, Brad." Her voice is muffled in my button down shirt.

Thinking there's not much I can say in this moment, I place a kiss on her head with the hopes it will calm her down.

"You aren't a guest; you're family," I insist, but her response is a huff. "You and Em are family."

Well, this is not how today is going to go, not on our first Thanksgiving.

I draw back, my finger resting on the bottom of her chin, urging it up so I can see her eyes. Those ocean blue hues are filled with despair.

"We are showing up as a family. You and Em are my family. Maybe not on paper yet, but in my heart. So, I never want to hear that again, got it?"

A slow grin spreads across her lips, but still she says nothing.

"Got it?" I repeat.

A slow nod matches her grin. "Okay."

"Settled. Let's clean up and get this girl in the car so she can sleep." I grab a roll of paper towels to wipe up the mess.

"What about the trifle?" She stares down at the discombobulated disaster spilled on the floor.

"It can stay here. Go finish getting ready. I got this."

She leans into me, her breasts rubbing against my arm. I reach around, gripping her ass when her lips meet mine. She falls back on her heels, and suddenly, I'm not thinking about cleaning, but rather getting messy.

"I'm sorry," she murmurs against my lips.

"You have nothing to be sorry for." I smack her ass and she scurries out of my hold and out of the room.

An hour and a half later, my daughter and girlfriend are asleep as I pull my truck into my parents' driveway. Wasn't I the one at Creadle's at six this morning with Cayden?

I park my truck alongside a rental sedan, and when I glance over to the McCain's driveway next door, I see Dylan's GTO is there. I'm guessing we're the last to arrive. Not that it matters, Thanksgiving around here is pretty casual.

I nudge Taylor lightly on the arm, but she only rolls her head to face the window. The two consecutive nights of love-making are taking their toll on both of us, but how am I expected to sleep next to her without being inside of her? Not possible. Seeing my nice attempts aren't working, I slowly and gently move my hand between her legs. The leggings are going to make this much easier on me. Moving my head to the curve of her neck, I kiss the smooth flesh as my finger slides along her center. After I apply a bit more pressure, she springs awake, almost hitting me with her flailing arm.

"Brad!" she screeches. "Em's in the car." She glances back to a comatose little girl.

"She's asleep, and I tried to be nice. You should be happy I didn't go further." I venture over to my side of the car, turning the ignition off.

"Should I be happy or disappointed?" she flirts back, surprising me every time she opens her mouth.

"Don't worry, I have plans for you tonight." I wink and her cheeks flush pink.

"We're at your parents'; Em will be in the room with us."

"She's going to spend some quality time with Grandma and Grandpa," I counter, and she rolls her eyes.

"That didn't work out so well last weekend."

"Then her aunt."

She shakes her head, probably not believing it can happen. I can't deny that a small part of me agrees with her line of thinking.

We both exit the truck and she rounds the back to retrieve Em while I grab our bags. Looking at the closed garage door, I'm surprised it hasn't been sprung open before I parked. Then again, the golden child is home.

I key in the code to the garage and the door opens. Taylor looks at me, and I give her a reassuring nod. She overthinks my family. We walk through the door, and in that moment, I hear Piper's scream.

"They're here!" She rushes over to us, punching me in the shoulder. Tanner arrives in the doorway, leaning on the frame, watching the scene unfold with a damn 'told you so' smirk on his face. It's still nice to see my best friend, especially when I'm no longer the fuck up I used to be.

"Nice to see you, too," I say, dropping our bags along the wall to pull her in for a hug. I wrap my arms tightly around her shoulders and sway back and forth.

She fights me, her small fists punching me in the stomach. "I'm mad at you."

"Oh, come on. You always forgive me." I release her and she stumbles back, right into her Prince Charming's arms.

"Oh jeez, you two. Let them come in first." My mom shows up in the doorway of the small hallway from the garage door.

Piper and Tanner back up, never taking their eyes off Taylor and Emerson. I wait for Taylor to step up to me, and then we walk in together. Emerson is tucked into her neck as normal, but when I hold my hands out for her, she easily switches spots.

"Taylor," Piper says and steps forward into an awkward hug. "It's good to see you."

"You too." Taylor's arms weirdly move around my sister.

"What's up, man?" Tanner holds his hand out for me, and I shake it with my free one as I shift Emerson in one arm. "Hi, Emerson." He peeks to get a good look, but she quickly tucks her head into my neck.

"Just give her some time."

He backs up and nods.

"Hey, Taylor. You look great." Tanner shifts his attention to her, and again, an awkward hug is exchanged.

They part, and I'm surprised she could wait this long, my mom swoops in. "Taylor," she gushes, holding her tight to her body. "I'm so happy you could join us."

"Thank you for inviting us. I had a dessert, but there was a mishap."

I exchange a look with her and we laugh. Piper glances back and forth between us.

"Ewe. You two haven't changed a bit," she groans.

"We have a two-year-old. One of the ingredients fell on the floor. Keep your dirty mind to yourself in front of my daughter." I pretend to cover her ears and walk into the kitchen.

"Whatever," she sneers.

All their footsteps follow and my dad walks out of his study to meet us. After some quick hello's, which lucky for Taylor do not include hugs, we settle in the family room, letting Emerson roam and play.

"She's a really good mix between both of you," Tanner comments, and I smile, thanking him for breaking the subject first. He's more tactful than Piper.

"That's kind, Tanner, but she's mostly Brad, even her demeanor," Taylor chimes in, and her body language more comfortable now that we're all seated.

"Don't say that. We do not need another Brad in this world," Tanner jokes, and I throw my candy wrapper at him. The demise of my parents' house, the candy dish.

Piper just sits there, inching a little closer to Emerson, wanting some of her attention. Figuring I need to make up for the fact that I kept the secret from her for so long, I intervene.

"Emerson," I call out, and she turns my way, her shopping cart in her hands. "Come here." I wave her over and she follows, her eyes in tunnel vision right to me.

Once she's secure in front of me, I twist her around to face Piper. "This is your Aunt Piper." I point to my sister, who shares our matching brown hair and eyes. "Can you say hi?" I ask her.

Emerson back steps into my lap, and I see why Taylor's always apprehensive when we meet new people with her. She makes them feel like they're venom.

"Hi, Emerson." My sister's usual voice turns sweet and welcoming. "Is this your shopping cart?" she asks, and Emerson does nothing but stare at her.

Seeing we aren't getting anywhere, Taylor slides up on the carpet and pulls something out of the shopping cart.

"Piper loves apples. Can you give her one?"

Emerson looks at her mom's hand, grabs the apple, and throws it at Piper, knocking it on her head.

The room laughs and Emerson slinks back into me.

"That's okay. Aunt Piper is used to people throwing stuff at her. See." I pick up an onion and it pings off her head.

"Your daddy is right. You can throw anything your little heart wants at me." She grabs a bunch of plastic grapes and bounces them off my head. "Your daddy likes it too."

"Ouch." I place my hand on my head and Emerson laughs.

Piper reaches in again, pulling out a potato, handing it out for Emerson.

She looks down at it and up at Piper. Twisting her small waist, she whips it at my face. I stare down at her stunned, and she laughs.

"Way to teach my daughter bad things." I jokingly glare at her, but she only hands Emerson another piece of plastic produce.

I urge Emerson off my lap and defensively grab my own piece, lightly touching her. She laughs, and then I chuck a cucumber at Piper's head. Soon all three of us are throwing plastic fruit and vegetables around the room. Once it's scattered along the floor, Emerson is in cahoots with Piper and a relationship has blossomed between the two.

I sit with my back against the couch next to Taylor, my fingers weaving figure eights in her palm. Tanner has now joined Piper on the floor and is pretending to play basketball with them. Emerson hasn't looked back at us in a few minutes, and it's nice that she's warmed to the people I love most in my life, after her and her mom.

Five o'clock strikes too fast, and we're all off to the McCain's. Tanner already left to spend some time with his parents and brother while Piper firmly told him she wouldn't be leaving her niece's side the entire weekend. Knowing my sister the best, he shrugged, kissed her, and left.

Taylor grabs the stack of my mom's desserts and I get the bag of wine while Piper dresses Emerson in her coat and hat. I'm actually surprised how much the little girl is letting her aunt do, but thankful at the same time.

The six of us file out the front door and trudge along the makeshift path Tanner's left for us to their driveway. We stand on the porch, waiting for the door to be answered. A second later, Tanner's mom, Laney, opens the door, her smile wide and welcoming.

"Happy Thanksgiving," she says loudly, as though we're in a wind tunnel. Piper walks in first with Emerson in her arms.

"Hi, Laney," she says, toeing out of her shoes before putting Emerson down.

We all follow, greeting her with hugs and kisses on the cheek. Patrick, Tanner's dad, steps into the room, taking the pies and wine from our hands. I briefly introduce him to Taylor and pleasantries are exchanged.

"Hi, Emerson." Laney claps her hands in front of Emerson's face, and her bottom lip quivers.

Her eyes seek me or her mom out, and she runs away to hug Taylor's legs.

"Oh, I'm sorry." Laney comes over and Taylor's already shaking her head.

"Don't be. She's just a little quiet at first. Give her some time and she'll be running circles around us all." Taylor swiftly picks up Emerson and soothes her with small back rubs.

I smile over at them. She's an amazing mom.

I'm not sure how long I've been staring at them, but Piper elbows me in the ribs and I'm snapped from my little bubble.

"You have it bad," she whispers, and I take my hand and give her a little push into the banister.

Tanner quickly rises from the couch to meet Piper as football blares from the television. Dylan joins us in the kitchen around the island where all the appetizers are, and I'm shocked there's no Bea.

"Thank God, she does have a family." I act like I'm praising the big guy upstairs.

"I was in the bathroom, jackass." Bea smacks the back of my head as she walks by on her way over to Dylan's side, no doubt.

"Hi, Emerson." She sticks her face millimeters from my little girl, and I watch her small hand fist her mom's sweater.

"She doesn't like you." I lean in close, smiling at Emerson to ease her discomfort.

"Some things never change." She narrows those cloudy eyes at me.

I grab a hold of a piece of her now all-blonde hair. "What, no orange for Thanksgiving?"

"Let's eat." Patrick interrupts the fight that's already brewing between me and Bea.

"Sounds like a great idea," my dad chimes in.

We walk into the dining room, and I see Emerson's high chair from my parents' house in the corner. On the plates are holders where each of us are supposed to sit. Nice new tradition the McCain's are doing, especially since I'm on the opposite side of Bea.

"Thank you for bringing her high chair." Taylor searches out Maggie and they share a smile.

"Chris remembered, actually."

My eyes move to my dad's, and he nods to us. I can't ask for things to go more smoothly right now.

We eat, and somewhere between the meal and dessert,

Creadle's comes up in discussion. I talk about what I'm thinking and Tanner brings up new ideas he has that could help, including him doing a commercial saying that's where he works out when he's home. The man is a saint I tell you.

"What does he do for advertising?" Bea asks, and I really don't want her involvement in this venture, but truthfully, she did come up with some pretty moneymaking ads at Deacon.

"Not much, because he doesn't have the money."

"You have to spend money to make money." A classic Advertising Exec answer. "He could start small, but precise. Make sure his advertising dollars are spent effectively. Like placing cards at pediatrician offices for the swim lessons, or better yet, a coupon flyer."

Damn, she's got a point.

"Yeah, my doctor would totally do it. Plus, they send out this newsletter twice a year, maybe you guys could ask to be included on the back," Taylor chimes in.

"You guys?" my dad asks. "Brad are you a part of this?"

"Um, I was going to talk to you later about it."

For some reason, my eyes instinctively move to Tanner's, who leans back in his chair, a smile quickly forming on his lips. He nods in approval to me.

"Are you thinking about getting involved in a failing business?" My dad picks up his wine glass, his eyes dead centered on me.

"I think it can be revived quickly. I've looked at his financials, his profit and loss since he first opened. He just needs to tweak a few things," I might be more liberal than I should be.

"A business doesn't fail if they only have to tweak a few things," he counters, guzzling down a hefty gulp of his wine. My mom's hand rests on his forearm.

"I have to agree with your dad, Brad. The last thing you want is to put money into something already sinking," Patrick adds, and I inhale a deep breath.

"Wes really is a good guy. He's knowledgeable, and I

think they'd work well together." Taylor squeezes my knee under the table.

"I, for one, think it's a good idea too." Tanner comes to my rescue, because if he thinks so, it could turn the tables.

"I'd gladly help with the advertising thing, for a minimal fee." Dylan winks, leaning back and placing his arm on the back of Bea's chair.

I'm not sure my heart could swell any more. It's like the Grinch on Christmas. But without my dad's blessing and loan, it's never a done deal.

"We can talk later about it," he says, ending the discussion.

"Oh, you know what? I have this friend in physical therapy. They might be interested in renting some time. I'll text her tonight."

"Thanks, Bea," I say begrudgingly, because it sucks that she's the one helping me.

"Act more grateful, otherwise I won't." The table laughs except for Taylor next to me.

I lift my head, pinning her gaze with mine. I widen my mouth as big as I can get it. "Thank you, Bea. You're the best."

She throws a roll at me, but it falls short. "Jackass."

"Little ears at the table," Laney says, her eyes pointed right at Dylan.

twenty-four

Taylor

BRAD'S BEEN HOLED UP IN his dad's office for most of the afternoon. I felt like Chris was just waiting for him and Tanner to return from Creadle's this morning. Tanner and Patrick were sequestered briefly, but have been dismissed now.

Brad gave me a sweet kiss before he went in, but I felt the tension in his body. I wish I could put him at ease, but it's out of my control. My only hope is for his dad to see how much he's changed recently.

Em is asleep on my lap because she refused to nap in her Pack 'n Play. Since I have to be at work tomorrow, this is her last day with Brad's family, and I think I'm as sad as she is to have it end.

"Hey, Taylor." Piper comes in, handing me a Diet Coke.

"Thank you. When she sleeps, I act like a mannequin, not even moving a finger."

She smiles, reaches over, and cracks open my can.

"She's really great." Piper stares down at Em on my lap with so much love, I'm grateful for who she's surrounded by.

"Yeah, she is," I agree, tempting my peace for a sip of Diet Coke.

"How is he?" She pulls her legs up to her chest, resting her chin on her hands. Oh, the sibling bond that I never truly was blessed to experience with my sister.

"He's doing really well." I nod. "Really well," I confirm because she has to notice it.

"I can see it. Love looks good on both of you." She smiles and I'm glad she's witnessing it. "I'm sorry about what happened in college. I was a bitch."

I shrug, because truthfully, she wasn't that bad. "You thought I was just one of his conquests. You were right to a point."

She vehemently shakes her head. "Taylor, you were never one of his conquests. Well . . ." She cringes. "Maybe the first night, but then he fell so hard for you. I was completely surprised."

"Wasted years." I stare off over her shoulder, hoping she doesn't notice how much I hate that we weren't a part of each other's lives.

"Hey, you and I are similar on that front. I spent way too much time regretting Tanner and I splitting, but honestly, all you do is waste the time in the future. Put all that shit behind you."

She's right. She and Tanner were split for years over what he did. I can't change it, so might as well accept it and move on.

"You're right." I glance at her ring, gleaming from the sun shining in the window. "Things worked out for you."

"And they will for you too. I bet you'll be wearing one of these by year's end."

I shake my head. We don't need to rush into anything.

"Okay, but you know my brother. Irrational and impatient. He'll want everyone to know who you belong to." Piper's eyes light up in the direction of the hallway, and I follow her gaze to find Tanner talking to her mom in the foyer.

"Hey, before we get interrupted."

Her lusty eyes come back to mine. "I'm sorry I hid Em

from you. It was wrong, and I shouldn't have done it that way."

"No, don't apologize. Like I said, the past is the past."

Tanner walks into the room and her eyes overflow with love.

"Love looks good on you, too," I whisper, and she smiles over to me.

"I think so, too." Tanner sits down next to her, his hand resting on her leg.

"Still in there, huh?" His head nods to Chris's office door.

"I figure there's no yelling, so that has to be a good sign," I say, and Piper nods quickly with wide eyes.

"Very good sign."

Tanner looks down at Emerson on my lap and then to Piper. "What do you think? It looks like fun."

"Are you talking about the kid on her lap, who's making her afraid to take a sip from her Diet Coke?" Piper raises her eyebrows at Tanner and he laughs.

"I guess we aren't there yet."

"Let's just get through the Olympics first." She pats his thigh and he nods. So easygoing, I wonder what it's like to date someone so smooth sailing.

The door opens and Brad walks out, papers in his hand, his computer nestled under his arm. His lips spread into a huge smile, and I'm hoping that's good news. He glances down at Em on my lap and nods when I know he'd rather scream.

Closing the distance, he leans across Em and gently kisses my lips.

"You got it?" I ask, wishing I could scream for both of us.

"I did." He backs up. "I'll be right back."

His footsteps steadily walk outside the back door. His arms flex to the side and just as I guessed, a roar of a scream escapes his lungs.

"He looks like the Incredible Hulk," Piper comments.

I laugh because he does, but his absurdity doesn't phase-out the fact that he's found his place. The best part is, I'm a part of it.

TWO WEEKS HAVE GONE BY, and if I thought raising a kid alone was hard, try it with two parents who have careers. Holy shit, Brad's had no choice but to pick Em up and take her back to Creadle's with him.

Tanner flew in and out in one day to shoot the commercial with the people Dylan hooked him up with. Of course, it was after hours on a Sunday, but it's going to air tonight. It turns out one of the guys who owns the company has five kids of his own, so in exchange for free swim lessons, billboards are being put up along the highway.

Brad's dad and Tanner both invested in Creadle's, but Chris demanded that Brad be equal partner, which was hard for Wes to swallow, but in the end, he agreed.

Everything seems to be looking up for us, and Christmas is just around the corner. Em and Brad's first together. Of course, we're going back to his parents' house, since my dad has currently cut off any contact with me completely. I have to work Christmas Eve, but I'm off Christmas Day. I knew there was a reason I'd worked last year.

I'm wrapping Brad's gift, which I'm hoping might be his favorite. The good thing is, it cost me nothing. My phone rings on the table and I stretch over Em's sleeping body to grab it before she wakes up. She's crawled out of her crib, so now naps are a struggle because she refuses to stay in her toddler bed.

"Hello?" I answer without even looking at the caller ID.

"Hey, Tay. I have great news." It's my friend Vivian from Arizona.

"Are you getting married?" I ask.

"No, but you're moving to Arizona." I choke down the lump in my throat. In all this chaos, it slipped my mind that I had asked her if I could get a job at her hospital. "I mean, you have to interview, but that's just a technicality. The girl you'll be replacing walked out with no notice, so they want to fill the position as soon as possible. I think you'd have to be here after New Year, can you swing it?"

I sit there, looking down at Em on the ground, the princess Brad bought her securely in her arms. I glance around and find his computer resting on the dining room table next to his bottle of water. Yesterday's baseball cap is hanging on the knob of the banister. All these things are making this home his too.

"Oh, Vivian, things have changed."

"What do you mean? You were begging me three months ago for this. What could have changed?" She doesn't sound angry, but she's not happy either.

"Brad."

"Brad? Taylor, what have I missed?"

My head falls between my shoulders, abandoning my wrapping for the time being.

"We're together again."

"Oh."

"I mean, thank you so much, Vivian. I appreciate you finding it for me and getting me the interview, but—"

"Can I interrupt you for a second?" When I don't say anything she continues. "Are you really prepared to give up a fresh start in a new city for someone who changes their mind as fast as the wind? I mean, seriously, Tay, do you really think he'll stick around?"

Vivian isn't mean, but she saw me at my worst that night, being stuck as my only confidant. She's kept my secret from all of the sorority girls she's still in contact with. So I know when she vocalizes her objection, she does so because she's a friend.

"Can I have a day to think about it?"

"They're going to call you to set up the interview. I'm not sure when, so I guess you have until you get that call. But, Tay, this is a great opportunity for you and Em. You need to really think about it."

"Thanks, Viv, I'll call you back in a bit." I hang up the phone, disturbed by her doubts of Brad. At the same time, can I blame her? I'd be the same if her ex came back in the picture with her.

She doesn't know the Brad now, the evolved one—the father, boyfriend, and worker he is. She's right when she brings up a new start. I'd love to live in a city so far away from Roosevelt. Maybe Brad would come with me, but then I remember, Creadle's and his new dream of making it the top Aquatic Center in the nation. He's kept me up most nights talking about expansion plans and how one day they'll be training Olympians. His ongoing mind dreams big and fierce.

The key clicks in the lock and I push my thoughts aside and scramble to finish wrapping his gift. I'm putting the last piece of tape on before he's able to reach me.

"What's that?" he whispers, already used to Em falling asleep wherever she lands.

"A gift . . . for you."

He grabs it before I can set it under our tree. Shaking the box, he'll never figure it out.

"Hmm . . . I have no idea." He chuckles, placing it where it should be under the tree. "But I have something else I want to open more."

He slowly lowers me to the ground, pressing my back down to the carpet.

"What would that be?"

He flicks open a button on my sweater, revealing a glimpse of my pink bra. "This hot nurse. Shh . . . don't tell my girlfriend." His hand slides under my sweater and he pulls the cup of my bra down.

Noticing something moving behind him, I watch her carefully, allowing Brad a quick feel before our fun time comes to a halt.

"I think she has some sort of radar on when you get home."

He lifts his head from devouring my neck and peeks

behind him.

"Jesus," he whispers, abandoning my breast and sitting up.

"Dada," she says sweetly and crawls into his lap. "Miss you."

His eyes overflow with love. It never gets old looking at the two of them together. "Miss you."

If Vivian called right now, I'd say no to the offer, but her words won't stop repeating. Do I want out of Roosevelt? The question needs an answer.

"I showered at the gym, so I could take you guys out to dinner." He stands up and Em moves back to her toys. He tosses the messy disarray of her toys in a bin and snags the scissors and tape from the floor before Em can get to them.

The small act brings an elation over me about the fact that we're making a home here. He looks back at me sitting on the floor and tilts his head.

"Am I missing something?"

"Why?"

"Because you look like you're about to cry. Are you okay?"

He steps over to me, holding out his hand.

"We need to talk," I say, and his lips turn down.

"I don't much care for those four words strung together in a row."

"Sit down." He moves to the couch, making sure my hand stays in his. Once we're both situated, I begin. "So, three months ago, I felt like I had to get out of here. I called my friend, Vivian, in Arizona."

"The quiet one, right?"

"Yeah. Well, she's a nurse at a big hospital down there, and she got me an interview." I bite my lip. "It would be four ten hour shifts with three days off with Em."

"Oh. More time with her. I get it." His eyes move past my shoulder, and I know I've probably lost him.

"She thinks it's a good opportunity for me."

"Are you taking it, Taylor?" He cuts to the chase, and I can't blame him.

"No."

His eyes shift to mine. "You're going to stay here for me?" He acts like he's not worthy of that decision.

"Yes."

"Is it what you want to do?"

"Yes."

"You're sure?"

I giggle. "Yes, but I wanted you to know."

His hand covers his heart and he falls back in the cushions. "You scared me half to death. I thought for sure I was going to piss my dad off by moving to Arizona and leaving Creadle's behind."

"You would have come with me?" I ask him, surprised.

He sits back up. His hand lands on my cheek, and I lean into his hold. "I told you, you're my family."

"That we are."

"We're in this together, and if you want to move, we will. We make decisions together now."

When did he become so rational?

"Now, let's go have dinner and watch the commercial."

Four hours later, we watched the commercial with Tanner endorsing Creadle's, confident that things are perfect and our futures will be just as perfect as our present. But the one thing Brad and I should both know is nothing stays that way, and unfortunately, when we wake the next morning, it's anything but perfect.

twenty-five

Brad

IF TAYLOR WASN'T IN THE room, I guarantee I'd be throwing some shit. My past is behind me. My future is with Taylor and Emerson. Hell, I have the damn ring for Taylor at my parents', but fuck if I can ask her to marry a loser.

Loser. That's exactly what I am. Taylor clicks off the television that I've been fixed on since she took Emerson to Mrs. Allan's. No need for her to see her dad as the failure he'll always be.

"Talk to me." She sits and the fact she called off work to babysit me makes me hate myself more.

"There's nothing to say, except you're never free of your past, are you?"

"I don't think it's as bad as we think. Maybe people won't care."

Hijacking the remote away from her hand, I click on Sports Center. There's the same anchor, Jeff Billings, who tore Tanner apart months ago.

"Brad Ashby, does anyone remember him? His five minutes of fame happened when he had to save his best friend from being torn to shreds by the media as an upcoming Olympian. He admitted Tanner McCain's innocence and his own guilt for the failed drug test two years prior at Michigan University. Now months later, Tanner McCain is on a commercial endorsing the gym he owns. Oh, excuse me, partially owns. The other owner happens to be Wes Jenkins, who was another Olympian hopeful who had a car accident his senior year, which ruined his shoulder. Cheaters and fakes are what Tanner McCain and Brad Ashby are to me."

I throw the remote across the room and it lands in the Christmas tree we bought a week ago.

"Sometimes negative press is just as good as positive press." Taylor's trying, I'll give her that, but there's no use.

"I'm going out." I grab my keys and jacket, slamming the door behind me. "Guess not," I mumble to myself. I'm not even at my truck yet, when my parents pull in the driveway, blocking my way.

"You aren't running." My dad climbs out, pointing his finger at me. "We're not going to take this lying down."

My mom joins him, wrapping her arms around my neck. "It's okay, sweetie. We'll get past this."

Taylor steps on the stoop, wrapping her sweater around her a little tighter. "Come in." She ushers my parents inside.

I give her a tight smile to acknowledge she hadn't run after me, but I see her purse and keys thrown on the table by the door. I should have known she's not about to let me hide from my problems now.

"Sit down and let's discuss it." Chris's eyes veer to the television. "Let's turn that shit off. Fucking asshole."

My phone rings and I click ignore, not in the mood for anyone. When my mom's phone rings a second later, I can guess it was Piper.

Mom retrieves it out of her purse and stands up. "Yeah, we're here," she whispers into the phone. "No, it's not good."

"First of all, why this guy gives a shit or how he even knew about the commercial is ludicrous. I talked to Rick on the way over, and we can file a slander suit against him."

"It's useless, Dad. It's over. I went too public and should have kept quiet. How can I expect people to trust a cheater?"

"People overcome mistakes." I'm surprised my dad of all people is willing to admit it.

I clench my fist to keep my hands from shaking, quickly shutting down to everything around me. They think I'm listening, my nodding head tells them I am, but I'm not. I'm sinking faster than they can reach me. Then without warning, I'm back two years ago when Tanner got the call and I didn't.

Taylor

HE SITS THERE NUMB TO everything around him. It's been eight hours, and the local stations have now picked up on the Sports Center's story. Things are getting worse, not better. Not that Brad knows because he just sits there in front of an off television.

At least he didn't disappear on me when I drove his parents to Mrs. Allan's to pick up Em. They've taken her to their house for the night because it's time for Brad and me to either rise up from the ashes, or well, I'd rather not think of the flip side.

I sit on my coffee table, so he has no choice but to look at me. Clicking on my photos on my phone, I display pictures of him and Em together outside in the snow, picking out the Christmas tree, and swimming together. "See this little girl? She's the reason you are going to stand up and face that asshole who's slandering her daddy. You are going to prove him wrong and that you've changed."

No answer, not that I expected one. Brad's stubbornness knows no end.

"If you want to run away, I'll take that job in Arizona and we'll make a life out there. The three of us. You can hide from it. The choice is yours, Brad. You have to decide if you are going to fight this or slither away like a weasel."

I stand and walk upstairs, crossing my fingers he chooses the right decision.

Brad

"WHAT DO YOU WANT ME to do? Fight a war I can't win? They only speak the truth, not lies. I can't defend that."

"Yes, you can." Taylor stops moving up the stairs and sits next to me. "People change, Brad, and all you have to do is show them."

I shake my head, unsure how I'm supposed to do that.

Dylan's name shows up on my vibrating phone next to me.

"Answer it," she urges. "Everyone's been calling for you all day, wanting to talk to you."

Before I can stop her, she swipes her finger across the screen and answers.

"Yes, he's right here." She holds the phone out to me, and I roll my eyes, but take it.

"No salt in the wounds, please."

"Never. I have an opportunity that I think might be good for you. First, I want to tell you, this is killer business for you guys, so don't be upset. You can't pay for something this big, so as much as that guy is the biggest prick of all-time, you're going to turn it around on him."

"What the hell are you talking about?"

"Damn, I wish I wasn't in Chicago, but I have this guy, a local news guy in Detroit who wants to interview you. I did some business with him while with Deacon, and he knows Tanner is my brother, so he reached out, which is a damn miracle for you."

"Why would I do an interview just for people to slam me?" He clicks it on speaker and suddenly Bea's voice comes on.

"It's perfect, Brad. You are going to have him come to the

house with Taylor and have Emerson nearby. You are going to publically apologize for your actions again, but show everyone how well second chances turn out by pouring your heart open on television. Quickly, news will spread and Creadle's will be famous," Bea says.

"You two are a team to be reckoned with," I say, pondering the idea. Taylor sits nearby me, waiting impatiently to know what they are saying.

"Who is the guy?"

"It's Hank Reed, down at ABC. He wants the exclusive, which I told him I'm not sure you'd agree to. So, just make sure he's the first and you're good. Seriously, Brad, this is the way to go. You have to put an end to it now," Dylan adds.

"You've made too much progress to let this ruin you and the center," Bea adds.

"Did that really just come from your mouth?"

"What can I say? I'm feeling nice today. Dylan is shooting over Hank's number to you now. Do it, Brad. Don't lay down. At least fight for them."

The phone clicks off, and I look over at Taylor. Bea's fucking right, I need to do this for them.

"They want me to do an interview with that Hank guy from ABC."

"Okay, let's do it." She's eager and willing to do whatever to pull me out of this funk.

My phone chimes with his number. "They think he should come to the house. That you and Emerson need to be a part of it."

"Okay."

"You're really willing to sit next to me and not be ashamed I'm your child's father and the man you love?"

She sighs, tears gathering in her eyes. "Do you really think that, Brad?" She closes the distance and takes my head in her hands. "I'd scream it from the rooftops that you're the man in my life. You're a wonderful father, lover, and partner. I'd never be ashamed of you. Never. I'm the exact opposite from ashamed."

I nod, still unsure about the interview, but if I want to live the happy life I want with Taylor and Emerson, my hands are tied.

With Taylor straddling me, I dial Hank's number. He picks up on the first ring.

"This is Brad Ashby, what do you need from me?"

24 hours later . . .

"IS THERE ANYTHING ELSE YOU'D care to express, Brad?" Hank asks.

My mind runs through my rehearsed speech before I speak. "Jeff Billings doesn't know me, nor does he know my best friend, Tanner McCain. Two and a half years ago, we were seniors in college. My life had crumpled in front of me. The dream I had strived and pushed toward, the light that led my way, ended without a warning. Maybe there were warnings, but I didn't see them. Suddenly, I was left confused and disoriented about what I should do with my life. I was desperate for one last straw. When that failed and I was about to cause myself more problems, Tanner sacrificed himself. I don't expect people like Mr. Billings to understand, because I'm guessing he wouldn't do the same for a friend. That's a shame, because although it was stupid of us to do what we did, it wasn't out of bad motivation, but good. We'd swam together our whole lives, and we were desperate for it to continue down that path. I made a lot of mistakes at that time in my life. Ones I've made amends for."

I look over to Taylor with Emerson on her lap. We smile. "I don't believe in cheating to get where you want to be in life. I regret the decisions I made back then, but I have no choice but to move forward for my family." Taylor scoots closer,

Emerson crawling onto my lap. "I'm sorry for what I did, and I hope others won't discount Creadle's Aquatics because of me. It has a lot to offer, and so do I. I swam for almost all my life, and my coaching can help even the most talented of swimmers. If Jeff Billings would like to actually have a conversation with me, rather than bully me through a television, I'm certain he knows how to find me."

"Okay, we're off." Hank claps my shoulder. "Good work."

"Thanks." I wrap my arm around Taylor, Emerson snuggling between us. Her nap was nonexistent today.

"What do you think?" I ask her.

"I think you'll win the world over just like you did me."

Em's hands land on each of our faces. "Mama and Dada." She sighs. "Love you," she says, patting our cheeks.

"Love you," we say at the same time before wrapping our arms around our daughter.

epilogue

Taylor

CHRISTMAS AT THE ASHBY'S IS like nothing I've ever experienced. A giant tree decorated in an array of homemade ornaments sits in front of their living room window. Garlands run up their staircase banister. An assortment of lights and moving figures are spread across their lawn with beautiful icicle lights falling from the roof. It's a magical image, and one I'm happy Emerson is blessed to enjoy.

"Oh, you made it." Maggie meets me at the door as I trudge in the snow and slush on my shoes from the storm that's coming down outside.

"I was late getting out of work, and then the roads are a disaster," I comment, being careful not to dump the snow from my coat on her expensive rug.

"Let me take your coat. She's putting out cookies and milk for Santa with Grandpa."

It so hard to miss the moments with her, but I'm grateful I have tomorrow off to spend with her.

"I promise this is your last Christmas Eve without us," Brad follows me in, dropping the bags of presents on the floor to remove his layers of clothes.

"It's okay." I enjoy being a nurse, and I have applications out to a few private practices. I might not make as much, but the time I'll have with Em is worth the sacrifice. Brad insists I'll be able to stay at home, but I'm not even sure I'd want to. I have to say, after the interview, Creadle's Aquatic Center has been busier. They've had some reservations for therapy sessions and a few teammates of Cayden's who want to work with Brad and Wes starting in January. Most of the parents of the children Brad and Wes teach wrote reviews online saying how great both instructors are. Things are improving, and although Jeff Billings hasn't had much to say about him and Tanner, we're sure the subject will come up with the Olympics approaching. All in all, there hasn't been much negativity from it, and it definitely didn't hurt the business.

"I'm going to take these to the basement before she figures out we're here." He goes in the opposite direction from where Em would come from, and not be spotted with her Santa gifts.

Maggie comes back from the laundry room and grabs Brad's jacket from my hands. "Go, go. Spend time with her," she urges, and I honestly couldn't ask for better grandparents for Em. Maggie and Chris are caring, nurturing, and loving to her, but they never overstep when it comes to Brad and myself.

I walk into the kitchen and Em's on her knees on one of their breakfast stools picking cookies out of a tin and placing them on the counter. Chris spots me and smiles. Tiptoeing, I slowly walk over to her and tickle her sides.

At first, she stills until I whisper, "Merry Christmas, Emelem."

She glances over her shoulder and smiles wide.

"Mama." She turns around and her small arms hold me tight around the neck.

"Are you picking out cookies for Santa Claus?" I ask her and she pulls back, nodding her head.

"With Pa." I release her and she goes back to her task. She picks them up one at a time, examines each one, and then either places it on the plate or back in the tin.

"Cookies. Did I miss cookie time?" Brad barrels in,

bending over with his mouth open for a bite.

"Dada, no." She shakes her head. "Santa's."

I suck my lips in, trying not to smile at how serious she is, but Chris is unable to hold back his own chuckle.

"Me want cookie," Brad mimics in his best Cookie Monster impression, which makes Em laugh like always.

"Cookie?" she asks.

"Me want," he continues the act, and she's loving every minute of it.

Her small fingers pick up a sugar cookie covered in icing and lots of toppings. I'm thinking she had her hand in the cookie preparation as well. She shoves it in Brad's mouth, and he shuts the tips of her fingers in.

"Mmm mmm, good cookie," he mumbles with crumbs falling from his mouth.

Em's hysterical laughter never ceases, her belly shaking uncontrollably. Brad grabs her hand, holding it to his mouth. "Cookie?" he asks.

"No," she answers like he really thinks her fingers could be a cookie.

Brad swallows the remaining part of the sugar cookie and probably needs a gallon of water to get down all the sugar.

"Dada funny," she says, and he swoops her up into his arms to put her to bed.

"Emerson sleepy," he tells her.

"No, not sleepy." She fights, which I knew she would.

"Just let her stay up a little longer." I'm the one changing routines because I need a little more of her tonight.

"But I had plans for us," Brad whines. "Thought we'd go to Brecker's. Tanner and Piper went over there."

"No, they're at the McCain's. The weather is horrible, so they didn't go out." Maggie moves to the family room and turns on the television.

Brad lets go of Em and she runs into the room with Maggie, happy to be freed from her bedtime. "That sucks," he says. "I thought it'd be good to get out."

"Actually, I'm super tired anyway. My feet are killing me." I sit on the breakfast stool and bring my right foot up on the seat and massage it.

"Looks like you have a job tonight." Chris clasps Brad on the shoulder and joins his wife and Em in the family room.

"You want me to draw you a bath?" He winks as though that's code for something else. He's insane, because we are not having sex in his parents' house.

"No, but thank you for the thought. I just want to cuddle up with you and Em and watch a Christmas movie." I wind my neck around, cracking it.

"Done. Let's go."

We sit down on the loveseat with his parents on the couch and Em on the floor. Maggie turns on *How the Grinch Stole Christmas* and it keeps her interest pretty well.

Halfway to Wooville, my eyes shut, and the next thing I know, it's Christmas morning.

"Wake her up, baby girl." Brad's voice urges our daughter.

I pretend to sleep, so she smacks me across the face.

"Ouch, okay. I'm up." I grab her hand and shake my head. "No hitting."

"Oh, don't yell at her on Christmas," Brad, the softy, says. "Let's go open presents."

"Presents? Santa?" Em's little head volleys between the two of us. "Go!" she yells and slides off the bed onto the floor.

"I think we better go before all the presents are unwrapped, including everyone else's." Brad jets out of the room as I put my hair into a ponytail.

"I'm just brushing my teeth," I scream out the door and run toward the bathroom. Brad will only be able to hold her back for so long.

Five minutes is all it took for me to look halfway presentable for his family and she's unwrapped one of her gifts already.

"I tried, but she cried and we just couldn't handle that," Chris takes the fall.

"She's stubborn." I raise my eyes at Brad, who laughs.

"Come sit down." He pats the spot next to him on the couch.

The door opens and all the McCains and Piper file into the house. Maggie walks in with coffee cups lined up on a tray and a carafe in the middle. She places it on the table and Laney sets down a coffee cake.

"We haven't done this for a while, huh?" Laney says to Maggie and she laughs.

"You all woke up early?" I glance at the clock. It's only six o'clock.

Dylan plops down in a chair and slides his baseball hat down his face to block out the light. Or go back to sleep. I don't blame him.

Piper hops on the floor next to Em, and the two of them scour the presents. "Grab one," she eggs her on. "Do you want the one from me?" Em's eyes open wide.

"And me," Tanner adds, and Piper laughs.

"And Uncle Tanner." She winks at him.

Piper digs through the over-the-top pile of presents for one two-year-old and hands it to her. Piper is more excited than Em, quickly unwrapping it for her. It's a Bitty Baby American girl.

"Baby," Em says.

"Baby." Piper sways it in her arms.

Em's eyes leave Piper and go back to the pile.

"That's my girl, see what's next," Brad encourages her and Em takes no time to open her next gift.

While she's busy and all the adults are pretending to be just as excited as she is, I notice Dylan texting on his phone. I nudge Brad in the ribs and eye Dylan.

"Dyl, where's your sidekick?"

Dylan shrugs, never looking up from his phone.

"She went to see her mom," Piper informs us.

"I didn't think she had parents," Brad says.

"Her mom, but she lives in London."

"Actually, she's in Italy now." Dylan decides to chime in now.

"I had no idea." Brad looks down at me.

"Yeah, it's kind of a messed-up situation," Piper begins talking again, but Dylan looks up from his phone and pins her with a look. "But it's her story to tell."

She sinks back into Tanner's arms and he kisses her temple. Whatever the situation, Dylan is more involved than Piper. If I had to bet money, it's Bea on the other end of the phone he's been on since he walked in the door.

Finally, Em is finished and Chris is busy putting a toy together for her to play with.

"Em, grab the one with the Candy Cane's for Daddy." I point to the gift and Maggie hands it to her to bring over.

"Dada," she says and plops it on his lap.

"This is from me." I pull out of his hold, so he has both hands to open it. Originally, I didn't plan for this in front of everyone, but these people are all his family, and I think they'll appreciate this as much as him.

"I hope you didn't pay a lot." He unwraps the end.

I grab Em on my lap because she should be here when he sees.

"No worries there."

He looks at me from the corner of his eye, judging what on Earth it could be.

My heart races as he lifts the box and moves the tissue paper out of the way. Adrenaline shoots through my veins, waiting for this moment.

He stares down at it and says nothing. I want to urge him to respond and jump up and down in happiness with him. I watch his Adam's apple move up and down, and when he finally looks up at me, there's wetness glistening in his eyes.

"Really?"

I nod. "Always. From day one."

He picks up Em's birth certificate and kisses the spot where his name is under father. "Emerson Ashby Delaney," he whispers.

"We just have to change her name to Ashby. They said it's simple, but we need you to be there to sign the forms."

"Done." He grabs Em and hugs her to his chest. "Not that I needed a piece of paper to say you're mine."

Her hands land on his stubbled cheeks and she rubs back and forth, not understanding what all the commotion is about.

"Thanks, Tay. This is the best gift ever." He leans over and kisses me.

"You're welcome," I murmur against his lips.

"Well, that only leaves one more thing." He claps his hands with a mischievous look in his eyes. "Although, in my opinion, paper means absolutely nothing, it's nice for proof. So, we just need one more piece to make this all provable."

He digs into the couch, pulling out a small box. He slides off the couch and falls on bended knee in front of me. My hands fly to my mouth and Em instantly rushes back over from the sound of my gasp. She stands between me and Brad, her head ping-ponging between the two of us.

"Taylor Delaney, I wasted too much of my time away from you. Be my wife and put me out of my misery, because a life without you is far worse than a life without competing."

Tears cascade down my cheeks and I nod. "Yes," I answer, and Brad takes a hold of my left hand, slowly lowering it as he slides the ring onto my shaky finger. The round diamond sparkles under the lights of the family room.

"We're getting married," Brad yells throughout the house and everyone throws a bunched up ball of wrapping paper at him.

As the room empties, Brad and I find ourselves cuddled on the couch, watching our daughter play with her presents.

"Never would I have guessed I'd be with you this Christmas, let alone be engaged," I admit, holding my hand out in front of me, admiring the ring.

"Stick with me, baby, and I'll keep you on your toes."

"I have no doubt our life together will be fun and spontaneous."

"And filled with love." Both our eyes shift to Em and back to one another, sharing a smile.

"Definitely love."

Meanwhile in an upstairs bedroom . . .

Piper

"COME HERE," TANNER SITS ON the edge of my childhood bed, his arms stretched out for me to come.

I slide the box behind my back and saunter over to my fiancée. Once I'm within reach, he pulls me between his legs and his hands rub up and down my hips.

"Pretty cool for Brad and Taylor," he says, his head falls to my stomach and usually my hands would be weaving through his hair.

My stomach is churning, turning, flipping, and fluttering, unable to stay calm because I'm nervous about how Tanner will respond to my gift. Knowing I can't keep this secret much longer, I bring the small rectangle box out from behind my back and place it under his face.

His head lifts, and his hands grab a hold of the box.

"I thought we already exchanged?"

He's right. The evening before we flew home, we opened our gifts to each other, but this was unexpected. If I'd done the math at that point, I could have told him in the comfort of our apartment rather than in my childhood bedroom. Not to say this isn't perfect in a way. The many hopes and dreams I had that Tanner and I would have a future were born in this room.

"This is just a little something for both of us." He raises one eyebrow and my hand grazes down his cheek. "Open it."

His fingers rip open one end and I fall to my knees in front of him. My heart pounds in my chest from the anticipation of this moment.

His eyes flicker to mine with every inch further in the unveiling as though he's worried about what could be resting in the box. He balls the wrapping paper into a ball and I roll my eyes. "Open it," I urge, my hands itching to flip the cover off myself.

"Patience," he says with a smile.

He lifts the top lid off the box and there, nestled inside, is the pregnancy test I took when we got here in all its plus-sign glory.

"You're, I mean we're . . . pregnant?" His eyes shine with bliss and I exhale a relieved breath. I assumed he'd be happy, but we didn't plan for this to happen until after the Olympics.

I nod, tears brimming my eyelids. "Man, I don't know what to say?"

Wait, what?

"We'll be three then," he continues.

My lips transform into a pouty frown and I look up at him through my eyelashes. "Yeah."

He places the test on the bed and slides to the floor, taking my hands in his. "Three is my unlucky number."

I remember every time he competes in lane three he's lost, deeming it his unlucky number.

"That really doesn't mean anything in regards to us."

He draws back, his eyes widen in shock. "Yes, it does, so unless you have more than one baby in that belly, we're gonna get cracking on number two right away." His lips curl into a devilish grin and I relax, moving into his arms.

I lean back into my fiancée's strong arms wrapped around me, his hands lovingly on my stomach. "You scared me for a second."

He kisses my shoulder. "How could you think I wouldn't be happy? We've talked about it."

I link my fingers with his as they cover the spot our baby is growing. "We said we'd wait."

"No, you said we should wait. I was following your lead."

A memory of the times we talked about it proves he's right. I was more sold on waiting until after the Olympics. Tanner's so casual I'm not sure he would have cared.

I shift in his hold, loving the feeling of safety he brings me. "We're going to be a family," I whisper and his arms tighten around me.

"So, how long do you have to wait after the baby is born to try for another," he says and I turn my head to see a dead serious expression on his face. "What? You thought I was joking? Nope, we'll need to have that second right away. We can't afford my luck to run out."

I laugh, not completely put off by the idea. "You're crazy."

"About you," he kisses my cheek.

Thank you for reading *Love Rekindled*. If you'd like to get the latest information on Michelle Lynn's releases, sales, and upcoming books, please join her newsletter.

about the author

MICHELLE LYNN IS A USA Today Bestselling Author. She moved around the Midwest most of her life, transferring from school to school before settling down in the outskirts of Chicago ten years ago, where she now resides with her husband and two kids. She developed a love of reading at a young age, which helped lay the foundation for her passion to write. With the encouragement of her family, she finally sat down and wrote one of the many stories that have been floating around in her head. When she isn't reading or writing, she can be found playing with her kids, talking to her mom on the phone, or hanging out with her family and friends. But after shuffling around her twins, she always cherishes her relaxation time with her husband after putting the kids to bed.

Please reach out. I love to hear from readers!

To get the latest new releases and sales from
Michelle Lynn, join her newsletter.

Visit her website at www.michellelynnbooks.com
Or connect on Facebook, Twitter or Goodreads.

acknowledgments

FIRST I NEED TO THANK all the readers that fell in love with Brad and Taylor in Love Surfaced. I had an idea his own book would come, but it was your messages and inquiries that brought their story to me. Thank you for being faithful and loyal readers of my work.

Sommer Stein from Perfect Pear Creative Covers. You never cease to amaze me. Thank you for another breathtaking cover.

To my betas, Karrie Puskas, Heather Davenport and Zsuzsi Teleki. Your words of wisdom helped make Brad and Taylor's story stronger. Thank you.

Heather Davenport, Book Plug Promotions, you get two thanks. For not only doing my promotions but being a great friend. I'd be lost without you.

To my editor, Hot Tree Editing, thank you for being understanding and efficient.

To my proofreader, Ultra Editing, I cannot thank you enough for polishing and glittering up Love Rekindled. You're a sweetheart and I'm so happy I met you.

Perfectly Publishable, you are timely, concise, and amazing. Thank you for the beautiful files.

To all the blogs who have supported me, not only with Love Rekindled, but also throughout the years. No one would find me without you helping me spread the word. I cannot thank you enough.

Mia Kayla, my Friday night date at Starbucks, and the girl that keeps me sane. Thank you for listening to my rambles, for brainstorming endlessly, and talking me off the ledge on more than one occasion.

Lastly, my family, the ones who understand why I'm holed up at my desk until late hours at night. I owe you a movie night, a date night, and a game night. Love you more than I'd ever be able to express.

books by michelle lynn

THE INVISIBLES SERIES
Don't Let Go
Let Me In
Let Me Love
Can't Let Go
Let Me Go
Love Me Always

LOVE SURFACED SERIES
Love Surfaced
Love Rekindled
Love Emerged (Coming Spring 2016)

STANDALONES
Love Me Back
Familiar Ground
Seeing You
Collaboration (co-wrote with Nevaeh Lee)
Love Grows in Alaska
(novella in The Washington Triplet Series)

Made in United States
North Haven, CT
10 November 2022